P. C. Doherty was born in Middlesbrough. He studied History at Liverpool and Oxford Universities and obtained a doctorate at Oxford for his thesis on Edward II and Queen Isabella. He is now the Headmaster of a school in North-East London, and lives with his wife and family near Epping Forest.

P. C. Doherty's Hugh Corbett medieval mysteries are also available from Headline, as are the first two books in this series, AN ANCIENT EVIL, being the Knight's Tale, and A TAPESTRY OF MURDERS, being the Man of Law's Tale.

Acclaim for P. C. Doherty's medieval novels:

'Wholly excellent, this is one of those books you hate to put down' *Prima*
'I really like these medieval whodunnits'
Bookseller
'A powerful compound of history and intrigue'
Redbridge Guardian
'Medieval London comes vividly to life ... Doherty's depictions of medieval characters and manners of thought, from the highest to the lowest, ringing true'
Publishers Weekly
'A romping good read' *Time Out*
'Historically informative, excellently plotted and, as ever, superbly entertaining' *CADS*

A Tournament of Murders

The Franklin's Tale of mystery
and murder as he goes on a pilgrimage
from London to Canterbury

P. C. Doherty

HEADLINE

First published in 1996
by HEADLINE BOOK PUBLISHING

First published in paperback in 1996
by HEADLINE BOOK PUBLISHING

10 9 8 7 6 5 4 3

ISBN 0 7472 4945 8

Printed and bound in Great Britain by
Clays Ltd, St Ives plc

HEADLINE BOOK PUBLISHING
A division of Hodder Headline PLC
338 Euston Road
London NW1 3BH

Dedicated to Mrs G. E. Fogarty

The Prologue

In the candlelit refectory of the Friars of the Sack, which lay outside the village of Singlewell, the Canterbury pilgrims were now resting their weary bones after a hard day's travel. The clouds had cleared. The sun had proven hot, drying the russet trackway which their horses' hooves turned to a powdery dust that clogged their mouths and nostrils. If the heat and dust hadn't been bad enough, a sheriff's tipstaff had come pounding along the highway. Eyes round in fear, he'd told them to be wary of Black Hod's gang, a group of outlaws who wandered the Weald of Kent: these villains ambushed travellers, stealing their jewellery, clothes, horses, anything of value.

'They even,' the tipstaff's voice had dropped, 'molested and ravished women!' He glanced quickly at the prim prioress who sat daintily in her side-saddle whilst her olive-skinned, handsome priest held the reins of her palfrey. 'Women of the Church are not safe,' the official had whispered loudly. 'To the Black Hod soft breasts and firm thighs are all that matter.'

'Well, he's in for a surprise when he attacks me!' the wife of Bath had bellowed back, her broad-brimmed hat tipped askew over her round, red, fat face. She opened her gap-toothed mouth to continue her description of what she would do to Black Hod when the knight, his gorgeous tabard covered in dust, leaned over and squeezed her hand.

'Madame, with me, you shall always be safe.'

The good wife of Bath simpered. The prioress looked archly at the knight, lips more pursed than ever. After all, she was a prioress conversant in French, albeit in the fashion of Stratford-le-Bow. She should have had first claim on the knight's attentions.

'Don't worry, my lady.'

The summoner, drunk as a sot, had pushed his horse alongside the prioress', his wart-covered face only a few inches from hers. Dame Eglantine smelt the stale ale fumes and the reek of his unwashed body and turned away in disgust so the summoner had raised himself in his stirrups, emitted a loud fart and returned to his wineskin.

Once the tipstaff had rode on, Mine Host, the owner of the 'Tabard' in Southwark, consulted with the knight and the yeoman, then organised his little troupe into what he termed 'a military formation in the manner of Alexander the Great'. No one had a clue what he was talking about. However, after a great deal of confusion, the knight, his son the squire, the yeoman, the summoner and the friar had taken the lead. The haberdasher, dyer, fuller and others on the flanks; the franklin and the merchant were at the rear with Mine Host, surrounded by the ladies of the party in the centre. In the end Black Hod did not make an appearance although they passed a gibbet where the yellowed cadaver of one of Hod's companions hung mouldering. Accordingly, apart from a hare loping across the road, the dull songs of the birds and the rustling in the thickets on either side, their journey had been uneventful.

2

Now they could relax: their horses were stabled and the good Friars of the Sack had provided accommodation in their guest house. Beds had been inspected and all were full of praise for the crisp, white sheets, the absence of any fleas or sign of any rat-dung amongst the rushes on the floor. They had supped well on turbot grilled over charcoal, fresh manchet loaves with honey cakes afterwards. Mine Host had organised a collection to pay the good brothers. True to his nature, he kept some of this back, in recompense, so he told himself, for organising everything and putting his companions at their ease.

After the meal, they sat around the refectory on stools or in the window embrasures drinking their wine, quietly gossiping with each other. Mine Host, sitting by himself in a corner, felt fresh and invigorated. He cradled his tankard of malmesy and studied his companions. By God's little toe, he thought, they are a motley lot.

'A penny for your thoughts, sir.'

The taverner looked up into the cheery face and merry eyes of Geoffrey Chaucer, poet and diplomat, a man who kept to himself. He also amused himself by watching his companions, studying their every mannerism, tone and speech. The taverner was convinced that Chaucer was making careful note of every one of the pilgrims and the stories they told each day. The taverner waved to the stool beside him.

'Sir Geoffrey, as always, you are most welcome.'

Chaucer sat down, stroking his snow-white beard and moustache.

'I have the penny, Mine Host.'

'My thoughts are free,' the taverner teased back though he tapped the side of his tankard 'I'd like to see this brimming.'

Chaucer called across to a servant who stood beside the door and pointed at the landlord's tankard. The boy came across, carefully avoiding the summoner who leered and lurched forward, one hand out to clasp his buttocks. The young lay brother was as quick as a whippet and the summoner fell flat on his face to a roar of appreciation from his companions. The servant, slightly out of breath, filled their cups then hurried back, stepping on the prostrate summoner's fingers and making him howl with pain.

For a while Chaucer and the landlord watched as the pardoner and the miller, not too steady on their feet, helped the summoner back on to his stool.

'He's never sober,' Chaucer remarked.

'He likes his drink,' Mine Host replied. 'Though he's not the fool he pretends to be.'

'That,' Chaucer commented, 'could apply to everyone in this room, Mine Host. Have you noticed,' he continued, 'how they all seem to know one another? The knight is wary of the monk. Ever since Sir Godfrey's story about the Strigoi, the blood-drinkers of Oxford, the monk constantly watches him but never dares draw him into conversation.'

'Aye,' Mine Host replied. 'And whenever the monk comes near the knight, the squire's hand falls to his dagger.'

'Then there's the prioress,' Chaucer declared. 'A lady of the Church, though very aware of her rights and privileges. Prim and proper she is, pert as a peacock, except where that lawyer is concerned.' Chaucer nodded to the far corner where the man of law was talking in grave, hushed tones to the franklin and merchant. 'When she looks at him, the prioress becomes all coy and hot-eyed.' Chaucer supped from his cup. 'God knows but I'd wager they were lovers many years ago. I have seen them both whispering together.'

'The man of law told a grand tale,' Mine Host replied, 'of secret passions and long lost love. Sir Geoffrey, you may well be right. I wonder if people only came on this pilgrimage because others were present?'

They stopped talking as the miller lurched to his feet and gave a strident blow to the bagpipes he always carried under his arm.

4

'That's what I think of reeves!' he bellowed. 'I hate bloody reeves!' the miller continued, swaying slightly on his feet. 'The bastards always want this or that for the master!'

The gentle-eyed village priest tried to intervene but the reeve, despite having the look of a frightened rabbit, sprang to his feet, his hand going to the dagger at his belt.

'Aye, pull your hanger, bully boy!' the miller shouted. 'And I'll knock the shit out of you!'

'Time for another story,' Chaucer whispered.

Mine Host sprang to his feet and banged his pewter cup against a brass plate hanging on the white plaster wall.

'By St Tristram and St Isolde!' he roared, advancing on the two would-be combatants. 'Who ever starts a fight here will feel my fist. The good brothers and their servants are not used to such discord.'

He looked so fierce and threatening that both the miller and the reeve hastily took their seats. Mine Host slurped from his tankard.

'Gentle pilgrims,' his harsh voice now a soft purr. 'Are we not good friends and companions united in devotion to the Blessed Thomas? We have had a good day's travelling, good rest, sweet food and fine drink. So now, before the hour becomes too late, let's hear another story.' He pointed to the window where the shutters were thrown back. 'Look, the sun is beginning to set.' He paused as a dog howled as if to emphasise his words. 'Even though the day be ever so long,' the landlord intoned. 'At last the bell rings for evening song.'

'And, after the struggle, the turmoil and the fight,' the franklin finished the poem for him. 'At last will fall the gentle night!'

The landlord smiled and beckoned the franklin forward. The worthy in question surprisingly obeyed. He stepped into the pool of candlelight, his dark brocaded robe, lined with fur, thrown elegantly over his shoulders, only partially concealing the white cambric shirt, dark-green, velvet hose and black riding boots of moroccan leather. The franklin looked a merry soul, with his twinkling eyes, nut-brown face and white beard. A man with a good knowledge of food and drink. How to cook a capon; how to grill a trout and what piece of venison was the most tender and succulent. Now he cradled his own drinking cup, a gold, jewel-encrusted goblet; the eyes of the summoner and the pardoner flared with greed. Nevertheless, the franklin seemed a shrewd man; as he brushed by the summoner and his party, he kept his hand on his purse of murrey velvet which, two or three times, the summoner had tried to cut. The landlord watched him curiously as he approached.

'Sir, you wish to tell a tale?'

The franklin removed his velvet cap and bowed mockingly.

'Sir, I have eaten and drunk well and the stories of Black Hod have sent my mind racing.' The franklin surveyed his companions. 'Now the sun is setting,' he declared. 'The shadows grow longer. I will take up Mine Host's challenge to tell a tale, to puzzle the mind and stir the blood. I have such a story, one laced with sorcery.'

'Is it true?' the carpenter shouted out from where he sat leaning against the wall.

'That's not fair,' Mine Host intervened. 'Each pilgrim must tell a tale, one to suit the night. He need not say whether it be true or not.'

'I was only asking,' the carpenter, resentful of Mine Host's superiority, bellowed back.

'Now, now!' The franklin raised his hand. 'Listen, all of you: as I talk, you decide whether my tale is fact or fable.'

He paused as the door suddenly swung open, making the wife of Bath jump and squeal. The friar swept into the room, his robes slightly awry, his face flushed and sweaty.

'I have just been to say my beads,' he slurred, as he slid along a bench.

'More likely in the stables with a wench,' the seaman whispered darkly, making his companions all snigger.

Mine Host, watching the friar brush his robes, could only agree. Lecherous as a sparrow the fellow is, he thought. He'd seen how the friar had scarcely slipped from his brown-berry palfry before he'd begun to sidle up, feeling the buttocks of the young goose girl. Yet, the landlord sipped from his tankard, it wasn't his business to tell men of the church how to run their houses or remind friars about their vows. Instead, he grasped the franklin by the hand and took him across to a high-backed chair which stood in the inglenook of the huge fireplace.

'Sit yourself down, sir,' the landlord grandly announced. He snapped his fingers at the servant to come across to refill their cups. Mine Host then looked around the refectory. 'There will be no more interruptions, not unless you want them. So come, sir, let's hear your dark tale.'

'My story,' the franklin began, 'happened many years ago. It had its roots in macabre murder. It came to full flower at the end of a bloody battle.' His face grew soft. 'And yet it was tinged with love, loyalty and a little magic. So, listen to me now.'

The Franklin's Tale

PART I

Chapter 1

At Poitiers, the bloody struggle between the massed armies of England and France was now drawing to a gory close. Ever since early evening, phalanx after phalanx of massed French knights had thrown themselves on the English position, only to be driven off by arrows which fell like a constant, angry rain from the darkening sky. The lines of English archers had not broken. Time and time again, behind their protective line of stakes, they had stood or knelt and loosed arrow after arrow into the gorgeously garbed French knights whose shining armour and glorious livery now turned a bloody red mixed with mud and slime. In some places the French dead lay two, three feet deep: horse and rider cast down by the accuracy and sheer fury of the English archers. The Black Prince, Edward III's eldest son and premier general, had stood and watched the carnage before ordering a general advance into the depleted French ranks. The carnage had continued. King John of France, clothed in his Milanese armour under a blue and gold surcoat emblazoned with the silver lilies of France, had been taken prisoner. Other French lords, his counts and generals, had surrendered. Those who didn't, died, pricked with arrows or lay gasping on the muddy soil. Some choked to death, others were despatched by English men-at-arms who pushed their misericord daggers through the cracks in their armour between visor and hauberk and slit their noble throats.

Nevertheless, the English, too, had suffered casualties. In a muddy ditch beneath a hedgerow, Sir Gilbert Savage, a poor knight, lay gasping as the blood seeped through his armour, forming a dark-red pool around him. In the gathering darkness, his squire, Richard Greenele, tried to make him comfortable.

'I should undo your straps, Sir Gilbert,' he whispered hoarsely. 'At least tend the wound.' He peered down at the knight's sad, weather-beaten face. 'Shall I fetch an apothecary or leech?'

'Damn all their eyes!' Sir Gilbert whispered. 'Let me at least die with dignity in my armour.' He caught Richard's wrist in a surprisingly firm grip and raised himself up. 'Listen,' the dying man hissed. 'No priest, no apothecary. Richard, you are to leave the battlefield now!'

'Now?' the young squire retorted. 'But, Sir Gilbert!'

'The battle is finished,' the older man replied. 'The Black Prince has his victory. I was commissioned to serve for six months and a day. My term is finished and my time is up. Sir Gilbert Savage is for the dark. Who will now care about an impoverished squire?'

Greenele looked at Sir Gilbert's face in surprise. He'd always thought his master was old. However, looking at him now in the pale moonlight, the noise of battle still echoing around them, the squire realised Sir Gilbert must be no more than forty summers old.

'I shouldn't have left you,' he confessed. 'But when the French broke through...'

'I sent you for help,' Sir Gilbert gasped. 'You only did my bidding.' He stopped and held his side. 'A French knight,' he continued, 'I thought I'd taken prisoner. Instead,' Sir Gilbert's hand went to the gap between his breastplate and the battered piece which protected his back, 'he thrust his sword in me. Now I have my death wound.'

'I should stay with you,' Richard insisted.

Sir Gilbert shook his head. 'Once I have finished with you, go. Send a leech back to tend me.' He smiled weakly. 'Though I'll not keep him long. Now, listen,' his grip on Richard's wrist tightened. 'You are not what you think you are.'

'What do you mean?' Richard asked.

'Never mind.' Sir Gilbert shook his head. 'Time is short. You are to return to England. Go to Colchester in Essex. Seek out the lawyer Hugo Coticol.' He paused and made Richard repeat the name at least five times.

'Who is Coticol?' Richard asked. 'Sir Gilbert, what does this all mean? You took me into your care when I was a baby, surely, after my parents died of the plague?'

Sir Gilbert's head went back as if he was listening to the fading sounds of battle around him.

'The Prince has won a great victory,' he whispered. 'They say the French king has been captured. Never again will the power of France make itself felt.'

'Aye,' Richard added bitterly. 'But it has cost me the life of my master, my father and my friend.'

He leaned over. In the dim light he found it difficult to make out Sir Gilbert's expression. He glanced up, pinpricks of light were appearing in the darkness as the English, now masters of the field, sent out archers carrying torches to search amongst the dead. Richard wondered whether to go across to seek assistance, at least a torch to dispel some of the darkness around him.

'Don't go,' Sir Gilbert rasped, as if reading his thoughts. 'I'll answer your questions. Richard, your parents did not die of the

11

plague. They were murdered, terribly and most mysteriously.'
He coughed. 'I do not know the details but Coticol will hand
over to you all the necessary documents.'

Richard sat back on his heels. He gaped, open-mouthed, into
the darkness. He'd begun the day as Sir Gilbert Savage's squire.
Oh, he knew he was an orphan, taken in by Sir Gilbert's
generosity. In time he hoped to advance himself, perhaps
receive knighthood from some great lord. Now that sword thrust
to Sir Gilbert had shattered his life. He had no master and he
was being told that the story he'd believed for eighteen years
masked a greater mystery. Richard rubbed the side of his face.

'Don't be angry with me,' Sir Gilbert whispered. 'I took a
great oath that before I died, or once you had passed your
eighteenth year, I would tell you the truth.'

'What will happen to you?' Richard exclaimed, pulling the
cloak around him against the biting wind chilling his sweat-
soaked body. 'Your possessions, your . . . ?'

Sir Gilbert laughed softly. Pulling himself further up the ditch,
he gasped, holding his side.

'What possessions, Richard? Battered armour? A horse that's
now dead? A few pennies in my purse?' He reached down and,
grasping the battered saddlebags which Richard had brought
with them, thrust these at his squire. 'After years of duty,' he
continued, 'in one castle after another that's all I have. As the
writer says, "we came out of the darkness naked, we go into the
darkness naked". I would want no other. Now, boy, for the love
of God, go! Take a horse, God knows there are many rider-less.
Make sure it has good harness. Ride to the coast.'

Richard, suddenly frightened at being alone, shook his head.

'You need help,' he whispered. 'I can obtain the services of a
leech.'

Sir Gilbert raised his sword in a surprising show of strength
and brought the flat down on Richard's shoulder, the sharp
blade only an inch away from his neck.

'I am your knight,' he rasped. 'It is the first duty of a squire to obey. Now, in the name of God, go! That is my last command!'

'And, if I don't?' Richard asked.

'Then you are a base-born rogue and a caitiff, disloyal, no longer my squire, my friend or the son I wished I'd had.'

Savage's face softened. 'Please, in the name of God, go and go now!'

Richard leaned forward, pressing away the sword and gently kissed Sir Gilbert on his weather-beaten cheeks and sweat-soaked forehead. As he did so, the tears started in his eyes, hot and scalding.

'Go on, boy!' Sir Gilbert ordered gruffly. 'Leave me to God.'

Without a backward glance, Richard scrambled out of the ditch. Clutching the saddlebag beneath his cloak, Richard Greenele, the poorest squire in Edward of England's army, staggered across the battlefield of Poitiers. Early in the day, the field had been a lush green meadow maturing under the late autumn sun. Now it was a hell on earth. A thick mist was beginning to roll across as if Nature itself was trying to hide the horror: decapitated corpses, horses threshing about in pain, battering, with their iron-shod hooves, the wounded and the dying piled thickly as leaves around them. The cold night air was turned horrid by the cries and moans of the wounded. Here a Frenchman cried for his mother. Next to him an English archer moaned for his wife and children.

The sound of fighting had now died away. The French were in full retreat, the English too exhausted to pursue. An occasional friar or priest moved across to give what consolation they could. Greenele sent one of these hastening in the direction of Sir Gilbert because the prospect of plunder had brought all the camp followers scurrying about with their little daggers to finish off the wounded and plunder the dead. Sometimes Richard would meet a party of these but the sight of his naked sword and the grim expression on his face afforded safe passage.

Occasionally he'd meet a group of English archers who'd hail him and ask his name and title. Richard's accent soon quietened such enquiries and he was left to his own devices. He would have liked to have stopped; twice he did, to offer his water bottle to men shrieking for a drink. As he did so, he collected weapons; a better sword, a buckler, a dagger, food and drink from a saddle-bag, even a cloak from a knight who would need it no more.

As he approached the edge of the battlefield, Richard came upon a beautiful, black war horse, tall and stately: it stood shaking its neck and pawing the ground. Now and again the horse would snicker at the corpse lying next to it. Richard approached slowly, talking gently to it. He dug into his purse and brought out some of the apple he'd gnawed at before the battle had begun. He held this forward. The horse took it gently, its ears going forward in pleasure. Still talking softly Richard mounted. The great war horse did not object though it snickered gently over the sprawled corpse. When the squire pulled at the reins and gently dug his heels in, the destrier turned and cantered off into the night.

Thankfully, the horse had been standing on the far edge of the battlefield near the road which wound down through the hedgerows. Richard had never experienced such horseflesh and, despite his abrupt and tragic departure from Sir Gilbert, he thrilled at the feeling of power and speed. At last, when he was some distance from the battlefield, Richard reined in, taking the horse off the road into a small copse of trees. He dismounted and, coming forward, held the horse's head between his hands, kissing it gently, murmuring endearments as he always did to any horse he worked with. The great destrier nuzzled him back. Richard examined the animal more closely. The war horse was jet-black from tip to tail, its coat sleek and soft: strong haunches, good legs, sharpened hooves with a beautifully proportioned head and neck. When Richard turned so did the horse, as if it, too, was glad of company. Richard laughed softly and dug into his wallet for the last bits of apple, letting the horse lick his fingers. Then the squire examined the harness: the reins and saddle were of dark-red, Spanish leather: the buckles, straps and stirrups of the finest workmanship.

'Your master must have been some rich lord,' the squire whispered. And, raising the saddle, exclaimed in surprise at the pouch which had been woven into the side. He undid the entire saddle, took it off and examined the pocket carefully. The horse immediately lay down and rolled over, scratching its back. Richard drew out the silver coins hidden in the secret pouch and whistled in amazement, counting at least a hundred pounds sterling. He reined the horse, threw the saddle back over it and returned the silver where he had found it. He rebuckled the harness, checking every strap and then re-mounted. Leaning over, he stroked the horse's neck and murmured in his ears.

'Perhaps both our luck has changed?'

Then he rode the horse back on to the road.

The further he travelled from Poitiers, the more Greenele was astonished how the news of the battle seemed to have preceded him. Villages and hamlets were deserted, the peasants already taking up their belongings and escaping to the woods. At the small walled towns the gates were firmly closed against him. The same was true of any fortified manor house and castle. The great English victory of Poitiers was already beginning to raise demons of its own. Time and again Richard encountered some of the free companies: mercenaries, organised gangs of English men-at-arms and archers now combing the countryside for plunder, pillage and rape. Eventually, Greenele decided to travel by night and sleep by day, keeping away from the black columns of smoke and the smell of burning. Occasionally, at some religious house or isolated farm, he was able to buy supplies for himself and fodder for his horse. No one dared accost him. An English milord, or so they thought, well armed and well mounted, was too dangerous to challenge.

Naturally, Greenele's mind kept going back to Sir Gilbert Savage lying in that muddy ditch, his life blood seeping out of him, his words shattering Richard's life. One night, as he lay in his blanket in some copse, the great war horse hobbled beside him, Greenele realised how much of his life had been bound by Sir Gilbert Savage. Ever since he could remember, Greenele had been Sir Gilbert's page, then his squire, as the impoverished knight journeyed around England signing indentures with this lord or that: a tour of duty in castles such as Bamborough on the Scottish march or at Dover overlooking the grey, sullen channel. Greenele had never questioned that. When he had asked Sir Gilbert about his parents, the knight had just shaken his grizzled head.

'They died of the plague,' he'd reply caustically.

'Where?' Richard would ask.

'In a small village in Kent. I was passing through, everyone had fled, then I heard a baby crying.' Sir Gilbert would lean over and ruffle his hair. 'St Michael and all his angels must have been watching over you. Your parents were dead, you were just sitting on the mud-packed floor, bawling your eyes out. I had a woman then, Mariotta. She looked after you. When she died of the sweating sickness, only the two of us were left.'

Greenele stirred and stared up at the starlit sky. And that had been his life. Up and down the dusty, narrow lanes and trackways of England: sleeping in smelly barns, the garrets of ramshackle inns or the gaunt, cold chambers of some castle. Nevertheless, it had been a good life. Sir Gilbert had fought in Prussia against the wild tribes so he was a never-ending source of fascinating stories about wet, green woods, macabre rites and tribes who took the heads of their enemies to decorate the lintels over their doors. At the same time Sir Gilbert had been an excellent tutor, teaching Richard the art of horsemanship, making him most skilled in the use of the bow, the sword, the lance and the dagger. Richard had expected such a life to go on for ever. Now and again he and Sir Gilbert would go to the great tournaments at Leicester, Nottingham, Salisbury, Winchester or Canterbury. His master had been brilliant with the lance. Time and again he would win a purse of silver or even the harness and horse of some luckless knight he toppled twice. These he'd sell and then they'd move on. Sometimes, however, at night Richard would suffer a terrible nightmare. It was always the same: he was in a room, all by himself, sleeping in a small cot. Outside he could hear a woman screaming, the clash of sword and mailed feet on the stairs. Sometimes the nightmare would be clearer: doors being thrown open, a man bending over him but then it would fade. One night when he had woke, soaked in sweat, he'd found Sir Gilbert watching him curiously.

'You suffer nightmares often, don't you, Richard?'

The squire nodded, gasping for air.

'Succubi,' Sir Gilbert would reply. 'Devils of the air: they spring up from hell to murder our sleep and plunge the soul into nightmares.'

'But this one's always the same,' Richard had protested. He'd close his eyes and describe it. Sir Gilbert looked at him strangely, shook his head and told him to go back to sleep. Now, all this was over and Richard wondered about Hugo Coticol. What were the secrets of his past? Of his parents? And why Colchester in Essex? Richard heard the horse whinny and, getting up, went to stroke and reassure it.

'You are beautiful,' he whispered. 'Brave-hearted and loyal.' He looked up at the skies. 'I shall call you Bayard. Yes, Bayard, a prince amongst destriers.'

The horse snickered softly, nudging at Richard's pouch.

'I have no more apples,' the squire laughed.

But, going back to his saddlebag, he took out a sugared plum he'd bought in a village they had passed through the previous evening. Bayard ate it from his hand. Why Colchester in Essex? Greenele thought. He withdrew his hand, making Bayard whinny in protest. Suddenly he realised, despite all Sir Gilbert's journeying up and down the kingdom, they had kept well away from the Essex towns or ports. Richard sighed. He let Bayard finish his plum, went back to his blanket, lay down and tried to sleep.

Eventually, after a few more days riding, Greenele reached the port of Bordeaux. The news of the Black Prince's victory at Poitiers had also reached there. The port, held by a strong English garrison, was now a hive of activity, as fat-bellied cogs and great, high-sterned merchantmen prepared armament to take them to sea to plunder French shipping. Everybody was coming into France, eager to seek their fortune, so Greenele found it easy to secure passage for himself and Bayard on board a wine cog sailing for Dover. They left one morning just, as the captain observed, the autumn winds made their presence felt. Richard was forced to agree. Bayard was well protected in the hold, hobbled securely with plenty of provender but he was given a sea-soaked bed between decks.

For the first time in his life, Richard knew what true misery was. The ship tossed and turned. The sea-water seemed to trickle everywhere, coating his clothes and skin with a fine dusty salt. The food was weevil-infested biscuit whilst the wine tasted like vinegar. The young squire spent most of his time staggering up and down the steps to vomit over the side. The sailors gently mocked him, clapping him on the back and saying this was nothing to what might come. Richard would smile weakly and stagger back down the steps to check on Bayard. Then, throwing himself down on the soaked mattress, he'd crouch in the darkness, cross his arms, close his eyes and pray the Lord would deliver him from all the perils of the deep.

At last they reached Dover, the great castle where Richard had spent some of his youth, soaring high on the cliffs dominating the busy port below. Richard, weak, unshaven and as filthy as a sewer rat, led a bedraggled Bayard off the ship. He entered the narrow, cobbled streets, searching until he found the best hostelry. Richard stayed there a week whilst he and Bayard recovered from the rough sea crossing. He stripped himself of his clothing, washed, shaved and ordered new raiment from a travelling journeyman. For the first three days the squire spent most of his time in bed or crouching in the inglenook before a roaring fire. Bayard was the first to recover: rested, groomed and well fed, he was soon kicking the wooden partition of his box, shaking his head with pleasure whenever his new-found master appeared. Naturally, with such a horse and being fresh from France, Greenele soon became the object of attention with people questioning him about what had happened at Poitiers. Richard answered as adroitly as he could, posing as a messenger of some great lord who held lands north of the Thames. He told his listeners what they wanted to know: the courage of the English archers, the stout hearts of the men-at-arms, the bravery of the knights, and the leopard-like qualities of their general, the Black Prince.

Most of the questioning was innocent, even naive, particularly from the young men, be they sailors, merchants or farm boys eager to cross to France to share in the plunder. Nevertheless, at times, Richard felt as if he was closely watched, scrutinised, whether he sat at the greasy-covered table of the tavern or strolled the streets, wondering when he could leave. A lonely man, used to danger and the deserted byways and trackways of England, Greenele also suspected he was being followed but, whenever he turned at a corner, or some booth, or stall he could see nothing untoward. The same was true in a tavern, at night the taproom filled with pedlars, relic-sellers, journeymen, sailors, men-at-arms, the red-headed whores and more elegant courtesans. Nevertheless, search as he would, Greenele could never find the mysterious watcher. By the time he left Dover, taking the road north for London, he was sure his imagination was playing tricks on him, perhaps the result of his hasty departure from France and bone-racking sea voyage.

Richard was glad to be out of Dover, free of its fetid streets and the pervasive smell of salted fish. The countryside was not yet in the grip of winter but autumn was beginning to die. Carpets of gold-brown leaves covered the trackways whilst a brisk, strong breeze stripped the trees and sent the birds wheeling against the sky. In the great fields on either side, the peasants prepared for the sowing; strong-backed farmers leaned over their great oxen-ploughs whilst, behind them, young boys, armed with slings, drove away marauding crows.

The roads were busy: friars and preachers, their tawdry wheelbarrows piled high with paltry belongings, hastened to London before winter arrived and turned the cobbled trackways into muddy morasses. Scholars of various nationalities, dressed in gawdy, tattered robes made their way to the Halls of Cambridge or Oxford. A pardoner, fresh from Avignon, rode with a string of bones round his neck. He claimed these were the sacred relics of St Thaxtus and his ten thousand companions. The squire kept well away from such villainy. Now and again he would join a troupe of mummers, moving from one village to another, or a party of merchants going towards Canterbury or up to London. Greenele, however, was desirous of avoiding London where anyone recently come from Poitiers might be dragged before the sheriffs, mayor or aldermen for interminable questioning. The squire realised he had no official letter allowing him to leave the Prince's forces, so he struck west. He crossed the Thames one evening by a muddy, deserted ford and headed towards the village of Woodforde. Greenele could only take directions from passing farmers or some lonely homestead and discovered he could not avoid the dark-green spread of Epping forest or the lonely pathways which ran through it. Greenele was not frightened but he was still wary of being followed. Only once, just after he crossed the ford, did he glimpse a mysterious rider cloaked and cowled, waiting under the trees. He tried to stay away from the woods yet, by the time he reached the manor of Wanstead, Greenele knew he had no choice but to take the forest pathway. He loaded the crossbow he had brought, swung it from his saddle horn and loosened his sword and dagger in their sheaths.

It was late afternoon before he was in the forest proper and his nervousness increased. The trees above him wound their branches together, blotting out the sky and the weak autumn sun. Thick rotting leaves coated the ground, deadening any sound. On every side came the sound of animals scuttling through the undergrowth, mingling with eerie bird-calls from high in the branches. Greenele's unease deepened. On one occasion, as darkness began to fall, he glimpsed dark shapes slipping through the forest on either side. Accordingly, he sighed with relief as the path became broader, the trees less dense and, in the far distance, Greenele glimpsed the twinkle of a welcoming light. So intent was he on reaching it, he relaxed his guard and the band of wolvesheads who had been tracking him, came streaming out of the wood. They ran soundlessly towards him, arrows notched to their bows, swords drawn, clubs raised. They were upon him almost before he realised.

There was no time to use the arbalest but he drew his sword, gripping Bayard's reins more tightly. The outlaws, hooded and masked, thronged about him, striking out. Greenele fought back, moving Bayard carefully, charging directly at the bowmen who danced around him looking for an advantage. At first the great destrier seemed puzzled by the dramatic change in events but then, one of the outlaws aiming for the squire's legs missed and caught the horse a blow on its withers. Bayard immediately retaliated. A trained war-horse, he reared up, flailing out his sharpened hooves, sending two of the outlaws sprawling. Given a respite, Greenele lifted the arbalest and loosed the bolt, turning one outlaw's face into a bloody mass. Then the others, perhaps desirous of the very horse who had caused so much damage, thronged in, lashing out desperately, trying to claw the young squire from the saddle. Time and again the squire escaped from their grip, Bayard moving adroitly away. Greenele's body became coated in sweat, his hands grew slippery and, after one blow, he moved too quickly and the sword slipped from his grasp. He dug his spurs in, hoping to break out, but one of the outlaws hung on for dear life to Bayard's harness, dodging the flailing hooves, screaming curses at his companions to pull the rider down. Suddenly, a horn blew, deep and rich from the forest. One short blast followed by another, long and trailing. Surprised, the outlaws stood back, then one of them seemed to leap in the air, arms out, as an arrow shaft whispered through the night air and took him full in the chest. Other shafts followed; two, three more outlaws fell. The rest took to their heels, slipping like rats back into the undergrowth.

For a while Greenele just bowed his head, sobbing for breath. He heard a sound, a gurgle and, looking up, saw a man, dressed from head to toe in lincoln green, bending over one of the outlaws and expertly slashing his throat. The man glanced up at Greenele's exclamation and came forward, pulling back the hood from his wiry, grey hair. He had a pleasant, square, sun-tanned face with a long dagger mark which ran the length of his left cheek. He moved quietly, effortlessly, like a cat. A sheath of grey goose quill arrows on his back, the long yew bow clasped in his right hand. The green tunic he wore was dirty and sweat-stained but the leather baldric and belt were a rich berry-brown colour. The sword which hung through a ring on his belt was clean and polished and Greenele noticed the thick leather guards on each wrist, the mark of a master bowman.

'You can dismount.' The man's face broke into a smile as he scratched the stubble on his cheek.

'How do I know you are not one of them?' the squire snapped back.

'Because, if I was, I would not have put an arrow in three of them. And, by now, you'd be dead as well! Now, be a good boy and do as I say. You can't leave a good sword lying on the forest floor.'

Somewhere in the trees a bird began to chatter, making Greenele jump.

'Don't worry,' the green-garbed man said softly, coming forward. 'They have all gone, at least for the moment.' He moved round the corpses, cutting their purses and taking any trophies they carried, putting them in his own leather pouch. 'Filth from the sewer!' he said.

'You know them?' Richard quietly drew his dagger from its sheath, steadying his still excitable war-horse.

'Oh, I know them all right. They call themselves the Houndsmen. Part of a large gang of wolfsheads, outlaws, rapists, blasphemers, pillagers. A finer body of men never graced the king's gallows.' He took a step closer and Greenele held up the dagger.

'How do you know all this?'

The man gave a mocking bow.

'My name is Cuthbert Barleycorn, huntsman, once royal verderer in the King's forest of Epping.'

'And now?' Greenele asked curiously.

'Well, master traveller, there are those who exist within the King's peace: there are others who live beyond it whilst a few, like me, live in the twilight between.'

'So you are an outlaw?'

'No, not really. I just refused the King's summons to join his armies in France.' Barleycorn stepped a little closer, his eyes narrowing. 'I wager you have come from there. A deserter yourself?'

Greenele gripped the dagger more tightly. 'How do you know that?'

'I was there over a dozen years ago. I fought at the carnage

23

they call the great victory of Crecy. I can recognise a French harness and saddle when I see one. Oh, by St Michael and all the Angels, and that's a prayer not a curse, you are sitting on that horse like a frightened rabbit. If I wanted to kill you, I could do.'

He moved with incredible speed; plucking an arrow from his quiver, he notched the bow and, before the young squire could even turn his horse, the arrow zipped through the air, a few inches above his head. Barleycorn came closer, picked up the sword and grinned as he handed it back.

'You're a good fighter,' he declared. 'Many a man would have been dragged from his horse. Where are you going?'

'Colchester in Essex.'

The smile faded from Barleycorn's face. 'Then you should be careful. The great pestilence has appeared there.'

Greenele looked up. Night was beginning to fall and he wanted to be off the woodland path, away from this sharp-eyed, skilful bowman. He jumped as, somewhere in the green darkness behind them, came the long mournful wail of a hunting horn. Without asking, Barleycorn grabbed the bridle of his horse.

'We'd best go,' he murmured.

He looked back over his shoulder and Greenele caught the fear in his eyes, even as the hunting horn sounded again.

'It's the Houndsmen!' the bowman muttered. 'They are gathering to hunt us!'

Chapter 2

The young squire did not resist Barleycorn's offer of help. The recent attack had reminded him how, in England, outlaws moved with greater impunity than some frightened peasant in France, hiding from the English milords. He and Barleycorn briskly made their way down the path, out of the forest and along the dusty high road of the village of Woodforde. Barleycorn led him along to the White Harte tavern, a rather grand, lofty hostelry which stood in its own grounds just as the trackway wound up to the church of St Mary's. Greenele remembered his manners and insisted that he pay for a meal and a mattress for his saviour. Barleycorn did not demur. Once Bayard had been properly stabled, he belched and rubbed his stomach.

'I could eat a pig and a half,' he muttered.

'Will the Houndsmen follow us here?' Greenele asked.

'Only if they are stupid. They are led by two men: villains: outlaws since the day of their birth, Dogwort and Ratsbane.' He pushed Greenele gently forward into the taproom. 'No, no, they much prefer the lonely trackway and the solitary traveller going that extra mile before darkness falls. But, to hell with them, let's eat!'

The fat-bellied landlord of the White Harte waved them to a table near the great fire. He served them a range of delicacies: spiced eels, leek soup and strips of beef from the haunch roasting on the spit, coated with pepper and mustard and covered with a thick brown onion sauce. Barleycorn ate like a man whose life depended on it and, no matter how much of the rich red claret he drank, his voice held firm. He told Richard, without being invited, how he had been raised in Essex, a trained archer and master bowman. He had been a huntsman in the royal household until he deserted from the king's army in France.

'Why?' Greenele asked.

Barleycorn sat back on his stool, cleaning his wolf-like teeth with a splinter of wood he'd washed in wine.

'You've come from Poitiers?'

'Yes.'

'And how did you find it?'

'Frightening.'

Barleycorn sat forward. 'I took my boy to France,' he murmured. 'He kept filling my quiver with arrows, just behind the stakes, where I stood in a line of archers. The French broke through. Great mailed men with their morning stars, axes, swords and daggers. It was every man for himself.' His eyes filled with tears. 'We drove them off, sent them packing but, when I looked round, young Alan was dead. I thought he was asleep except for the great blue-black bruise on the side of his head. He had lovely hair, like ripe wheat: eyes blue as a summer sky. I sat cradling his head in my lap and wondered in God's name what it was all about. Who cares if Edward wears the crown of France? It wasn't worth a fig, a frog's spit, if boys like Alan died. So I left. I came back to England.' He paused and stared into the fire. 'My wife had died shortly after Alan's birth.'

He continued slowly. 'I returned to my duties as verderer but, of course, you make your enemies. Someone went before the Justices in Chelmsford and laid information against me as a deserter. I was summoned to appear before them and I refused.' He shrugged. 'Nothing happened. Eighteen months later, fresh writs were served by the Commissioners of Array, telling me to join the King's forces when they mustered at Colchester. I refused; I fled to the forest, where I am now.' He smiled thinly. 'I still play the part of royal verderer.'

'And no one pursued you?'

'You have seen the forest? Who'd leave a trackway and follow a man like me into the darkness?'

'But these outlaws, the Houndsmen?'

'Ah!' Barleycorn sipped from the battered, pewter cup. 'You see, young sir—'

'Richard,' the squire replied testily. 'My name is Richard Greenele. I've told you that.'

'Of course you have. Well, young sir, when I was a verderer, I hunted Ratsbane and Dogwort. They are evil, their souls are full of malice. They have no compassion and fear neither God nor man. Now, I am on the wrong side of the law, they hunt me.'

'For revenge?'

'No.' Barleycorn put the cup down. 'But for the reward, fifty pounds dead or alive, we play a game of cat and mouse in the woods. Since last Michaelmas I've killed ten of their men.'

Greenele gazed anxiously round the crowded taproom.

'And you are safe here?'

'Of course. No one knows me. Now you,' Barleycorn stretched out. 'Why did you leave the King's armies in France? Riding a horse far too good for you, equipped with expensive harness? And why, in God's name, go to Colchester?'

Greenele stared into his wine cup. Barleycorn seemed trustworthy: a tough, weather-beaten, hard-bitten soldier. He breathed in quickly, yet, it seemed most fortuitous that he had appeared when he had. How did he know Barleycorn's story was true? What happened if he had followed him from France? Was this master bowman his mysterious pursuer?

'I am not a liar,' Barleycorn whispered hoarsely. 'I have told you the truth.'

Greenele lifted his head and smiled. 'And then, sir, the truth you shall have back.'

And, pulling his stool closer, the young squire quickly described his early life, the journey to France, Sir Gilbert's sudden death and his return to England. Barleycorn watched him intently: when he had finished, he shook his head.

'It seems strange that a dying man should change the story of your life. Your heart is set on Colchester?'

Greenele nodded. 'I have nothing else to do. Sir Gilbert is dead. All my possessions are what you see. I intend to resolve the mystery.' He paused. He'd glimpsed something in Barleycorn's eyes. Nothing sinister but, as if the man was quietly smiling to himself. Richard felt the hairs on the back of his neck prickle with fear. He pushed his stool back. 'I'd best retire. I still have some distance to go. I thank you for your help and assistance.'

'Sit down. Sit down.'

Barleycorn leaned over and, picking up the wine jug, refilled his companion's cup. The young squire slumped back on the stool.

'I'll come with you,' Barleycorn offered. He lifted a hand. 'I'd value your company: winter's drawing in and sooner or later my luck will run out.'

'It's still yet autumn,' Greenele protested. 'Oh, a cold and biting wind there may be but, the forest's still full of game.'

Barleycorn disagreed. 'I know the weather, within a week it will be freezing. Before St Crispin's Day, the snows will be here. If you don't mind, I'll come with you.'

Greenele couldn't refuse. After all, he reasoned, Barleycorn was a good man in a fight and he preferred to have him with him than, perhaps, trailing quietly behind. So he agreed, finished his wine and said he'd retire to bed. Barleycorn, however, said he would stay downstairs. He had espied a group of pedlars and, grinning from ear to ear, had a pair of dice in his battered wallet.

'Fools and their money are soon parted,' he whispered. 'You go to sleep, young master. I'll see if I can recoup the cost of our meal.'

In the garret on the top storey of the tavern, Greenele undressed, pulling off his boots and securing his money in a secret place. He put a bolt in the arbalest and placed it on the floor, pushing his dagger under the dirty bolster and the sword within hands' reach. He lay down, his mind teeming with the events of the day: the outlaws loping like wolves through the trees; the crash of arms; Barleycorn appearing like the avenging angel. Greenele slipped into sleep and his nightmare re-emerged. He was back in that chamber, this time everything was more finely etched: a well-furnished room with damask tapestries on the walls, woollen rugs on the floor, a night lamp burning beside the small cot bed. He was small, a little boy, yet he could think like an adult. He was crouching in the darkness listening to the fearful shouts from below, cries of murder and treason. The sound of mailed feet on the stairs, a woman bending over him, she had the most beautiful skin, golden with sea-grey eyes but behind the beauty, panic, terror. The gruff tones of a man's voice could be heard. He was snatched up: the woman was holding him; they were going towards the door, swords were flashing . . .

Richard sat up in bed and stared around. He had to remind himself that he was in the garret of the White Harte in the village of Woodforde and that he had just been visited by a succubus, a night demon. He fumbled for the tinder and struck the tallow candle in its pewter holder on the table beside the bed. The mattress across the room was unoccupied. Barleycorn was apparently still gambling in the taproom. Richard felt cold.

Getting out of bed, he tiptoed across the icy boards, to close the shutters. He jumped as a rat, fat and brown, scuttled across to disappear into some hole in the dark corner. Richard closed the shutters. There were no sounds from the taproom below.

He took the blanket from the bed, wrapped it round his shoulders and opened the door. It was pitch dark on the stairs leading down. He could hear nothing but the squeak of foraging rats. He went to the top of the stairs and glimpsed the amber eyes of a cat staring up at him. If the taproom was empty, Richard thought; if the tavern was all asleep, the rats were bold enough to forage and the cats to hunt. Where was Barleycorn? He tiptoed back to his room, closed the door and re-opened the shutters. The garret window, no more than a small lattice door covered with fly-blown horn paper, overlooked the trackway. Richard opened this, flinching as the cold night air burst in. He could see the glow of light from the lantern horn which swung on a hook outside the tavern door but little else. The night sky was clear and the stars, glinting like jewels on a velvet cushion. Everything else was black. Richard stood and shivered, ears straining into the darkness. Then he heard it. The gentle clop of a horse but different as if the rider had placed woollen cloths over his mount's hooves to muffle any sound. Richard went across, blew out the candle and returned to stand by the window. Out of the darkness a rider came, cloaked and cowled, a shadow darker than the rest and there, slightly in front of him, Cuthbert Barleycorn. There was a murmur of voices. Straining his eyes, Richard saw Cuthbert raise his hands, then the mysterious rider turned and disappeared into the night.

By the time Cuthbert, as soft-footed as a cat, entered the chamber, Richard was back in bed pretending to be asleep, blankets pulled well over his head. He lay there, breathing deeply, even as he listened to the faint sounds of his companion preparing for bed. Richard's eyes grew heavy, his breathing slower. Nevertheless, even as he slipped once again into sleep, he wondered if his meeting with Cuthbert was accidental? Had Barleycorn arranged that attack? Was Barleycorn one of the outlaws?

The same questions nagged at him the next morning when he and the master bowman broke their fast in the taproom on greasy smoked bacon, bread and rather curdled cheese. There was none of the bonhomie from the night before. The room was cold, the landlord less genial and the fire didn't burn so merrily in the great hearth.

'Did you win at dice last night?' Richard asked innocently.

'Some coins,' Barleycorn answered, not raising his head. 'But not enough. So I decided to walk up to the church and back, clear my head of the fug.'

Richard nodded understandingly but, as he saddled up Bayard in the cobbled courtyard, he began to wonder at the wisdom of allowing Barleycorn to accompany him. It was still dark when they left the tavern with only faint streaks of light in the sky. The bells of St Mary's were tolling out across the village so Richard decided to stop for Mass. He knelt, just within the rood screen of the simple, rough-hewn church, whilst the parson, dressed in gorgeous robes, celebrated a low Mass. Throughout the service Greenele watched Barleycorn intently, noticing how the archer's lips moved in answer to the prayers. An educated man, Greenele concluded, with some knowledge of Latin: devout in his devotions. Like Richard, he took the communion wafer and drank from the chalice. Nor did the venerable, ascetic-looking priest show any surprise at his presence so Greenele felt a little comforted. A village priest would know most of the men and women who lived in his area and would certainly refuse the sacrament to a known outlaw. After Mass they stopped for a while to chat to the priest, discussing the war in France and the king's demands for supplies and fresh men. Then they left the village, taking the Epping road as the sun grew higher and stronger in a pale blue sky.

Barleycorn proved to be an ideal companion, a source of amusing stories on forest lore. He chattered like a magpie, putting Richard more at his ease. Just before mid-day they reined in and stopped at a ramshackle ale-house which stood in a small clearing on the edge of the forest. Once again Richard noticed how the landlord and his slatterns and servants showed no recognition of Barleycorn.

'What's the matter?' The bowman licked his horn spoon clean: he pushed the earthenware bowl away from him and placed his horn spoon back in his pouch. 'All morning you have been watching me like a cat does a mouse.'

'I just wondered,' Richard retorted, 'how is it that, an outlaw, a man like yourself, a verderer, is not known or recognised either by the priest in Woodforde, the landlord there or anyone here?'

'Because I am also a stranger,' his companion replied. 'And we are off the beaten path here.' Barleycorn beat his fingers on the grease-laden table. He stared up at a leg of ham hanging from the rafters to be cured by the smoke which spiralled like mist across the taproom. 'I keep well away from the villages,' he said softly. 'God's open air is better than the fug of man. Come, we ought to go.'

The squire could not object so they continued along the path to the small village of Theydon Bois. As soon as they were past the first cottages, Greenele sensed there was something wrong. Dogs barked from within locked doors but no children played; no old people sat on the rough, wooden benches trying to catch the last of the autumn sun; no women worked in the small garden plots with hoe or mattock. An eerie silence held, broken now and again by the occasional cry or shout. Barleycorn, walking slightly in front of Greenele, raised his hand.

'What is it?' the squire asked. 'Pestilence? Outlaws?'

Barleycorn shook his head. 'No, no, listen.'

Greenele leaned forward on his horse. The cries were more

distinct: shouts, curses, then he caught the smell of wood-smoke, thick and heavy on the air.

'They are burning someone,' Barleycorn declared. 'You can always tell.' He pointed up and Richard saw great black puffs of smoke against the autumn sky. 'It's none of our business,' the bowman muttered. 'We can take another path.'

Greenele shook his head. 'I am curious.' He smiled bleakly. 'Who knows, it might be someone innocent.'

They walked on along the dirty, rutted trackway which served as a high street and round the corner. Here the path ran into a broad expanse where the market would usually stand but now it was thronged with people: men from the fields, women with bare-footed children clinging to their dusty skirts. They were all gathered round a tall column of wood heaped high with brushwood, about five yards in front of the village cross. On a high-wheeled cart next to it, stood a cluster of men, all holding a prisoner. They watched as their fellows heaped more brush-wood against the execution stake. On the other side, a blacksmith, with poker and bellows, had set a huge fire raging in a great iron brazier. Now and again he would place more brushwood on, sending the flames and smoke soaring into the sky.

'What's happening?' Greenele murmured, reining in, ignoring the curious looks as some of the villagers turned.

'They are going to burn the prisoner,' Barleycorn replied. 'And they intend to do it fast. He will be lashed to the beam, that brazier will be dragged towards the brushwood and its contents thrown on.'

'What crime has he committed?' Greenele asked a man resting on a staff, a small mongrel dog lying between his feet.

'I am just passing through,' the man replied. 'Looking for work.' He nodded towards the cart. 'But I think they have caught a warlock and intend to burn him.'

'I'm innocent!' the man in the cart shouted, breaking free

33

from his captors. He grasped the edge of the tumbril and stared wildly at the crowd. He was tall, thin as a bean-pole, ashen-faced, his eyes rounded in terror, his red greasy hair stood up in spikes. His clothes were dirty, weather-stained; his jerkin greasy with threadbare hose pushed into battered boots. 'I'm innocent!' he screamed. His eyes caught those of Greenele. 'All I did was cure the old woman!'

'No one could do that!' someone shouted back. 'Unless he's in league with Satan!'

'You've got the sign on your face!' a woman shouted and Greenele, peering closer, saw the 'W' for warlock branded on the man's right cheek.

'That was a mistake too,' the prisoner pleaded despairingly.

The crowd just roared with laughter; they began to throw rotten vegetables and clods of mud towards the cart. The prisoner, his arms now more firmly pinioned by his captors, stared beseechingly at Greenele. His gaze reminded the squire of a frightened child. He leaned down, patting Bayard's neck.

'He's innocent,' the squire whispered. 'He's probably some travelling quack who has performed a miraculous cure. Now someone has decided to settle scores.'

Richard edged his horse through the crowd, not caring whether Barleycorn followed or not. The men and women, tough, seamed faces burnt brown by the sun, glared suspiciously at him, almost aware that the stranger was going to spoil their day's fun. After all, such burnings were rare. The execution of a warlock, the destruction of his body and the scattering of his ashes on the crossroads at midnight would keep them talking till Yuletide. Greenele reined in before the cart and stared at the prisoner's face.

'What's your name?' he asked.

'Gildas.'

Greenele could see the man's face was bruised and bloody froth bubbled at the corner of his mouth. He was lean visaged, dirty, yet his speech was good. Greenele glimpsed the intelligence in the man's eyes though his face showed a consummate actor, a man used to lying and deception.

'Where did you get the brand?' Greenele asked.

'At Hertford,' the fellow replied, trying to struggle free from the burly peasants who hung onto his arms. 'I was a priest,' Gildas continued. His face cracked into a smile, 'I was thrown out of my living because of a woman. I received the brand because I cured a merchant when his physician could not.'

'What's all this then?'

A small, fat, pompous man clothed in a green robe, came from behind the prisoner, pushing back his shabby beaver hat. His little eyes, snub nose, pert mouth and clean-shaven, quivering cheeks reminded the squire of a pig's face. Around his neck hung some seal of office. He stuck his thumbs into the torn, leather belt round his bulging middle and stood at the rails of the cart glaring malevolently at the newcomer.

'What's all this then?' he repeated. 'Who are you?'

Behind him Greenele felt the people closing in. Gildas, licking his lips, stared nervously at the thickset blacksmith who stood feeding the brazier like some demon from hell.

'My name's Richard Greenele, I am the King's messenger, taking news of his son's great victory at Poitiers to the town of Colchester.' Greenele drew his sword and pushed the tip of the blade close to Pig-Face's chin. 'How dare you speak to a royal messenger like that, sir?'

'I am John Southgate, apothecary and leech,' Pig-Face stuttered. 'This man is landless, with no parish or letters of approval. He came into the village, practised medicine and gave Goodwoman Bartleby magic potions and herbs. He cured her of the sickness when, by all rights, she should be dead. Isn't that right, Robert?' Pig-Face turned and stared at a mean-eyed, choleric-faced man who stood at the tail of the cart.

35

'I am the reeve,' Mean-Face explained. 'I have the authority to arrest in this village.'

'But not to execute a man without trial!'

The reeve's grimy face broke into a sneer. 'We are not simpletons, sir.' He bent down and dragged from beneath the cart a set of battered saddlebags. He opened one and drew out a yellowing skull, amulets, small bags of powder, a crude drawing of a demon carved on a piece of rock and, finally, the shrunken head of a cat. 'He's a black magician,' the reeve continued, throwing the stuff back into the bag and offering it to Greenele.

The squire snatched it from him.

'I just carry them,' Gildas whimpered. 'To perform tricks and to earn a penny to buy a crust.'

'The fire's ready!' the blacksmith bellowed.

The peasants began to pull Gildas from the cart. Suddenly an arrow zipped over their heads, smacking into the market cross behind. Cuthbert Barleycorn, another arrow to his bow, came swaggering through the crowd, who quickly drew away. He took up position, lifted the how, pointing the arrow straight at Pig-Face's fat belly.

'We are king's men,' the bowman said quietly. 'This man is to be executed without fair trial. He should be questioned by the royal justices who have the right to condemn. If he's guilty, he also has the right to be shriven by a priest.'

Greenele stared round the crowd. 'Where is your priest?'

'He's in his church,' the reeve sneered. 'Locked himself in he has.' His sneer faded as he realised the implications of his words.

Greenele saw the look of sheer terror in the prisoner's eyes.

'Release the man!' he urged. 'Give him into our care and, I swear, I'll take him to Colchester, to the king's gaol.'

'The great pestilence rages there,' the reeve screamed.

'In which case,' the squire replied. 'You have a choice. You can kill your prisoner and I'll arrest you for murder and take you there. Or, you can release him into my custody and I'll see justice done.'

The fat reeve almost scrambled from the cart, shouting out orders. The crowd murmured its disapproval but others, perhaps not so eager to see a man burn, supported Greenele. The squire threw the saddlebags over the horn of his saddle and ordered Gildas' hands to be bound.

A short while later, he and Barleycorn, their prisoner in tow, were out of Theydon Bois and back along the forest road to Colchester. They travelled in silence for a while. Greenele knew that some of the villagers might become suspicious and follow them, or even send a rider to demand warrants, proof of identity. Gildas, however, was delighted to be free.

'Curse them!' he roared. 'May their lot be as the Amalekites! May the Lord strike them hip and thigh. May they fall in the pit of Dathan and may their lot be with the dogs of Bashan!'

'Shut up!' Barleycorn snapped and jerked at the rope. Greenele reined in, dismounted and drew his dagger. He cut the rope, went back to his horse and tossed the battered saddlebags at Gildas' feet.

'You are free to go!' he declared.

Gildas fell to his knees, clasping his hands before him, eyes closed. He pulled such a pitiful face, Greenele found it hard not to laugh.

'I am a worm and no man,' Gildas intoned. 'A mere scratch on God's creation.' He opened one eye. 'I have no money, master. No friends, no food, no horse.'

'And, if you don't start running,' Barleycorn snarled, 'you'll have no nose!'

Gildas opened the other eye. 'I set my face like flint,' he continued lugubriously. 'Against those who taunt me. The Lord will rescue me from the hunters' snare and he will...'

'Quite. Quite.' Greenele came over and pulled the man to his feet. 'What is it you want?'

Gildas smiled. Greenele realised he was a very young man, a mummer who could change his appearance to suit his needs.

'What is it you want?' the squire repeated.

'To be your friend, master.' He stepped back, studying Greenele closely. 'You have a man's eyes but a boy's face. Your mouth is kind and those green eyes have no malice in them.' He pointed to Richard's auburn hair. 'An old witch told me that such a person would save me.' His eyes grew wider. 'Accompanied by a warrior, a veritable David to take on Goliath.'

Greenele laughed and stepped back. 'So, you are a warlock?'

Gildas shook his head. 'No, master, no, just someone who knows all the tricks of the fair. I'd like to accompany you, where you go, I follow.' He suddenly pulled down his ragged jerkin. Greenele flinched at the red cord mark which circled the man's throat like a purple necklace. 'Twice, master, I have looked into the face of death: the midnight destroyer, the demon which prowls at mid-day. Next time I will not be so fortunate.' He clasped his hands as if he was about to sink to his knees again.

Greenele looked at Barleycorn who shrugged, hawked and spat into the bushes.

'I am a good cook,' Gildas pleaded. 'Sharp with the knife.'

'Oh, for Lord's sake, you can come with us!'

Greenele remounted and, with Gildas singing his praises, they rode on, the squire wondering how many others would join him on his journey to Colchester.

They spent that night out in the open, under the trees, keeping close to a roaring fire. Greenele recalled Barleycorn's warning about the change in weather. The night proved bitterly cold and, even with their thick cloaks and constant feeding of the flames, they woke freezing, teeth chattering, eager to move on. Later that day they left the forest, spent the night at a tavern and then took the road to Colchester. Progress became slow as crowds thronged the highway, fleeing from the pestilence now raging in the city; carts piled high with possessions, the old and sick being removed in wheelbarrows. Proud ladies in their clumsy carriages, powerful merchants on palfreys. All had just one ambition; to put as much distance between themselves and the plague. People kept to themselves, cloaks pulled high over nose and mouth against the contagion in the air. Roadside taverns were closed. Farmhouses and the solitary, peasants' cottages were firmly boarded up. Anyone who approached would be driven off with curses, threats, sticks, stones or snarling guard dogs. So thick was the crush that, at last, Barleycorn said they would have to take a different route into the city and led them off down narrow, winding country lanes.

Gildas was now quiet though, now and again, he'd sniff the air and exclaim about the fetid, sickening fumes. Greenele ignored him but, at last, he, too, caught a strange stench and became uneasy. The day was beginning to die. A thick mist came swirling over deserted fields. Greenele wondered how difficult it would be to find their way when darkness fell when, through the fog, appeared a dull red glow. He heard the crackle and hiss of flames and suddenly came upon a bonfire built up in the centre of a track. They passed this, the fire had burnt off some of the fog and they glimpsed small houses; one, with an ale-stake pushed under its eaves, showed they were entering some lonely village. Along the trackway other fires burnt, giving off an oily, suffocating smoke which drifted through the air, writhing its tendrils around them.

'It smells of brimstone,' Gildas exclaimed, covering his mouth and pinching his nose with his fingers. 'They are stupid if they think this will drive off the plague.'

Greenele lifted himself up in his stirrups and pointed further down the trackway.

'There are other fires down there,' he noticed. 'And a small fortified manor house.'

He turned away, coughing, his eyes watering, fighting hard to keep a restless Bayard quiet. They moved on. No living thing moved in the village streets. As Gildas commented, it was like entering the land of the dead. No sound, no light, no open window or door. At last the trackway wound towards the manor walls and the shallow, dry moat around it. The wooden drawbridge, however, was raised flat against the portcullis.

'God and his Angels!' said Gildas in shock. 'Look! May the Lord shield us, Master Barleycorn!'

On the side of the drawbridge was painted a red cross at least four feet high.

'There's plaque in the manor,' Greenele declared. He dragged his eyes from the plague cross and listened, his hands on Bayard's reins trembling a little. Suddenly a shutter above the drawbridge opened and a man's helmeted head came out.

'What do you want?' the man shouted. 'We have no kiss of welcome to give you. Death lives here!'

'By all that's holy!' Richard cried. 'What's happened?'

'Sixteen of us are dead. God shrive them for we have no priest. The chaplain died first, five nights ago, and the others followed him.'

Richard drew back.

'It's the same throughout the village!' the man continued. 'At the top of the hill you'll find a farm house. God knows if they are dead or not!'

Richard thanked the man and rode on. The mist and fires gave the village a garish, demonic look. All the houses were shuttered, many of them with red crosses daubed on their doors. Now and again a shape would pad quietly through the darkness. The road began to climb and at the top they passed through the half-open gate of the farm and into the yard. On the cobblestones near a well, more plague fires burned. An old woman, in a soot-tarnished red and grey dress, was throwing handfuls of yellow sulphur on to smouldering logs. She raised her shaggy head and looked at them dully. Two other figures moved across the yard. They were hooded and masked in black cloth and carried shovels in their hands. Some of the cobblestones had been lifted. Richard pushed Bayard closer: he saw a long ditch had been dug. On its rim lay a bumpy pile of corpses covered by a blood-stained, tattered sheet. The stench from this heap was noisome and bitter despite the sulphur fumes from the fire.

Richard sat, fascinated by that terrible pyre of corpses. One of the hooded men brought a little hand-bell from beneath his cloak and jingled it. He put the bell on the ground as two more hooded figures came out of the mist. They silently dragged a lean figure with long, black hair from the pile. A blue spotted hand protruded from beneath the death cloth as the masked figures tossed it into the ditch.

Greenele had seen enough and, turning his horse, he and his companions fled through the night.

Chapter 3

They passed similar scenes all along the way to Colchester; deserted villages, boarded-up houses. In one village they passed through, the people seemed to have gone mad. In the small market place they had found a group of young people naked, except for their shifts, their faces covered by goat masks, dancing drunkenly and coupling on the ground as if this pursuit of pleasure would drive the plague away. The squire and his group hastened on.

'I've seen the same thing happen in France,' Barleycorn muttered. He glanced at Gildas who had fallen strangely quiet since they'd entered this valley of death. 'I thought you were the great healer? Can't you do anything?'

'Not with the buboes or yellow pus,' the charlatan replied. 'Certain fevers and sickness, yes. I make a philtre out of the juice of crushed fern moss and mix it with stale milk. I learnt it from a Berber who comes from the land south of the pillars of Hercules. Sometimes it works and sometimes it doesn't.'

Colchester was no different; its stinking streets, the sky

blocked out by high, leaning houses, were inhabited by ghosts. No church bells rang. No market or stalls stood open. Nothing, but an eerie silence broken, now and again, by the rattling of the death cart or the howl of some dog. Occasionally they would pass a friar, cowl pulled over his head, slipping along the alley to give spiritual comfort to the families imprisoned behind their red-daubed doors. Some soldiers from the castle patrolled the streets but they looked like phantasms out of hell, their faces hidden behind visored helmets. They all carried crossbows and, when Richard and his party drew closer, drove them off with muffled curses. The plunderers were also there. The outlaws, wolvesheads and villains: they flitted like bats through the streets, preying on the helpless, stealthily entering houses to finish off the dying and plunder their goods. At last the young squire drew his party into a cemetery and, whilst Bayard cropped the grass, sat on a weather-beaten tombstone and gazed bleakly at Barleycorn.

'How do I find Hugo Coticol?' he demanded. 'No one will stop. No one will talk.'

Smoke and mist billowed across the derelict graveyard.

'I should have stayed in France,' he added bitterly, then stared round: 'Where's Gildas?'

He heard a sound from behind the lych-gate: the warlock reappeared, dragging a thin, greasy-haired, rat-faced man. Gildas' dagger was pressed firmly into the side of his hapless victim's neck.

'Who's your friend?' Barleycorn asked.

'It's just a matter of where you look,' Gildas replied. His voice rose. 'The Lord will look after his own. He will deliver us from the hand of the ...!'

'Shut up!' Barleycorn growled.

'This is Simpkin,' Gildas replied. 'He's a thief and should hang. I caught him plundering the stores of a tavern just across the street.'

Simpkin's protruding front teeth made him even more rat-like in appearance.

'I am hungry,' he wailed. 'A man has to eat.'

'And you can eat what you want,' Gildas replied. 'Once you have taken us to the lawyer, Hugo Coticol.'

Simpkin quickly agreed. He led Greenele and his companions out of the graveyard and through a maze of streets. Now and again they stopped, Simpkin would call out to some cowled figure creeping along an alleyway, ask directions then they'd move on. They returned to the market place past the church and down a narrow alleyway. On one side was an apothecary's shop, all boarded up. On the other, a large three-storeyed house with a brick base, the upper tiers a mixture of white gleaming plaster and smart black beams. Nevertheless, every window was shuttered. On the front door was a great red cross with the words, 'JESU MISERERE' daubed beneath.

'This is Hugo Coticol's house, the lawyer?' Gildas shook Simpkin by the scruff of his neck.

'Yes!' the man yelped. 'I have kept my promise. Keep yours!'

Gildas let go of him and Simpkin disappeared like a whippet down the alleyway. For a while they hammered on the door but there was no reply.

'They are all gone,' Gildas murmured. 'Or dead as nails.'

'I must speak to Coticol,' Greenele answered. 'Or his representative and see what papers he holds for me. I have travelled far and hard. I am not going away empty-handed.'

He went down a narrow lane at the side of the house. The gate at the bottom was open and he entered a large, pleasant garden with flower beds and herb patches. At the far end was a small orchard with apples and pear trees: their leaves were heaped in a wet, soggy mess and the squire noticed how the fruit lay rotting on the ground. Barleycorn, leading Bayard, joined him. They hammered on the small postern door. Again there was no answer. So, after they had hobbled Bayard, Richard organised

Barleycorn and Gildas to take a garden bench from a small arbour and used this to force the door open. After a great deal of hammering and knocking, the hinges snapped back. The three men stepped carefully into a white-washed, stone, paved passageway. The air was clean, rather fragrant.

'There's someone here,' Greenele whispered. 'There's no smell of death.'

Cautiously they walked past a small, clean-swept scullery and kitchen, up a small flight of stairs towards what must be the door of the parlour. Richard was about to push this open with his sword when he heard a yell: he turned and a crossbow bolt missed his face by a few inches. He flung himself against the wall. Gildas scampered back down the passageway whilst Barleycorn notched an arrow to his bow and hid in the shadow of the stairwell.

'We are friends,' Greenele called up into the darkness. He could just make out a dark shape standing there. 'We mean you no harm.'

Another bolt zipped through the air and Barleycorn, breaking from his hiding-place, sent an arrow whirring up the stairs. Richard heard a scream but the arrow must have missed as he heard it smack into the wood.

'We are friends!' he added hastily. 'We seek Hugo Coticol, the lawyer. Once our visit is done we will go.'

The dark shape reappeared at the top of the stairs.

'Then put your sword down!' The woman's voice was clear and sweet. 'And the bowman, I want him standing next to you!'

'Agreed.'

The dark shape came down the stairs. As she drew closer, Greenele saw a thin but very pretty, oval face, well-arched eyebrows, lustrous lively eyes and a sweet mouth whose lips were quivering, either from anger or fear, he couldn't tell.

'I am Richard Greenele, squire.' He stretched his hand out.

The woman stopped, one hand on the stair-rail. She was

dressed like a nun. A dark-blue veil covered jet-black hair. Her gown was of the finest sarcanet, light-blue and edged with ermine: her slender waist was bound by a silver chain though the boots she wore were scuffed and dirty whilst the dress was stained on the bodice and around the cuffs. Embarrassed by the squire's careful scrutiny, the woman self-consciously wrapped her cloak more closely about her.

'We mean you no harm,' Barleycorn offered. 'But my companion speaks the truth, he seeks Hugo Coticol, lawyer.'

'He's dead.' The woman came down the stairs. 'My father has been gone two weeks. Dead of the plague, his body buried in the great burial pits beyond the walls.' She shook her head. 'I cannot help you.'

'But you must,' Greenele insisted. 'Please, I have travelled from France.'

'I don't have the plague.' She half smiled as Gildas nervously made his appearance. 'All the servants have fled. The death cart man said that if I had no symptoms within a week I was safe. I keep the house clean,' she murmured, rushing her words. 'But there's little food left and there are others who've tried to break in.' Her eyes filled with tears. 'They know I grow weak and they'll be back.'

'Don't you have any kin?' Gildas asked.

'In the north, yes. My father was a widower. Oh, we had clerks and scriveners, maids and tap-boys.' She flailed her hands beneath her cloak. 'But now there's no one.' She sat down on the stairs and leaned her head against the wall. 'I am very hungry,' she declared. 'And slightly drunk. Nothing left but cheese and wine!'

Gildas drew a linen parcel from beneath his cloak and, leaning down before her, opened it. It contained strips of dried salty bacon, two rather stale manchet loaves, an apple, a bruised pear and three or four plums. The woman looked at him.

'Eat,' Gildas offered. 'Don't worry, I took it from a villain called Simpkin.' He smiled over his shoulder at Greenele. 'I am sure her needs are greater than his.'

The woman needed no second bidding. She thanked Gildas, told Richard her name was Emmeline and, without a care in the world, daintily devoured everything in sight. When she had finished, she elegantly wiped her mouth with the tips of her fingers. She then stood up, preening herself, and stared boldly at Greenele who noticed how her large, grey eyes were fringed by dark eye-lashes: her skin was silky smooth with a rose flush high on her cheekbones; her lips were now smiling and Greenele was immediately smitten by the woman's courage and beauty.

'What are you staring at, sir?' she asked coolly.

'Oh, nothing,' he stammered. 'I just wish you could help us.'

'And help I will.'

She opened the door they had first tried to enter and led them into a comfortable but rather darkened parlour. In the far corner she turned the key of a small door and ushered them into a musty chamber where only a narrow, arrow slit window high in the wall provided any light.

'My father's chancery,' she explained, her voice sounding hollow in the darkness.

Greenele heard a tinder strike and the room flared into light as the woman silently lit candles, both in the wall and those which stood under their metal caps in the centre of a small, oval table. The room was bigger than Greenele had expected. It was filled with small coffers and chests, most of them locked; a few, open, spilled their contents out on to the floor: sheaths of documents, rolls of parchments. On the shelves were more documents, indentures, charters and countless letters. Greenele groaned quietly. How on earth, he thought, in all this confusion could he find anything referring to the great mystery Sir Gilbert Savage had gasped out only a few weeks earlier. The squire now felt as if it were years since he had left that muddy, blood-drenched field at Poitiers. He sat down on the chair before the great writing desk, despondently moving aside the ink horns, pumice stones, quills, parchment knives, seals and long strips of red wax. Emmeline, however, more pragmatic, opened up a battered, yellowing folio and ran her finger along a page. Barleycorn and Gildas, realising this was not their business, retreated back into the parlour.

'It'll take an age,' Richard breathed, staring round the dusty chancery room, 'to find anything here concerning me.'

'What are you looking for?' Emmeline asked. 'I never heard Father mention your name.' She looked up archly. 'Which is?'

'Richard Greenele,' he replied. 'Squire to Sir Gilbert Savage.' He smiled bleakly. 'A poor knight, not from these parts.'

'Well, well, well!' she replied caustically. 'Richard Greenele, squire to the late Sir Gilbert Savage, a poor knight, not from these parts.'

She glanced up again, the squire grinned at her perfect mimicry.

'It is important,' he declared, getting to his feet. 'Sir Gilbert, whilst he lay dying at Poitiers, told me that I was to come to Master Hugo Coticol, lawyer of Colchester: he would give me the true secrets of my birth and family.' He pointed to the folio. 'What are you looking at?'

'My father was most meticulous. He kept good records and this was his index. I never heard him mention your name. However,' she turned to the back of the folio and jabbed at the title, 'RES SECRETAE, secret matters,' she explained and ran her finger down the page. 'Oh, yes, here: Item thirteen – R.G. and G.S.'

'Richard Greenele and Gilbert Savage!' the squire exclaimed.

He peered over her shoulder, not only interested in the item but rather excited at being so close, able to study the soft curves of her cheek and savour her faint perfume. He glanced at the date next to the entry: Anno Domini 1340.

'Sixteen years ago!' he said excitedly.

Emmeline closed the folio with a snap then, finger to her lips, looked at the shelves around her. She pointed to a small set of steps in the corner.

'Bring those across, please!'

Richard obeyed. Emmeline daintily climbed the steps, fingers to her lips, looking up at the darkened shelves. She sighed and came back down carrying a dusty, canvas bag, tied at the neck by a white cord with three seals attached. On one of these was a small tag. Emmeline took this over to the counter.

'Yes, this belongs to you, Richard Greenele.' She tossed it across.

Richard caught it and sat down at the desk. Taking up a knife, he cut the cord, opened the neck of the sack and sneezed at the dust which blew up into his face. He drew out a small roll of parchment and unwound it. He studied the roll quickly: five sheets, all sewn together, covered in neat, precise writing. The blue-green ink was beginning to fade though the parchment was of the best quality.

'It's in my father's hand,' Emmeline declared, looking over his shoulder. 'He was well known for his calligraphy.'

Richard smiled up at her. She blushed.

'As well as his honesty.' She looked round the chancery room. 'God knows what secrets are kept here.' She pressed Richard on the shoulder. 'I will leave you. Do you want some wine?'

'Yes, yes,' Richard replied absentmindedly. 'Mixed with some water please.' He pulled the manuscript roll closer and began to read.

'In the name of the Father and of the Son and of the Holy Ghost, I, Roger Greenele, knight, baron, member of the King's Privy Council, Lord of the manor of Crokehurst in Essex with all its fields, barns, granges and appurtenances

50

do now take the Holy Trinity and the blessed Virgin Mary as my witness that, what I dictate here to Hugo Coticol, my attorney, is the truth.'

The squire stopped reading and his jaw fell.
'Crokehurst!' he breathed.
'It's further north,' Emmeline declared, putting the wine down on the table. 'On the Essex coast. Father once told me. It's haunted and deserted. According to royal edict, no man can go there. The house and its demesne have fallen into decay.' She saw how pale Richard's face had become. 'I'd best leave you,' she murmured.
Greenele picked up the cup, gulped from it and continued reading.

'I write this letter to my heir. I have already given instructions to my trusty yeoman, Gilbert Savage whom I myself have knighted, to look after my baby son. However, God willing, once my son has passed his eighteenth year, Gilbert, as his mortal soul depends on it, is to instruct him to come to Hugo Coticol, my attorney in Colchester. He will then learn the truth about his inheritance as well as the foulsome treachery which killed his mother and plunged his father into terrible disgrace.

I love you, my son, only two years old. I have held you in my arms and pressed my face against yours. I, and your mother Maria, would have dearly loved to see you grow to manhood, carry on the family name and inherit the title, manor and lands of Crokehurst. Satan, however, has risen up from hell. He has taken camp, set up his standard in my world and the Gates of Hell have prevailed against me. Time is short but, before I begin, remember three things: first, your mother and I loved you deeply; secondly, I am innocent of all charges levelled against me; finally, I am

51

prepared to lay my life down and spend eternity demanding that the good Lord sees justice done. Remember me.'

Richard stopped. Try as he might, the hot scalding tears began to run down his face. He threw the paper aside and put his face in his hands and, for a while, sobbed bitterly. He had a presentiment about what he was about to read. He now realised those nightmares were not phantasms or the work of some succubus but a brief flicker of what once had been. Tattered memories when, as a child, his world had smashed to pieces. He dried his cheeks and picked the parchment.

'The name Greenele is an ancient one. And the manor of Crokehurst has always been in our tenure, even before the days of the Conqueror. My grandfather, and his father before him, were the most loyal knights of the Crown. Never once in our history did the King ever ask for our sword or support and was refused. I was no different. The King's own knight, his friend and body companion. I was with him in all his trials, both at home and abroad. I grew strong and powerful in the royal service. I was allowed to marry a woman I loved. She bore me the son I'd always prayed for. Life was pleasant, rich and full. Perhaps that's where I committed my sin. Proud and ambitious, I was unaware of the shadows gathering around me.

My Lord, Baron Simon Fitzalan and his Lady Catherine, were constant companions and visitors to Crokehurst. We jousted, gambled, hunted and hawked whilst our ladies chattered, gossiped and teased us mercilessly. I was proud of my retinue, five knights bold and courageous: Sir Philip Ferrers, Sir Lionel Beaumont, Sir Walter Manning, Sir John Bremner and Sir Henry Grantham. These were my men, both in peace and war, each holding manors and lands in Essex. Baron Simon and myself, together with the

above-mentioned knights, had won great honour on the
battlefields of France.

I came home early in 1340 when you were two years old.
The summer proved to be a glorious one, the crops were
ripe and plentiful. We coursed the golden hare and hunted
its enemy, the russet fox. I checked my fields, barns and
granges and feasted at my table. Perhaps I did not thank
God for all the great gifts he had sent me. However, not
everything in my life was clear and pure. His Grace the
King had sent messages to both myself and Baron Simon
Fitzalan: how fishermen on the Essex coast had seen
French galleys nosing in and out of the deserted inlets
there. Accordingly, the King believed, as did his principal
ministers, that there was a traitor in Essex, one of the lords
of the soil selling secrets to his enemies abroad.

Now, in mid-summer of 1340, Baron Simon and the Lady
Catherine came to stay with us; this time we had business as
well as pleasure to pursue. Baron Simon believed that one
of my knights was the traitor. He pointed out that all five
held lands near the Essex coast and, being Commissioners
of Array and men of stature in the county, were well placed
to pass on the King's secrets, the movement of his troops
and the strength of his castles to his enemies. At first I was
aghast, loud in my protests of innocence. Lord Simon,
however, was adamant. He would sit in my chancery office
or, in the evening, walk with me through the cool orchards
of Crokehurst. We studied maps, the reports of these
galleys and, slowly, grudgingly, I accepted the truth. At the
King's request, I summoned all five knights to my manor.
Oh, I hailed them as friends. I treated them like honoured
guests, we feasted and tourneyed. On the evening of their
second week at Crokehurst, however, after supper when
the ladies had withdrawn, the servants dismissed, the doors
closed, I told them the real purpose of my summons. How

they raged, demanding proof, hands going to swords and daggers but Lord Simon intervened: coolly and incisively, he presented the same facts as he had to me. They protested their innocence and I could make no sense of it. The meeting broke up: that night, and for the rest of the following day, we did not meet again. Each knight stayed in his chamber, writing out, at my request, a careful reflection of the charges levelled against them all...'

'Richard, Richard, are you all right?'
The squire looked up. Barleycorn was standing in the doorway, hands on his dagger, looking at him strangely.
'Good Lord!' the bowman whispered. 'You look as if you've seen a ghost!'
'I have,' Richard breathed back. 'Lord have mercy, Cuthbert, leave me alone!'
He went back to the manuscript.

'On the following night, the atmosphere in the manor was so tense everyone stayed away from each other. I grew concerned. I spoke with Lord Simon and asked if troops should be sent for or that I should arm some of my own retainers. Lord Simon said there was no need.

Now, every night, before I retired, I always walked out to the edge of the island. I would stand staring at the water: the sweet smell of the lake, the night cries of the birds and the beautiful sunset always calmed my soul. That last terrible night was no different. I was near the Causeway which was invariably flooded when I heard a sound in the trees behind me. I knew that island like the palm of my hand. I became nervous and watchful, believing that someone was in the trees behind me. Oh, I wish I had immediately acted on the warning given. Someone attacked me, struck me a blow on the back of my head. When I awoke I was lying on the straw in one of my outhouses. My five knights and members of Lord Simon's retinue, swords drawn, were standing over me. I was pulled roughly to my feet. My head ached, my mouth felt sour. In my hand was my dagger, covered in blood from tip to handle. There was blood on my clothes and I stank of wine fumes, beside me in the straw lay an earthenware jug. Lord Simon's retainers were in a murderous rage. One of them pushed me in the chest and called me an assassin, I was too confused to understand what he was saying. Philip Ferrers, my leading household knight, had tears in his eyes.

"Lord Roger," he exclaimed, "do you know what you have done?"

Outside, from the manor house I could hear my own wife scream. I tried to push them away but my arms were held fast.

"Show him!" someone cried. "Show the assassin what he has done!"

They dragged me out. Being summer, the day had begun and the sun was already rising in the sky. I was led out into the manor yard and back down towards the Causeway. My head still throbbed and, despite my questions, I could not find out why my clothes were stained with wine and blood. Or why my dagger had been clutched in my hand? They pushed me on into the trees along the small path leading down to the lake. Lord be my witness, I almost swooned at the sight! Lying on the grass, eyes staring, head thrown back, sprawled Lady Catherine Fitzalan. Her dress was pulled over her knees: her throat had been cut from ear to ear, her face was a blueish-white. I shall never forget the terror in those eyes whilst, by the disgraceful sprawl of her body, I could see she had been ravished before being murdered. Fitzalan's retainers began to curse and even strike me. My own knights protected me. I was led back to the manor, now aware that, because of the state of my clothes and the dagger in my hand, I was cast as Lady Catherine's murderer.

I was loud in my protests of innocence, demanding to see the Lord Simon. At this, even my own knights betrayed their feelings with fearful looks and whispering amongst themselves. Once back in the manor I found the reason why. Lord Simon's corpse, a death wound in his chest, lay on his chanter floor where, one of my knights explained, he had been found.

God be my witness, for the first time in my life I swooned out of sheer terror. When I awoke I was a prisoner in my own chamber. Your mother, distraught beside me. Now the Lady Maria was as gentle as a fawn, she lived a golden life, well protected from the horrors of life. Even then, only a few hours after those two dreadful murders had taken place, her mind was already unhinged. I did what I could to comfort her. I demanded my baby son be brought to me but all such pleas and entreaties were ignored.

Later that day the sheriff and his posse arrived. I was arrested for the murder of Lord Simon and his wife, loaded with chains and taken to Colchester Castle. The Lady Maria, her wits now wandering, was sent to a convent. The only man I could really trust, my yeoman Gilbert Savage, plucked you from your bed and took you as his own. What could I say? How could I plead? Not even the king himself could save me. I had been found stained with the Fitzalans' blood, apparently as drunk as a sot, still carrying the murder knife.

I was committed for trial before the Justices of Eyre. I pleaded my innocence but could offer no proof whilst the royal serjeant of law implied that not only was I an assassin but the traitor conveying information to the French. The verdict was that I should suffer the full rigours of the penalty for treason as well as the destruction of my family name and the seizure of my property. I was to be taken to the common scaffold where I would be hanged until half-dead then cut down, disembowelled, my head struck off and my body quartered. During the trial my five knights protested my innocence, taking great oaths that I was a good and honourable man. Yet, even as they swore, I realised one, or more, must be a liar. But what proof did I have? Not a shred, not a whit. Nevertheless, one of these five men must have ravished and murdered the Lady Catherine, killed her husband, struck me unconscious and then arranged the evidence to render me guilty. Even as I dictate this letter I still do not know. I cannot lay the finger of blame against any of them.

Once sentence was passed, I was committed to Colchester castle to await the day of execution. All five knights visited me. Each offered comfort and solace. Gilbert Savage came last. I knighted him there in my prison cell. I had the power to do this. Only on the day of execution, when my spurs would be hacked off, would I lose that right. Gilbert brought me ill news. My wife, your mother, the Lady Maria, had died in the convent. At first I thought it was suicide but Gilbert assured me that the good nuns at Amhurst said she simply slipped away and fell in to a deep sleep from which she never woke. Who says you cannot die of a broken heart?

Gilbert's head was full of madcap schemes. He brought me a knife, a purse of gold and, on the evening after he left, I bribed the gaoler and made my escape from Colchester castle. God knows what story the fellow told his masters. I left with one desire, to find the true assassin, bring him to justice and clear my name. I fled to the house of my good friend Hugo Coticol. He had heard the news. I swore a great oath on his Bible that I was innocent of any crime and he believed me. He provided me with a change of clothing, money and arms. I also thought of the future. My wife, God rest her, was dead. My family escutcheon taken down from the King's chapel in Windsor. The charge of treason and murder lay against my family name and so, before I left this house, I dictated this letter.

I have told you the truth. I can say no more. If God is good. If there is a time under heaven for justice to flourish, I will clear my name. I have taken a great oath on this, the Feast of St Michael, St Raphael and St Gabriel, the three angel lords who lead the heavenly host. If justice is done, I shall journey to Jerusalem and spend my life defending the pilgrims of God. Given this day, 29th September in the 13th year of King Edward III's reign 1340.'

There was another sheet attached. Richard heard a sound at the door. He lifted his head, not daring to turn because of the tears in his eyes.

'Go away,' he whispered. 'Please go away.'

He looked down at what was written in Hugo Coticol's hand: a Memorandum dated the 13th October, the same year, on the Feast of Edward the Confessor.

'Ill news has come to us,' Coticol wrote. 'Sir Roger Greenele did not see justice done. His body was plucked from the river Stour near Blacklock Mill. The face and body were bruised and marked but his corpse was recognised by two of his retainers. He lies buried in St Mary's church, Colchester, in an unmarked grave. May God have mercy on his soul!'

The squire blinked as he heard the footfall behind him.

'What is it?' he snapped.

'Sir,' Barleycorn hissed. 'I am sorry to intrude but Dogwort and Ratsbane are in Colchester!'

Chapter 4

Richard put the documents down and followed Barleycorn up the stairs into a bed chamber. The shutters on the window were open, the mullion glass had been cleaned. Greenele stared down into the darkening street: in the pool of light from a sconce torch pushed into a wall, he glimpsed a group of figures. They stepped closer into the light. Greenele gasped. They were phantasms out of a nightmare. Five men, dressed in motley garb, were heavily armed with swords, dirks and daggers swinging from leather baldrics and belts. They all wore good riding boots; bows and arbalests were slung across their backs. All, except one, had their faces hidden behind leather, metal-studded masks which made them look grotesque. One even had the antler horns of a deer on his head. The unmasked man had a lean, cruel visage, one eye covered with a patch. The men were talking and pointing across the street to the houses.

'Are they hunting you?' Greenele whispered, drawing back from the window.

'I doubt it,' Barleycorn answered. 'If they knew I was here

they would attack. The contagion has drawn them out of the forest. The day I rescued you, I wondered where the rest were. The prospect of easy plunder, food and drink, particularly as winter draws on, has brought them into the towns. Once the contagion passes and law and order is re-imposed, they will disappear like shadows in the sunlight.'

'They have been here before.'

Greenele whirled round. Emmeline stood in the centre of the room, a hand resting on one of the bedposts.

'They look fearsome, don't they? Two days ago they broke into a house further down the street. The city watch says it's impossible to stop them.'

'Are you sure it's Dogwort and Ratsbane?' Greenele urged.

'I'd know that face anywhere!' Barleycorn snapped.

'We have to leave,' Greenele declared. 'The sooner the better.' He pressed his face against the window again. 'Barleycorn, you are right.' He stared up at the roof opposite and saw the first, small flakes of snow beginning to lie there. 'The weather has changed.'

'Where are we going?' Barleycorn asked.

'Further north to an island, a manor house called Crokehurst. I'll explain later.'

'We'll need supplies,' Barleycorn added.

'I can get them,' Gildas declared from where he stood in the doorway. 'And don't worry about Dogwort and Ratsbane.' His lean face broke into a smile. 'I have given them the slip before.'

'Do you know them?' Barleycorn walked towards him.

'All those who wander the roads of Essex know Ratsbane and Dogwort,' the warlock replied. 'They impose tolls and levies, especially if you are wandering by yourself. They offer me no harm. Rats tend to leave other rats alone.'

'I'm coming as well.' Emmeline Coticol sat down on the edge of the bed, primly pushing down her skirts and smoothing the wrinkles out.

'There's nothing for you at Crokehurst.'

'There's nothing for me here,' she retorted. 'Apart from slow starvation, possible death or rape, if the gentlemen down in the street break in.'

Greenele looked at her determined face and sighed, though secretly he was delighted. He liked the young woman, her common sense and lack of any air or graces. Moreover, his father and hers had been close friends. He had a debt of honour to repay.

'Then let's pack,' he said, going towards the door.

'Mistress Emmeline, are there horses?'

'My father kept them in the stables on the corner of the alleyway,' Emmeline replied. 'Mine Host at the "Dovecote" is a good, honest man. He stabled my father's horse and two sumpter ponies.'

Greenele nodded at Gildas. 'Get them and whatever else you can steal.'

Gildas and Barleycorn waited until the outlaws had moved, then slipped out of the small postern gate. Richard went back to the chancery, studying his father's last will and testament. Emmeline brought him wine, then leaned on the table looking down at him.

'I'd like to know,' she declared.

So Richard told her, reading out extracts. Emmeline, arms crossed, listened intently.

'Did your father ever mention my father's name and what happened at Crokehurst?' he asked.

She shook her head. 'Never.' Then her fingers flew to her lips. 'But he kept a careful watch on those five knights. I remember that. Journeymen and travellers often came here because my father could draft a letter or keep money for them.' She shrugged. 'I never eavesdropped but, sometimes, Father entertained them and those five names always cropped up in his conversation. What were they doing? What preferment had they received? How were their crops and their profits? And, when his visitors were gone, Father always came here and wrote everything they said into a ledger. Nothing much, tittle-tattle, shire gossip.'

'Where is this book?' Richard asked.

'My father kept it in his own chamber. I'll collect it for you. Do you mind me accompanying you?' she continued in a rush. 'I can ride, write and cook.' She smiled sweetly. In the soft candlelight she became even more beautiful, her eyes taking on an elfish, mischievous look. 'I am not one of your elegant ladies of the court.'

Richard grasped her hand and kissed it; her fingers were warm and sweet-smelling.

'My lady,' he teased back, 'if you had not agreed to come, I'd have seized and taken you by force.'

She withdrew her hand quickly but winked impishly at him.

'Ladies don't flirt,' she murmured. 'I will get you the ledger.'

Emmeline left. Richard sat, a little nonplussed about her abrupt change of mood. She came back and pushed a calf-skin leather tome into his hand. She smiled down at him.

'If I am leaving, I have to pack.' She looked round the chancery office and blinked. 'And, if I am to go, well, Father had a secret place in the cellar. I'll have to hide certain things away.'

She left Richard to study the ledger, returning now and again to light more candles. At first Richard couldn't make sense of the different entries until he realised how the dead lawyer had kept this as a summary of the gossip and chatter he'd collected from the traders, journeymen and chapmen. Hugo Coticol, Richard concluded, was a born lawyer. A man who probably never stirred from his own house, street or ward. Yet he was shrewd enough to keep his ear close to the wall and learn what was happening around the shire. The entries included ships visiting ports: the profits of a wool merchant; the building of a manor house; the business of the courts. There were also entries against his father's five knights. Richard wryly noted how each of them had prospered, living well on the fat of the land, investing monies in different trading places, creating marriage alliances between their families. At the back of the ledger, Richard found the names of the five knights listed together and where they lived. He heard a sound from the back of the house; the door opening, Emmeline's merry laugh, Barleycorn's deep voice and Gildas' sharp, caustic comments, Emmeline again laughed and all three came into the chancery office.

'What are you doing?' Barleycorn asked, staring curiously at the quill in Richard's fingers.

'I have to write five letters,' the squire replied. 'Mistress Emmeline, did your father have a map of Essex?'

She opened a trunk and brought out a greasy roll of vellum. Richard cleared the table, using inkhorns to hold down the corners of the manuscript. The map was cleverly done, showing the roads to and from Colchester. He glanced up at Gildas.

'We will eat tonight?'

'Like kings,' the fellow replied. 'The Lord looks after his own. He fills them with good things.'

'Yes, I am sure he does,' Richard answered. 'Look, whilst we sup I will tell you a tale.' He pointed to the road going north from Colchester towards the coast, then a small trackway leading to a circle bearing the name Crokehurst. 'I have to go there,' Richard explained. 'But,' he traced his fingers along the coast, 'here are different places, the residences of five knights. I must speak to them: Ferrers, Beaumont, Manning, Bremner and Grantham.'

'I know some of them,' Gildas declared. 'Lords of the soil they are: owners of good, comfortable houses with windows full of glass. Fat-tailed sheep graze in their meadows. Cattle in their fields with barns and granges fit to burst.'

'Then you'll take my invitation to them?' Greenele replied.

'Not yet, but once we are on the island. How long would it take you?'

'No more than a day.'

'That's if we get there,' Barleycorn intervened. 'Master,' he smiled and Richard realised this was not the first time he had used such a title. 'The snow is beginning to fall. Ratsbane and Dogwort have probably brought their whole coven here.'

Richard rolled up the map. 'Then let's sup. By daybreak we'll be gone.'

Words between the pilgrims

The franklin stopped speaking and stared round the priory refectory. He hid his smile as his eyes quickly caught those of his fellow pilgrims who had a part to play in his tale. He watched the pardoner in particular, that seller of relics with his flaxen hair and ghostly white face, his nose constantly stretched in the air like a bird with its beak. The pardoner, however, seemed engrossed in the string of tawdry relics slung round his neck and refused to lift his head. The knight, however, was listening avidly, smiling to himself as if the franklin's tale had touched something in his own memory. His son, the squire was looking at him curiously and, leaning forward, whispered in his father's ear but Sir Godfrey shook his head, lost in his own reverie. The man of law also stirred himself, chewing the corner of his lip. He watched the franklin, narrow-eyed, but his close, dark features revealed no emotion.

Ah well! the franklin thought and scratched his luxurious, white beard which more than covered the lower half of his face.

'What's this then?' Mine Host spoke up. 'Is this fact or fable, franklin?'

'Shush!' Chaucer caught Mine Host by the sleeve. 'You know the rules, good fellow. We'll hear the tale through to its end; no digressions.'

'I have heard about Dogwort and Ratsbane,' the poor priest spoke up, his voice clear as a bell on a summer's morning. 'Evil men, wolves amongst Christ's sheep.'

'Yes, yes, quite so,' the franklin replied. 'And they have had their just deserts, gone into the pit they dug for others.'

The knight's smile widened.

'But is your story true?' the prioress piped up. She sat comfortably in the corner, feeding her lap-dog small morsels of bread dipped in milk. 'I mean,' she continued hastily, ignoring Chaucer's warning look, 'Master franklin, as your tale unfolds, is it fable or is it truth? It whets the appetite.'

'What do you think, Master summoner?'

But the summoner simply scratched his wart-covered face.

'It awakes memories,' he murmured. His cruel eyes held those of the franklin. 'But go on, sir. I'll tell you how the pie tasted when I've eaten it.'

PART II

Chapter 1

Richard Greenele and his party left just before dawn the following day. They had supped well on what Gildas had stolen but slept little. Instead they'd huddled round the kitchen table to listen to the young squire's tale of his father's fate and his journey to Crokehurst.

'A journey ordained by God,' Gildas solemnly declared when the squire had finished. 'A pilgrimage to truth, a search for justice.'

'Yes, quite so,' Barleycorn interrupted. 'But what do you intend to do when you get there? These terrible events happened some sixteen years ago. How could you find the truth when your father couldn't?'

'He can at least try,' Emmeline spoke up. 'He must try. My father kept that secret for him.'

'Is that why you are going to invite the five knights?' Gildas asked. 'And, if you do, do you think they'll come?'

Richard tapped the five letters beside him. 'Oh, yes, they'll come.' The young squire smiled. 'I have told them,' he added, 'that certain evidence has come into my hands to clear my father's name. Oh, yes, they'll come. However, tomorrow we leave and, before we do, there's work to be done!'

They finished their wine, packed their own fardels and bundles and then helped Emmeline take her father's manuscripts, family silver and other precious possessions to a secret store room in the cellar. They slept for a while then rose, washed and broke their fast on strips of greasy bacon and cups of water. Afterwards they went out into the garden. Bayard and the lawyer's three horses had been stabled in a little arbour, sufficient protection against the freezing cold. More snow had fallen to carpet the ground in a crisp white sheet. At Richard's instructions they saddled the horses, loading their possessions on to the sumpter ponies. They spoke in whispers, their breath like clouds of steam in the clear, dawn air. Emmeline was dressed in a thick, woollen cloak, her head protected by an ermine-lined cowl. She looked even more beautiful, the cold bringing a colour to her cheeks, reddening her lips and making her eyes sparkle. She caught Richard watching her and smiled shyly back. A look which sent his heart pounding; now Emmeline was with them he'd travel to the mountain of the Golden Horn! They went down the alleyway and into the street. The town still slept. The people not only hiding from the plague but keeping warm against the increasing cold. A thin-ribbed mongrel came out, yapping at them, but then slunk away. Now and again they caught dark shadows slipping in and out of the runnels and narrow alleyways. They crossed the market place, passed a deserted church, heading for the northern gates. They rounded a corner and almost rode on to the huge bonfire burning there. The men sleeping on the ground sprang to their feet, hands going to knives and daggers.

'Peace,' Richard lifted his hand. 'Simple travellers leaving the city,' he declared, but his heart sank.

The men were armed and a few wore those terrible masks he

had glimpsed the day before. He looked quickly at Barleycorn who strode beside him but the bowman had already pulled his cowl well over his head. The outlaws, followers, as Richard knew, of Ratsbane and Dogwort, stood back and allowed them to pass. After all, they'd glimpsed Richard's sword and dagger. Gildas, too, was armed whilst the long yew bow slung across Barleycorn's shoulder was sufficient warning to leave them alone. They murmured under their breath, faces snarling but they did not interfere. Richard heaved a sigh of relief. They were through them, riding down towards the city gate when a voice called out, 'Barleycorn, you caitiff!'

Before Greenele could stop him, the bowman turned.

'It is him!' one of the outlaws cried and began to run towards him.

'Ride on!' Cuthbert shouted, waving at Greenele. 'Protect the Lady Emmeline!'

He knelt down. Gildas was going to flee but then changed his mind and came back, a loaded arbalest in his hand. Richard and Emmeline, leading on their sumpter ponies, headed towards the gate. Greenele heaved a sigh of relief as he saw the guards running towards him.

'Outlaws!' he cried. 'They've attacked us!'

The hard-bitten soldiers, veterans from the castle, went to join Cuthbert. Greenele turned in the saddle. Cuthbert needed very little help. A master archer, he had already released five arrows and each had found their mark. Gildas, too, had brought one down though he was having difficulty winching back the cord for a second bolt. Six corpses lay twitching, spreading pools of blood across the snow. The rest of the outlaws had decided retreat was the better part of valour and were falling back out of arrow-shot, their curses and threats rang clearly on the cold, frosty air. The city soldiers took up the pursuit. Barleycorn and Gildas, sweating and breathing heavily, but grinning from ear to ear, rejoined Richard and Emmeline.

'You did well,' the squire observed. 'Five shafts in three minutes!'

'At my best,' Barleycorn boasted, 'it could have been six shafts in one minute. But the cold and the frost,' he twanged the cord of his bow, 'they have their effect.'

'Listen to the chanting of the victorious!' Gildas bellowed. 'See how the Lord has brought the mighty down, smiting them hip and thigh! The Lord's vengeance on earth. A veritable Gideon has risen amongst us!' Gildas' smile faded. 'I played my part as well,' he protested.

Barleycorn brought his hand slapping down on the warlock's shoulder.

'A veritable Ajax!' he declared. 'A true companion of Achilles!'

Barleycorn stared up at Greenele. 'What's the matter!' he asked.

The squire shook his head but decided to keep his thoughts to himself. 'Nothing,' he murmured. 'Come, we should go.'

They rode on through the city gates and into the open Essex countryside.

'We are heading out into the wilds and wastes,' Gildas declared. 'You'll find few travellers on the road we take.'

'We should hurry,' Barleycorn urged, striding ahead. 'Once Ratsbane and Dogwort know I am here, they'll take up the pursuit.'

'Why?' Emmeline asked, leaning down from the horse. 'Why do they hate you so much?'

Barleycorn stopped and looked up at her. 'Because, my beautiful lady,' he murmured, not sparing Emmeline's blushes, 'I killed their kith and kin and they have sworn to take my head as an ornament for the cave, their lair in the heart of the forest.' He played with the bridle of her horse, tightening its straps. 'They also know,' he added, 'if they don't kill me, as God is my witness, I'll certainly kill them!'

'Let's go,' Richard snapped, more harshly than he intended. He looked up at the iron-grey skies. 'The weather has definitely changed and there's more snow to come.'

Within the hour his prophecy was proved correct. The snow

began to fall, muffling all sound, driving birds back into their nests, covering the hedgerows, filling the ditches, blanketing the hard brown earth. They were now into the wastes of Essex. Occasionally they saw a column of smoke on the horizon but, otherwise, they felt as if they were alone in the world, moving across a snow-white desert. The trees stood black and stark. The banks on either side of the trackway blocked out any view. Sometimes the silence would be broken by a burst of raucously cawing rooks as a fox, soft-footed, flitted across their path. On another occasion Emmeline started as a snowy-white owl burst out of the trees and glided like a ghost above them. Now and again Barleycorn stopped, especially when they broke cover or climbed to the top of a hill. He'd turn and stare back.

'They won't follow us!' Gildas scoffed. 'They'll stay in Colchester till the plague ends and the city fathers re-impose law and order.'

'Oh, they'll come,' Cuthbert muttered. 'They'll dog our footsteps like the hounds of hell.'

The day grew on. The horses began to falter and, despite their thick cloaks and heavy gauntlets of fur, the cold and frost made its presence felt.

'It will be dark soon,' Gildas observed. He pointed to a small copse of trees. 'That is no tavern or farm. We'd best stay there. Don't worry. It will be all right,' he added sheepishly.

Greenele was tempted to ask him why he said that about a copse of trees clustered on the top of a hill but it was cold, and darkness was drawing in. They left the trackway, dismounted and led their horses across the field, up the small hill and into the copse. There was a little clearing and Gildas soon had a fire crackling merrily, the flames leaping boisterously up. The trees also served as a breaker against the biting wind. They opened their provisions and, as they sat around the fire, filling their bellies, all agreed that their resting place was as good as any draughty tavern. Nevertheless, now and again, Gildas would stop eating and stare into the darkness. Richard watched him intently. The self-confessed warlock seemed unusually withdrawn. Greenele also became aware of how quiet the copse was. Despite the cold and snow, foxes, badgers, stoats and weasels should be hunting but there was nothing. No rustling in the undergrowth and, when he stared up into the gaunt, black branches, he could see no nests or hear any bird call. Gildas then pulled his battered saddlebags nearer to him: he took out a rough-hewn cross and laid it in front of him. He placed some rosary beads around the cross and, clasping his hands together, began to pray silently. He then got to his feet, having taken a small stoup of holy water, a flask with a stoppered top out of his saddlebags and began to sprinkle the water over his companions. Barleycorn and Richard watched him curiously.

'What is the matter?' Barleycorn snapped. 'Scared of the goblins and elves are we?'

Gildas sat down near the fire. He stared into the flames, lips moving soundlessly.

'Gildas, stop frightening us!' Richard declared. 'What's so special about these trees?'

'It's the warmest and safest place to be,' Gildas replied curtly. 'As long as you take care to protect yourself.'

'You've been here before, haven't you?' Barleycorn accused. 'Come on, you little charlatan!'

'I've been here before,' Gildas confessed. 'And, yes,' he struck his breast in mock sorrow. 'Mea culpa, mea culpa, I have dabbled in the black arts.' He raised his hand dramatically. 'Though I have now forsaken these but, years ago I was here with a coven.'

'Why?' Richard asked. 'Why did they come here?'

'This is not a natural hill,' Gildas replied slowly. 'Many, many years ago, long before the Conqueror came with his Normans, a great battle was fought here between the Saxons and foreigners from across the sea. According to the old stories, the dead lay piled in heaps and the ravens feasted for days. So many died, they stacked the corpses on the top of each other and covered the pyre with earth.'

'And this is the place?'

Gildas nodded. 'Aye and strange things have been seen here. Ghosts, the sound of battle, the cries of the dying. When, in my foolishness, I joined a coven,' he smiled weakly at the flickering flames of the fire. 'It was here,' he tapped the soil. 'If you dig deep enough you'll find the remains of the great fire they built.'

'What happened?' Emmeline asked.

'My lady, I am not too sure.'

'Did a ghost appear?' Barleycorn scoffed, though he drew his cloak closer around him, fearful of the mist now swirling in the darkness amongst the trees. 'Well, come on, charlatan, did a demon spin up from Hell?'

Gildas shook his head. 'No,' he muttered. He pointed to the trees around him. 'But, afterwards, when the fire was dying, I looked around and, Heaven be my witness, tall, dark figures were standing amongst the trees staring in at us. It was a summer's night but the air turned cold and reeked of the stench of rotting corpses.' Gildas pulled his blanket closer and lay down, resting his head on the saddlebags. 'Now you know why I blessed the place and pray that daybreak comes soon.'

'Then why did you bring us here?' Barleycorn asked.

'Because I know it's haunted,' Gildas replied sleepily. 'And so will Dogwort and Ratsbane.'

Richard sighed and threw more logs on the fire. 'It's time we all slept,' he declared. He glanced sideways at Emmeline. 'My lady, for safety's sake I suggest you sleep between myself and Master Gildas.'

'Oh Lord save us!' Emmeline's fingers flew to her lips in mock surprise. 'If my old nurse could see me now.' She laughed. 'Sleeping between two men!'

'That,' Richard teased back, 'is a story you can tell your grandchildren.'

They settled down, using pannier bags and saddles as pillows, wrapping their blankets tightly about them. Richard found it difficult to sleep. He would have loved to have turned around and gazed at Emmeline but that would have been too forward and what would he do if she turned her back on him? Instead, he lay and wondered what was waiting for him at Crokehurst. How could he clear his father's name on a lonely deserted island in a derelict manor house full of ghosts with winter drawing on? And would the outlaws follow? What was their real reason for pursuing Cuthbert Barleycorn? Richard wondered about the bowman. Whom had he met that night on the Epping road? Why hadn't Gildas recognised him? The fellow apparently wandered the lanes and byeways of Essex yet he was sure they were strangers to each other. Richard recalled Cuthbert's reference to Achilles and Ajax. How could a common archer have benefited from a classical education? Or had he listened to some courtly songs; the deeds of some great paladin, and picked up the reference there? The fire crackled merrily, the logs bursting under the heat. Richard remembered Gildas' story and stared into the darkness. There was a magic here, he thought. Indeed, his whole journey to Crokehurst and the mystery awaiting him reminded him of the stories of Arthur's knights and their quest for the Holy Grail. From across the frozen field, an owl hooted as it searched the hedgerows for prey. Richard began to recite the Pater Noster and was asleep by the time he was halfway through.

They were up early the next morning. A heavy mist now rolled amongst the trees and the place still held an air of quiet menace. The fire had burnt low but Gildas cooked some oats, steaming hot, sprinkling in a little sugar and honey to warm their insides. Once they had eaten, they were back on the track following the dead lawyer's map to the island of Crokehurst.

Thankfully, despite the mist, the trackways were still fairly clear for no snow had fallen during the night. They travelled for most of the day. Later in the afternoon they passed through a small village. Here they stopped at a stinking, leaking ale-house to get some meagre warmth from a smoky fire and soup, supposedly made out of chicken bones, served by a taciturn, greasy ale-wife. Gildas whispered that it was more cat than chicken but at least it was hot. When Richard produced a penny, the ale-wife's dirty, seamed face broke into a smile and, in a strange outlandish accent, she explained to Gildas that, yes, they were on the road to Crokehurst and would be at the island within the hour. She then asked Gildas a question.

'Oh no,' he shook his head. 'We intend to go on to the island.'

The ale-wife's smile disappeared. She muttered something under her breath and stamped off.

'What was the matter with her?' Richard asked as they collected their horses and made their way down the muddy street and out of the village.

'Well, at first she was pleasant enough,' the charlatan replied. 'There's no news of the plague here, nor have they heard anything about an outlaw band. However, when I told her that we were going to cross to Crokehurst, she said it was devil-cursed, haunted. No fit abode for any christian soul.'

'Perhaps Ratsbane and Dogwort will learn that,' Cuthbert added cheerily.

Richard, leading his horse and the Lady Emmeline's, was all eager to press on. He didn't care about the cloying, freezing mist which was beginning to gather as daylight faded. He just wanted to see this island, visit the house where his parents had lived and from where he had been snatched so abruptly. For the first time in his life, despite his wanderings with Sir Gilbert Savage, the young squire felt he was going home. They reached the brow of the hill, the land sloping away below them. For a moment the mist parted in the chill evening breeze.

'Crokehurst!' Gildas exclaimed.

Richard, his heart in his mouth, stared down, The island was thickly wooded, the water of the circling lake grey and sullen. He strained his eyes. He glimpsed the roof tiles and gables of a house, almost hidden by the trees, and a derelict bridge which connected the island to the snow-covered fields around it.

'There's a causeway somewhere,' Gildas whispered.

'Have you been here before?' Greenele asked.

The charlatan turned away. 'Now and again,' he murmured. But then he glanced up at Richard. 'The old ale-wife didn't tell me anything I didn't know already.' He shuffled over to Richard, his face only a few inches from his. 'Are you sure you want to cross, Master? Not even the masters of the gibbet, the lords of the Sabbath, the witches and warlocks visit Crokehurst.' Gildas' long face now had a gentle, caring expression.

'How old are you, Gildas?' Richard asked.

'No more than twenty-three summers,' the charlatan replied. 'I was ordained young. I've dabbled much in my short life. Why?'

'I am eighteen,' Richard replied, pointing down into the mist. 'Sixteen years ago, that was my home, not even the Lord Satan and all the powers of Hell will stop me going there.'

And, leading Bayard on, he went down the hill and on to a narrow, muddy trackway to the bridge. He heard the rest following behind, talking and whispering amongst themselves. Richard reached the entrance of the bridge and stared across. The island looked even more dark and forbidding, the trees coming down almost to the water line.

'The bridge does not look too safe,' Barleycorn volunteered.

Richard had to agree: the bridge was a wooden structure, no rail on either side, just wooden slats though with supporting beams. Some of these were missing, others cracked and buckled. He closed his eyes, said a prayer and led Bayard on to it. Emmeline and the rest followed. The bridge squeaked and groaned beneath them. Bayard's hooves slipped, a plank split, another broke. Richard stopped. He stared longingly at the far end of the bridge. As he did so, he saw a figure, cloaked and cowled, move further back into the trees: the island was not deserted!

Chapter 2

Eventually they arrived safely across the bridge. They moved up the shingle into the wet darkness of the trees. Richard stopped and drew his sword, telling Gildas to slip a bolt into his arbalest whilst Barleycorn, an arrow notched to his bow, went ahead.

'There's someone here,' Richard declared. 'I definitely saw someone watching us cross.'

They moved on along the line of trees. Barleycorn found a path almost hidden by the snow-covered undergrowth and they followed this up through the woods. Richard felt strange. It might have been here where his father, sixteen years ago had come on that pleasant summer evening, just before his descent into hell had begun. He felt a lump in his throat and tears started in his eyes.

'So much ruin,' he whispered. 'What demon could have caused that?'

The trees thinned, the path grew wider and suddenly they were in a snow-covered field which stretched up towards the great manor house. In its prime, Crokehurst must have been a small palace with its red-tiled roof, chequer-board gables, large bay windows, grand entrance, chimney stacks, cornices, corbels and gargoyles along the front. The house was large and sweeping with wings on either side. Nevertheless, the years had taken their toll. The roof was holed, the windows gazed out like sightless eyes. The plasterwork scored by wind and rain, the paint peeling on the beams. The red brick foundation was covered in lichen. A great, sprawling building, it lay like some wounded animal and Richard felt the sadness and sorrow of the place. He moved across the grass, still leading Bayard, and realised that, in his father's time, there would have been a path through the field gardens, herb beds, bowers and garden seats and benches. Now everything was overgrown, breaking down, covered by the wetness of winter. A shutter in one of the upper storey windows suddenly clattered open, banging in the icy wind. Gildas gave a small yelp. Richard stopped, stroking the side of Bayard's muzzle, quietening the horse who had also grown strangely restless at the eerie atmosphere. The squire studied the building carefully, noting how the front door was locked and padlocked The house was three storeys high, all the windows of the lower storey were gone, no doubt passing tinkers and traders had broken in to plunder what was left.

'Do you remember any of it?' Emmeline asked, coming up beside him.

Richard closed his eyes. 'No, none of it. But perhaps it will come back.'

They went round the manor house and into the stable yard formed by the house and its two wings. The gate leading into it had long rusted from its hinges and lay mouldering on the overgrown, cobbled yard. The outhouses were in a similar state of disrepair: roofs falling in, doors gone.

'Your father must have been a great lord,' Barleycorn declared. 'There's a smithy, forge, outhouse, storerooms.' He pointed to the centre where the cover of the well had collapsed, revealing a red bricked hole. 'I don't think anyone has been here for years. It's a long time since anyone drew water from that!'

They hobbled the horses and forced a door into the small buttery, its white-washed walls were dirty and covered in mildew, then into a kitchen, a large spacious room with a great canopied fireplace built against the walls. The fleshing table still stood there, covered in cobwebs and dust, but everything else, pans, skillets, spoons and ladles had long gone. The rows of rusting hooks against the wall were now bent, showing the great force used when the manor house had been ransacked. Gildas crept into the hearth and peered up the chimney stack.

'This is still clear,' he said and coughed as dust fell down into his face. He came out, shaking his head, smiling wryly at the laughter he had caused.

'Get some wood,' Richard ordered. 'Build up a fire.' He drew his sword and smiled thinly at his companions. 'I would prefer,' he said, 'if I went through the house by myself. You can understand?'

They all agreed. Richard went out into the stone-paved passageway. As he went from room to room: parlour, solar and chancery, he experienced a deep sense of sadness. Images flitted across his mind. There was something familiar about a door, a large hooded fireplace in one room, the large bay window which over-looked the side of the house and the snow-covered fields.

He went up the great staircase, absentmindedly shifting the dust with his hand from the carved newel post and balustrade. The wood was in good repair, the stairs still firm. As he climbed, Richard realised that the house must have a reputation of being haunted otherwise local peasants would have stripped it bare. He stopped at the top of the stairs and listened. Was it true, he wondered? Was the house haunted? Did his parents' ghosts and those of Lord and Lady Fitzalan stand in the shadowy, cobwebbed corners and stare piteously out at him? The white-washed walls above the battered wooden wainscoting were covered in grime but he could see where pictures and tapestries had hung. The sconce-holders, the brass turned green, would have once bathed the gallery in light, turning it into a place of beauty, warmth and security. There were six bedchambers along the first gallery. All were large, spacious rooms but stripped of any furniture. Richard, however, seemed to sense which was his parents' bedroom. For a few minutes he sat in the window seat, his back to the shutters, and stared round the dusty, mildewed room before putting his face in his hands and sobbing softly. For a while he sat and cried. He wept, not so much for himself as for his parents and raged at the cruel demon who had smashed the cup of happiness from their lips.

At last Richard dried his eyes, whispered a requiem for their souls and wondered what to do next. He felt sad and, for the first time since leaving France, realised how much he missed Sir Gilbert Savage. How deeply he had loved him, grown used to his taciturn ways. The knight had treated him as well as any father. He had cared for Richard, tending him when he was ill, teaching him all he knew about the world and its ways. Sir Gilbert had been thrifty in his speech but generous and warm-hearted in everything he had done. As Richard had grown older, a certain distance had grown up between them. Often Richard would catch the knight staring at him sadly, now he knew the reason why.

'I wish you were here,' Richard whispered into the darkness. 'And, when this is all done, I'll erect a memorial to you. I'll never forget you.'

He went out into the gallery and inspected the rest of the rooms. One chamber further down the passageway, was, he was sure, the guest room where Lord Simon Fitzalan had been stabbed. Indeed, when he shifted the dust from the floor with the toe of his boot, Richard was certain he could make out the dark blood stain which still marked the floorboards. As he went from room to room the sadness gave way to anger and, for the first time in his life, Richard knew how to hate. The house was derelict, dusty, the home of bat, rat and mouse. Cobwebs and dust coated everything but, beneath it all, Richard sensed the happiness which had once thrived there. He went up the stairs to the third floor. The light was poor here and he had to open the battered shutters. He went into one room and immediately knew that he was in the same chamber which figured so prominently in his nightmares. So sharp was his recall that he felt frightened and had to sit crouched in a corner, fist to his mouth. He closed his eyes, remembering his dreams.

'Over there,' he whispered to himself. 'That's where my bed was. There were tables and chairs, a carpet on the floor, and a mattress here.'

He got up and opened the window, a sliver of grey light poured in. Richard stared round. There was a faded painting on the wall. He could make out the outlines of the figure of Christ. Richard could take no more. He almost ran from the chamber down the stairs and back into the kitchen.

For a while he stood with his back to the door, gulping in air, trying to calm the thudding of his heart and the sharp catching pain in his belly. The others, gathered round the fire roaring in the hearth, looked at him strangely.

'I did it myself,' Gildas cried. His grin faded as he saw Richard's pallid, drawn face. 'Come on,' the charlatan briskly came over and, grasping Richard by the arm, pulled him over to an upturned cask. 'Sit down,' he ordered and, going outside, came back with a wineskin. Taking out the stopper he pushed it into Richard's hand. 'Drink,' Gildas urged. 'It helps the blood flow.'

Richard obeyed. Gildas had apparently been busy as other kegs and casks were brought in.

'There's a cellar,' Barleycorn explained. 'We found them there. They'll serve as stools and chairs.'

Emmeline stretched across and touched Richard's hand. It was cold as ice.

'You have been here before?' she asked.

'Yes. Yes,' he murmured.

He drained the cup and Gildas, seeing Cuthbert's warning glance, refilled it. For a while they just sat sipping at the pewter goblets they had taken from Emmeline's house. The wine soon had an effect. Richard felt calm but sleepy, his eyes growing heavy. He gratefully accepted Gildas' invitation to sleep on a blanket in the corner of the kitchen. He did not dream but slept for hours.

It was dark when he awoke but he could see at one glance how busy the rest had been. Water had been boiled, the fleshing table was clean and scrubbed as was the floor, cups and jugs had been unloaded from their baggage. Richard rose and stretched; he went across and grasped Emmeline by the hands. She did not resist but looked up, eyes shining.

'A lawyer and a housewife,' he teased. 'I thank you. I am sorry if I was selfish but, going round this house . . .' He pulled a face.

'More of a journey for the soul?' Emmeline asked.

He did not reply. Emmeline drew closer, stood on tiptoe and kissed him on the cheek then almost jumped away as the door crashed open and Barleycorn and Gildas came into the kitchen.

'There's not a rabbit in Essex, not a rabbit on four legs that can escape Gildas. The woods are teeming with them.'

The animals were soon skinned, gutted and roasting on a make-shift spit over the fire. They ate and drank well that night. Afterwards Richard went out to the stables to check on Bayard and the other horses. Feed had been brought with them. Barleycorn had supplemented this by cutting grass and drying it in front of the kitchen fire as well as collecting some fruit from the orchard. Richard went back into the yard and stared up at the sky. Gildas had reported how the clouds had broken but now they were massing together again. A cold wind had risen and whipped at Richard's hair.

'There'll be more snow,' he murmured.

'Do you want me to summon the five knights?' Barleycorn stood in the doorway. 'I can go with Gildas and think we'd best go tonight,' Barleycorn continued. 'When the snow comes, it'll be thick and fast.'

'You are tired.' Richard walked towards him.

'It's best now,' Barleycorn retorted. 'The roads are still clear. I've just looked at the map. We could have them all here by tomorrow evening, if they'll come.'

'Do you know what to say?'

Barleycorn nodded.

'Tell them of our situation,' Richard said. 'Tell them it's urgent. Ask them to bring supplies, on allegiance to my father; they, at least, owe me that.'

Cuthbert nodded and went inside. Richard followed. Apparently Gildas also thought it was a good idea to leave for he was already packing. The charlatan glanced slyly at Emmeline.

'Is it wise to leave you here?' he teased. He gazed around. 'I mean the wine, the fire, a lusty young squire.'

Emmeline laughed from where she sat in the ingle-nook, studying the map laid out across her lap.

'Don't worry about me, Gildas. Better here, than with Ratsbane and Dogwort.'

For a while the kitchen was chaotic, Barleycorn and Gildas collecting their belongings and arms. Richard and Emmeline accompanied them to the stables where they took the horses and, with shouts of farewell, disappeared into the darkness.

After they had gone Emmeline became strangely silent. She returned to the kitchen and lay down on a makeshift bed in the far corner. For a while Richard just stood watching her and wondering about the strange moods of women; she lay with her back to him, the blanket pulled well up over her face. He began to tiptoe over.

'I am fast asleep,' she declared. 'And I think you should be.'

The next morning Richard woke late to find Emmeline already up, cheerful as a sparrow.

'Out of bed, lazy bones!' she urged. 'I have bathed and changed.' She pointed to the pot bubbling over the fire she was building up. 'Oatmeal for breakfast, some watered wine and more rabbit stew. You should wash.' She wagged a finger. 'You haven't shaven and your hair is greasy. Barleycorn said you owned a change of raiment.'

She chattered on, nagging him so insistently, that Richard was glad to escape to the stable yard to draw fresh water from the well. The morning was grey but clear, the wind still biting.

'We'll have snow,' Emmeline shouted from the kitchen. 'You wait and see. Later this afternoon, Barleycorn told me the signs.'

Richard returned with a pail of freezing water. He took this into the parlour. He stripped, washed and shaved himself, put on fresh clothes and returned to the kitchen to break his fast.

'I am going out,' he declared as he left the table. 'Bar the door behind me.' He pointed to a second crossbow standing in the corner. 'If necessary,' he added, not meeting her eye, 'use that.'

'Can't I come with you?' Emmeline stamped her foot.

Richard grinned at her. 'Woman, just this once, let me see what else my father's manor holds.' He strapped on his war belt and swung his cloak around him.

'Do you really think there's someone else on the island?' Emmeline asked, coming up.

Richard grasped her hand and, pulling her closer, kissed her vigorously on each cheek. She stepped back, blushing slightly.

'What was that for?' she asked.

'I forgot to do it last night,' he replied.

And, before she could respond, he was through the kitchen door, striding across the yard. He followed the trackway through the woods, noticing how the orchard of apple, pear and plum trees was overgrown. The leaves and fruit lay everywhere, coating the ground in a wet soggy mess. The loose snow had begun to melt, making the ground slippery underfoot. Once or twice he missed his footing and, swearing under his breath, had to make his way more carefully. As he did, he listened to the crackle as rabbits scrabbled through the undergrowth. Richard realised that the island had once had its own warren. He passed a dovecote standing in a small clearing, its roof holed and part of the wall decaying. Further on there was a piggery, derelict chicken coops which showed that, in its day, the island must have been self-sufficient: small wonder, Richard reasoned, his ancestors had taken it as the safest place to build their house. He thought of the fields they had passed through on their way to the island. Were these once part of the manor? He heard a branch snap in the woods alongside him. He stopped, hand going to the dagger of his belt. He tried to control his breathing. Once again, even in that moment of danger, he realised how much he missed Gilbert Savage. He quickly turned round and stared through the trees. Nothing. His sense of loneliness increased and the words of his dead comrade echoed in his mind: 'When you have a friend, Richard, a real friend who walks beside you, you are never alone. You are never vulnerable. All the armour in the world, the sharpest sword and the fleetest horse are no match for a good friend.'

'I wish you were here,' Richard murmured.

He continued his walk. He recalled the dark shape he had seen flitting through the trees on the edge of the lake. Was there someone on the island? Someone who was part of his father's dreadful nightmare? So intent was he on his own thoughts, Richard hardly realised where he was until he found himself on the edge of the trees, staring out across a great meadow.

'By St Michael!' he exclaimed loudly, stirring the crows above him. 'In the name of all that's good!'

He couldn't believe his eyes. The meadow was so unexpected, a large, almost perfectly oval field ringed by trees, not a bush, or hillock broke its white smoothness. Richard blinked. Was it a field, he wondered? Or a small lake within the island? He began to walk across gingerly, marvelling at its strangeness. The dark skies above him, the blackness of the trees on every side, the brilliant dazzle of the undisturbed snow.

'It's a jousting field!' he exclaimed.

Perhaps his father was one of those tournament champions, a knight skilled in the joust and the tourney? The owner of a great war horse like Bayard? Used to the crash of lances, the cries of spectators and the acclamations of the crowds as the garland of victory was lowered on to his helmeted head?

Richard had seen all this in the different castles and towns he and Gilbert had stayed at. He had served as his companion's squire, learning every trick of the trade: how to hold a lance; how to sit on the saddle of a charging horse; the use of stirrups and reins; the cool nerve and sharp eye behind the great jousting helm; the constant search for the opponent's weakness. Time and again Richard had broken lances with Sir Gilbert. Indeed, just before they had assembled at Portsmouth with the Black Prince's army, Richard had even begun to get the better of his master.

'But I won't let you joust,' Sir Gilbert had warned. 'You are not a knight and you are still too young. Moreover, if you lost, we wouldn't be able to pay the fine.'

Richard smiled at the memory and continued across the field. He walked carefully, still believing that there must be some trap, some hole, some hidden dip. At last he was across and he stared back over his footprints.

'Beautiful,' he whispered.

He felt a thrill of excitement. When Barleycorn and Gildas

returned, they would bring his father's companions. They would be able to tell him everything about that shadowy figure, Sir Roger, his beloved wife and this mysterious island and all it once held. Richard entered the trees and noticed the ground began to slope away. As he struggled through the icy brambles, he glimpsed the water of the lake and, at last, he reached its edge. Apparently he had now walked the whole width of the island. He stared across the freezing water to the far shore; the flat, Essex countryside was now hidden under a rolling blanket of mist.

'It will freeze!' he exclaimed.

The water was now sluggish, so flat, Richard could even glimpse where the ice was forming. For a while he stared at the mist seeping across. He felt drops of water on his face and realised it was beginning to snow: thick, heavy, white flakes were floating lazily down. He guiltily recalled Emmeline and, retracing his footsteps, went back into the trees and across, what he already called, the tournament field. This time he felt the eerie silence of the island oppressive, as if in the trees around him were watching ghosts. He heard the clink of harness but dismissed it as a figment of his imagination. He heard it again and looked up. In front of him nothing. To his right just a snow-covered field. Slowly he turned, his jaw sagged, his heart began to thud like a drum: at the far end of the field, just outside the edge of the trees, was a knight in full armour bestride a great war horse.

'I'm dreaming,' Richard gasped. 'Oh Lord, have mercy on me!'

He stared unbelievingly. The knight was dressed in black armour from head to toe. A great, jet-black plume jutted out from the helm. In his left hand he held a shield, also painted black except for a small silver cross in the centre. In his other hand, not a lance, but a great sword held up threateningly. The horse, larger even than Bayard, was also caparisoned in black harness, whilst the cloths beneath the saddle were as dark as night. Even the faintly falling snow offered no relief to this vision of hell. Just sitting there, the face completely hidden by a steel-pointed visor. Richard looked around, the snow was still thin. It would offer little obstacle to a horse though. If he began to run, it might cause him to slip and the trees were so far away. Richard knew enough about the speed of a charging destrier to realise he'd never reach safety in time. He drew his sword and dagger and began to edge sideways. Neither horse nor rider moved.

'Who are you?' Richard shouted.

The horse whinnied, shaking its head.

'Well, at least, I know you are no ghost,' Richard whispered. 'I am Richard Greenele!' he shouted. 'Son of Sir Roger, once lord of this island. Why do you threaten me?'

The knight never moved. He still held his sword point up. Richard kept walking sideways, one eye on the line of trees, the other on this ominous, sinister knight. He glanced back, heart in his throat. The knight was beginning to move, the flat of his blade against his shoulder. He gently dug his spurs in and the great war horse, dainty in its movements, began to move across the field. Richard walked faster, now and again slipping. He looked up, the horse was coming at a quick trot. Richard stopped, re-sheathed his dagger and gripped his sword with both hands.

'Then by St Michael and all his Angels!' he shouted. 'Charge me, you coward!'

The horse was now moving to a gallop. The air was alive with the drumming of great iron hooves as horse and rider bore down on the squire who could do nothing but hold his sword out in front of him. Faster and faster the horse came on: neck forward, great legs moving in a terrible harmony, the drumming of the hooves echoed by the creak of harness.

Richard drew in a deep breath. The knight had not yet

lowered his sword. The horse was drawing near. Richard forced himself to keep his eyes open: he measured distances, stepped forward, the knight was almost upon him. Richard's world now shrunk to this terrible war horse with its awesome, sinister rider, the great, black helmet, the armour, the shield and that terrible sword which came swooping at him. Richard tried to parry this with his own blade. There was a clash of steel, his sword spun out of his hand and then the rider was by him. Richard, sobbing for breath, half crouching, waited for the rider to turn. He had seen knights do this, turning quickly to come back for the killing blow. Yet the knight didn't do this. He charged on across the field. The drumming of the hooves faded and he disappeared into the shadows of the trees. Richard scrambled for his sword where it lay a few feet away. He picked it up and ran as fast as he could to the edge of the field. Once inside the protective darkness of the trees, he threw himself down on the ground, retching and sobbing, fighting for breath, lips moving in a wordless prayer, ears straining for the return of those throbbing hooves.

At last he grew calm, aware of how the cold air was chilling the sweat which bathed his body. He picked himself up and, with sword in hand, stumbled back along the path towards the manor house. But he had to stop. His stomach was still heaving and he couldn't understand whether he had dreamed that phantasm or had he been attacked by a real knight? He bound his cloak more firmly about him and sat on a fallen tree stump, head in hands, trying to calm himself.

'Who was he?' he whispered. 'Where had he come from? What was he doing on the island? What was he waiting for? Where did he hide?' Richard's numerous questions were shouted at the silence around him. He heard a crackling. 'That's no bloody rabbit!' he muttered and, spinning round, saw a dark cowled figure, his back to him, hobbling away.

Richard, his fear now replaced by anger, chased after like a hunting dog. His quarry tried to run but Richard could see whoever it was was hobbling lame. Eventually the figure turned, drawing back the tattered cowl of his dirty cloak revealing tousled grey hair, a seamed face and watchful, shrewd eyes above a straggling beard and moustache.

'Who are you?' Richard snarled, venting all his anger on this hapless wanderer. 'Who are you? And why do you sneak up on good Christian folk?' Richard edged forward, sword out. His victim was nervous, mouth gaping to reveal red, toothless gums.

'Do you have any cheese?'

The question stopped Richard in his tracks. The man's hand came out, the fingers thin, the nails long and dirty, like the claw of some animal.

'What?' Richard exclaimed.

The man stepped forward. 'The name's Buthlac. I am a hermit.'

Richard watched him carefully. Madcap, he thought, or someone just pretending to be mad? The hermit edged closer.

'Cheese,' he pleaded. 'Please, I need some cheese. Thick and creamy with a hard rind.' He stopped, screwing his face up, eyes closed, sniffing the air. 'I'll say prayers for your soul and for the pretty thing at the manor house. I thought of asking her, but the doors are all locked. Cheese, please, a piece of cheese?'

Richard was about to lower his sword when the man's arm moved under his cloak. The squire stepped back and, as he did so, the self-proclaimed hermit darted towards him, the hand beneath the cloak coming out, the Welsh stabbing dagger aiming straight for Richard's heart. The squire brought his sword up just in time. There was a clash of steel which pealed like ringing bells amongst the trees. Now the hermit did not look so mad. His eyes had a closed, calculating look. He stepped back, thick, slobbering tongue wetting his lips.

'For the love of God!' he growled. 'All I want is cheese.'

Then he closed again. Despite his hobbled gait, he could

move quickly. Richard found it difficult to feint and parry the cunning strokes of the knife. He edged his way back carefully, letting Buthlac come on. The way his assailant moved showed that he had some military training: never too close, striking with his dagger, but then quickly drawing back, well away from Richard's sword. The squire kept feinting and parrying, blocking that wicked blade, giving his opponent the impression that he was a mediocre swordsman. The squire recalled the advice of Sir Gilbert.

'Don't watch the weapons, Richard,' he'd always warned. 'Watch the eyes, they'll tell you when he plans the killing stroke.'

Buthlac grinned. He stepped back, clasping his dagger in both hands, then he darted in, quicker than expected, the dagger point jabbing at his opponent's face. Richard moved abruptly sideways, foot out and, as Buthlac aimed what he thought would be his killing blow, he tripped over Richard's outstretched leg and fell flat on his face, the dagger spinning from his hand. Richard now pressed his boot in the back of the man's head, pushing his face down, pricking the side of his neck with his sword.

'All I wanted,' Buthlac moaned, 'was a thick piece of cheese. I've lived for cheese,' he wailed. 'And now I'm going to die for cheese!'

Richard withdrew his blade. 'Turn over, on your back. Keep your hands out!'

Buthlac obeyed, arms outstretched, face now fearful, eyes never leaving the tip of Richard's sword. The squire looked at his attacker, the dirty, soiled, leather jerkin, its buttons all broken. His woollen hose were held up by a piece of rope and the boots were not a matching pair, one heel being higher than the other.

'Clubfoot,' Buthlac moaned, following Richard's gaze. 'Been like that since I was born. Marked with the devil, you see.

Served in the Lord Mortimer's wars in Wales but, everywhere I went, people said the devil followed, so I came here.'

'How long?' Richard asked curiously.

'Twenty years in all.'

'Twenty!' Richard exclaimed.

Buthlac now propped himself up on his elbows and stared curiously at the squire.

'Aye,' he whispered. 'The good Lord Roger, God bless his soul, and that of his fair wife Maria. They let a poor soul be, they let me have a cottage in the woods. They let me say my prayers and, above all, they gave me cheese.' Buthlac licked his lips. 'Soft and white it was: sometimes a creamy yellow.' Buthlac swallowed hard. 'And soft bread, not to mention little capons rolled and roasted.' His stomach grumbled and he dropped back, banging his head on the snow-covered ground. 'Now the Lord Roger and the Lady Maria have gone, and poor old Buthlac is to follow them. Cruelly murdered for a piece of cheese!'

'Get up!' Richard snarled. 'If my father helped you why should I kill you?'

Buthlac sat up so quickly he took Richard by surprise.

'Your father!' he exclaimed, one bony finger outstretched. 'Aye, you have his face, the Lady Maria's eyes. I thought that when I first saw you.'

'So, why did you try to kill me?'

'I protect the island,' Buthlac replied defiantly. 'Oh, they come across the bridge there, looking for plunder, wanting to set up house, even though royal proclamations say this island and all on it belong to the Crown.' The hermit's face broke into a wicked smile. 'But I scares them off. You see, I am the ghost. I am the spirit of the woods. If they shelter in the house, strange fires begin, strange sounds at night.'

'You didn't try that last night,' Richard commented.

'There were too many of you and I was curious. You didn't

92

look like Moon-people or outlaws and old Buthlac was curious. I
sits and I watches.'

'Did you see the knight?' Richard interrupted.

Buthlac's eyes grew cunning.

'Did you see the knight?' Richard repeated. 'He charged me
across the open field.'

'Oh, I sees him all right,' Buthlac replied slowly. 'But, there
again, you see, Master, just because I play at ghosts and
demons, doesn't mean...' He stared round the trees fearfully.
'Oh, no, you take Buthlac's words seriously, it doesn't mean the
real demons don't prowl here.'

Chapter 3

Richard stared down at the prostrate man.

'What do you mean?' he asked.

'Can I get up?' Buthlac pleaded. 'I assure you, sir, now I know who you are...' The hermit's eyes now had a direct, honest look.

Richard nodded. Buthlac staggered to his feet and picked up his dagger.

'So, you don't know who the knight is?'

'I saw him,' Buthlac replied. 'As God is my witness, sir, I don't know where he came from or where he went to. This island is so thickly wooded, there are places where you could conceal a stableful of horses.' He grinned slyly. 'Even I find it difficult to find my little cottage. Come, I'll take you there.'

Richard waved him on. The hermit, quietly cursing at the bruises he had sustained, led him into the trees. For a while they wound about, sometimes leaving the path to struggle through the snow-covered bracken. The snow was now falling heavily, quickly covering the branches and ground beneath.

'You can see why your ancestors chose this island,' Buthlac

called back. He stopped and waved a hand. 'The woods teem with wild life. Moreover, if the manor was attacked and over-run, it would be a very rash horseman who followed you into these trees.'

Richard agreed: he knew enough about sortie and ambus-cades to recognise these woods were a death trap.

'But what about the field?' he asked.

'Oh, that's Mother Nature,' Buthlac replied. 'Always been like that. Your father used to love it in the grand days of the Hall.' He grinned over his shoulder. 'That's what we called the manor. On May Day a maypole would be put up, people would flock to the island to set up a fair and market. On the feast of St George and St Michael, your father's patron saints, a great joust would be held there. The field would be covered with pavilions and tents with great, leather-covered lists set up down the centre. Grand days, grand days,' he whispered. 'But, come.' They entered a small clearing. 'There's my cottage.'

Richard really had to stare before he glimpsed the wooden hut built on the far edge of the clearing carefully concealed between the two trees.

'There's a small brook behind it,' Buthlac said. 'So I always have fresh water and everything I need: rabbit, pheasant, quail, pigeon, some truffles from the wood.' He shook his head dolefully. 'But no cheese. Oh, sir, I have a passion for cheese, it's beyond understanding.'

He led Richard into the hut, slamming the rickety door behind them. He quickly lit a candle and two oil lamps on the rough-hewn table. The cottage was spacious and clean: the mud-packed floor covered with fresh rushes. There was an upper loft containing a bed and stool, a battered leather trunk and a set of steps leading downstairs to the large room which served as both kitchen and parlour. The far wall of the cottage was of stone with a small hearth built into it where pine logs crackled and glowed on a fiery bed of charcoal.

'As comfortable as the King's own chamber,' Buthlac said and then pointed to the stone wall. 'Your father did that for me. Came here once he did and complained of the smoke. All I had at the time was a fire in the centre with a hole in the roof. Here, sit down, sit down.' He pushed a stool near the fireplace. 'A grand man, your father.' Buthlac stamped away and came back with a pewter cup brimming with a sweet-tasting white wine. 'Took it off a pedlar, I did,' Buthlac boasted. 'I scared him off so quickly he left his property behind.'

He sat down opposite Richard, cradling his own cracked pewter cup between his hands. 'But there's not much left now, so some cheese, sir, would be gratefully received.' The hermit stared at his cup. 'I am sorry I attacked you,' he muttered. 'I didn't . . .'

'Did you know my father well?' Richard asked sharply.

'Oh yes, sir. Tall he was, little bigger than yourself. Broad across the shoulders and slim-waisted. Keen-eyed with a voice like a bell.' Buthlac spread his fingers out towards the warmth from the fire. 'He was a truly good man.'

'Then why did it happen?' Richard asked.

'Jealousy,' Buthlac replied. 'Hatred.'

'On whose part?'

Buthlac scratched his grey hair and stared up at the light streaming through the shuttered window

'You know about his five council knights, sir?'

'I have invited them here.' Richard saw the change in Buthlac's eyes: just a glance, like a shadow, across his face.

'One of them's the killer,' Buthlac declared. 'You must realise that, don't you, sir? On the night Lord Fitzalan and his wife were murdered, there were the usual servants and retainers here. But they, like your father and mother, were innocent. That leaves those five knights.'

'But why?' Richard insisted. 'Buthlac, you must have heard, seen, learnt something?'

'Oh, I did,' the hermit replied. 'Your father always let me into his hall. I'd sit by the fire, always a gentleman your father. If he ate well, old Buthlac ate well. If your father cut cheese then so did old Buthlac.' He tapped his nose slightly. 'Everybody else ignored old Buthlac, treated me like a dog or the family cat.'

'And?' Richard asked.

'Well, those were the war years, sir. Before the King's great victories at Crécy and elsewhere. French galleys roamed the Narrow Seas and prowled along the Essex coast. They attacked shipping, slipping into the narrow islets, sacking and plundering the farms and villages. My Lord Fitzalan and your own father were Commissioners of Array.' He winked at Richard. 'For a hermit I knows a lot. I used to sit and listen. Now, your father and Lord Fitzalan were very concerned about this. During that fateful summer, they would talk for hours, wondering about who the spy could be.'

'Spy!' Richard asked innocently, as if he was learning about this for the first time.

'Oh yes. You see, from what I could gather. By the way I tried to tell the sheriff this when he came to arrest your father but the bastard drove me off with curses and kicks.' Buthlac paused and sipped from his wine cup. 'Anyway the French always knew where to land: which villages had their menfolk away; which castles were insecure. If Lord Fitzalan moved troops to the north the French would attack the south. If troops were taken to a place like Bradwell, the French would go north to Walton-on-Naze or Holderness. Somebody must have been passing such information to them.'

'Someone in authority?' Richard asked.

'Yes, sir, but the only people who knew that information were the Lord Fitzalan, your father and his household knights. All five of them held land along the Essex coast. Somehow Fitzalan had narrowed it down to a small group; himself, your father and the five knights. Certain information was given only to these.

Yet the French still thrived. I heard your father mention that, when he and Lord Fitzalan were walking in the woods not far from here.'

'Was there any evidence?' Richard leaned closer. 'Any shred of proof of who it could be? Think, man!'

Buthlac shook his head. 'Nothing, nothing at all. Except...'

'What?' Richard asked.

'Lord Fitzalan said, and I remember it well: "Eyes can be tested by fire." Your father laughed. "No, no," he replied. "It can't be he."' The hermit shook his head. 'That was all.'

'Are you sure he said that?' Richard asked. 'Eyes can be tested by fire? What does it mean?'

Buthlac pulled a face.

'So, my father and Fitzalan were close to the traitor?'

'I don't think so. If anything,' Buthlac replied, 'your father didn't believe the traitor was amongst his household. He considered all five men his friends and boon companions.' He looked up from under his bushy eyebrows. 'All five will come, you know. The traitor and killer must be amongst them. Whoever he is he'll come to protect his name but the other four they will come out of loyalty and love to your dead father's memory.'

'And the night Lord Fitzalan was killed?'

Buthlac swilled the wine round in his cup. 'I was here sleeping like a pig. My belly full of sweet pork and your father's best claret. The first I knows of it was the next morning. People running, shouting and screaming. When I heard about it I couldn't believe it. I thought it was all a nightmare and the real killer would soon be found. But then your father was sent to Colchester, your mother died and the sheriff's men came back. They took everything. Furniture, stores, the hunting dogs, your father's wines, tapestries, books, all piled high on carts. After that the plunderers swept in. If it moved, they stole it. They cleared the farmyard and piggeries.' Buthlac glanced at the young squire and shrugged. 'Only then did I intervene, spreading stories that the island was haunted.' He grinned. 'As well as helping matters along myself. It wasn't hard. The island and manor still belong to the Crown, trespass is forbidden. The bridge is not too secure and you have to be of these parts to be able to ford that treacherous causeway.'

Richard gazed into the fire. He knew he was trespassing. In reality, he had no more claim on this island or manor house than old Buthlac here. His father had been condemned as a traitor: consequently all his lands and belongings were forfeit to the Crown.

'But why this knight?' he asked abruptly. 'Why should a knight in full armour be riding round the island?'

Buthlac stretched and yawned. 'I don't know,' he replied. 'But I tell you this, master. Old Buthlac sits here and watches. Oh, I spread the stories about ghosts and ghouls but this is an eerie place. It frightens even me.' He paused, listening to the wind rattling outside.

'I know this island now, or at least I think I do. Ever since your father's death, strange things have happened. Now and again, particularly on fine evenings, I have glimpsed strangers, whether it's the same person or not I don't know. Masked, cowled, hooded like an outlaw, usually in or near the great manor house.' Buthlac screwed up his eyes in concentration. 'Not regularly, just now and again. I have also glimpsed a horse, hobbled near the causeway, and a figure entering or leaving the hall. Different type of dress, sometimes in black, sometimes green or brown. He's not like some plunderer, he carries no bag.' Buthlac paused and licked his lips. 'Now people say I'm fey, a madcap, but I am sure that person comes back looking for something, something to do with the terrible murders here. You see, sir, over the years I have sat with one thought. Your father's trial was a mockery, a sham. Yet, no one ever stopped to ask what was Lady Fitzalan doing out in the middle of the night, away from her husband's bed chamber, walking in the woods fully dressed?'

Richard glanced across at Buthlac. 'You're not fey or a madcap,' he flattered. 'But very shrewd.'

'Oh and there's other things.' Buthlac drew himself up proudly. 'Which a proper inquest would have established.'

'Such as?' Richard asked.

'Well, according to those who knew, the tittle-tattle and gossip of the servants, Lady Fitzalan had been ravished: her skirts were all awry. Now, why should someone rape then murder her? Remember, Master, whoever was behind these macabre acts had to move quickly: her murder, I understand, but why the rape?' Buthlac, now really proud of himself, emphasised his points on his stubby fingers. 'So, why was the Lady Fitzalan in the woods? Why didn't anyone hear her scream?'

'What was she like?' Richard interrupted.

'Aye, that's another matter. Your mother was small and slight, pretty as a picture. Beside your father she looked like a little doll. The Lady Fitzalan, however, was robust and plump. Surely she would have struggled, not only screamed but left scratches on her attacker's face? Yet none were noted.'

'Continue.' Richard delved into his purse and passed one of his precious silver coins across. Buthlac hesitated then grabbed it greedily.

'Well, the Lord Simon Fitzalan, he was a warrior born and bred. Yet, once again, he allowed someone to come into his chamber and stick a dagger into him without protest or struggle. Don't forget, young sir,' Buthlac leaned across and wagged a finger, 'no disturbance was reported until after daybreak. There was no commotion during the night. Yet, would you allow someone to come into your chamber and stab you in the chest?'

'But I thought he was found in his bed?' Richard replied.

Buthlac shook his head and tapped the side of his nose, now

growing a bright red from the flames of the fire. 'Ah no, sir. Lord Fitzalan was found on the floor. He was in a swoon, close to death but his soul hadn't gone.'

Richard looked up in surprise.

'Ask them,' Buthlac volunteered. 'When the knights come, ask them. No one ever reported that.'

'And what else?'

'Nothing,' Buthlac muttered. 'Nothing but suspicions and questions.'

Richard put his cup down and got to his feet. He pointed at the fire.

'Douse that!' he ordered. 'Buthlac, would you like to meet the pretty one? Have some wine?' He bent down. 'And the creamiest of cheeses?'

The hermit needed no further urging. A few minutes later, swinging a great ash pole, he led Richard out of his hut into the growing snowstorm and back along the forest path to the manor house. They had to knock hard to gain entry and, when Emmeline opened the door, she sighed with relief.

'Where have you been?' she cried, pointing to the hour candle burning on the table. 'I thought something had happened to you.' She stared hard at Buthlac. 'And it looks as if it has. Who's he?'

Richard made the introductions, explaining that Buthlac was a hermit and had been since his father's day. Behind Emmeline's back he winked at the old hermit, not bothering to tell Emmeline about their violent clash and subsequent struggle. Buthlac, however, was sniffing the air like a dog, closing his eyes and moaning with pleasure.

'Is there something wrong?' Emmeline asked anxiously.

'Cheese, Mistress. I can smell it from here.'

A short while later, Buthlac was sitting in the ingle-nook, a piece of cheese between his fingers. He was staring at it so passionately Richard wondered whether he was going to eat it or pray to it. He then told Emmeline about what had really happened: the appearance of the knight; Buthlac's misapprehension and attack; and, above all, what the hermit had told him about the fateful night when the Fitzalans had been murdered.

'There must be something here?' Emmeline whispered. 'Something the assassin overlooked.' She stared through the cracks of the shuttered window. 'But do you think they'll come? The snow is falling thick and fast.'

'Oh, they'll come,' Buthlac bellowed. 'And my hearing's better than you think. Mark my words, they'll come!'

They spent the rest of the day, Buthlac helping, making the kitchen more habitable. They even cleaned the parlour and two of the bedchambers upstairs, wiping away the dust as well as going out into the swirling snow to collect wood which they dried before the great kitchen fire. Richard kept well away from his parents' bedchamber and the room where he knew he had slept as a child. He worked hard to control his mounting excitement. Darkness fell. The snow continued to fall. Richard began to wonder if Barleycorn and Gildas would not return until the following day when he heard sounds outside. He ran to the door, glimpsed the torchlight and heard the whinny and clip-clop of horses. Dark shapes began to fill the yard. Men cursing and shouting, shaking the snow off their cloaks. Richard drew a deep breath and stepped back into the kitchen.

'They are here,' he breathed. 'Thank God!'

'Oh yes, they're here,' Buthlac echoed. 'I knew they'd come: dying time is near.'

Richard looked at him strangely. He didn't know whether he was mistaken about Buthlac. Was the man witless or very shrewd and cunning? He recalled the murderous attack upon him earlier that day. Was that just fear or something else? Had Buthlac anything to hide? He heard Barleycorn telling Gildas to stable the horse and unload the sumpter ponies. Then the visitors strode into the kitchen. Buthlac continued to crouch in the corner. Emmeline stood near the door as each of the knights came up and introduced themselves. Sir Philip Ferrers; his broad, craggy face was clean-shaven, his greying hair shorn close to his head. He had a firm grip, deep voice, the look of a fighting man. Sir Lionel Beaumont; thin and narrow-faced, his cheeks scored by furrows, sad eyes, a crooked nose and a mouth constantly open as if he was about to speak. Unlike Sir Philip, he simply mumbled a greeting, his watery eyes never met those of Richard. Sir Walter Manning was squat, thickset and podgy-faced, his merry eyes almost hidden by rolls of fat. He sported a thick moustache which he constantly stroked with his fleshy fingers. Sir John Bremner; soft-spoken, grey-faced, his hair so black Richard suspected it was dyed. Quite the court fop, for under his military cloak, he wore an ornate brocaded jerkin and Richard noticed with some amusement how his riding boots had pointed toes and high heels. Finally, Sir Henry Grantham, he towered above the rest and looked rather odd with his completely bald head, broad fleshy face, yet his eyes were small, little black pebbles which never seemed to blink.

Richard couldn't decide whether all five were pleased to see him or not. Oh, they clasped his hand but he noticed their nervousness. They toyed with the brooches of their cloaks or the pommel of their daggers; they looked over their shoulders at Lady Emmeline, Buthlac in the ingle-nook or round the kitchen as if they couldn't really believe that they were back at the scene of the tragedy. For a while there was confusion as cloaks were doffed and Gildas staggered in carrying the provisions the knights had brought. Meat, chickens and capons recently slaughtered, the blood still dripping on the floor, bread, salted meat, small tuns of wine, even a keg of malmsey. Sacks of vegetables, not to mention bedding, clothes and saddle bags. All of this was heaped on the kitchen floor.

'Your man told us,' Ferrers declared, 'how you had just

arrived here. We have enough provisions to last us through Yuletide and my manor's close. Send a messenger and more will come.'

'We brought no servants,' Sir Lionel spoke up from where he lounged against the wall, slapping his gauntlets against his leg. He smiled at Richard. 'More mouths to feed and, what we've come to discuss, is best not heard by others.'

'It was good of you to come,' Richard replied. 'As you know, I have no authority to command you. This is not my house or land and, since my father's forfeiture, you have no allegiance to me.'

'It's the least we could do.' Bremner had already unstoppered a tun of wine which he began to pour into cups. 'Hey you, you lazy bugger!' He turned to Buthlac. 'Give us a hand here!'

'I'm not your servant and I'm not a lazy bugger!' the hermit shouted back.

'Please,' Emmeline came forward, smiling at Buthlac. 'Please help; our visitors must be tired.'

The young woman's face was slightly red, eyes sparkling as if she was embarrassed to be in the presence of so many men. The visitors, however, clustered about her. Richard explained who she was and there were muttered compliments. Manning seized her hand and kissed it.

'Another reason for coming,' he murmured.

Emmeline threw her head back and laughed in an attempt to lessen the tension.

'All of you!' she ordered in a mocking voice. 'There is work to do.'

For the next two hours more provisions and supplies moved in the kitchen and torches were lit along the passageways and galleries. The knights were old campaigners used to sleeping rough. As Beaumont reminded Emmeline time and time again: they did not mind the chaos. By the time they had finished, each knight had a chamber on the first or second gallery above. Emmeline agreed to sleep near the scullery. Richard, Buthlac and Gildas on the other side of the kitchen whilst Barleycorn muttered something about the stables being as warm and as friendly as any room.

Despite the jokes and banter and the compliments offered and taken by Emmeline, Richard felt the tension. He studied the knights closely. Now and again he would also catch Buthlac's eye and read the expression there. One, or more, of these men was a bloody-handed assassin responsible for his parents' disgrace and death, not to mention the brutal murders of Lord and Lady Fitzalan. Why, Richard kept thinking, why had they come?

Once the kitchen was cleared and each person knew where he was sleeping, beeswax candles were lit. Traunchers and a motley collection of goblets were laid out on the great fleshing tables. Then Emmeline and Barleycorn served each person a portion of salted meat, bread, cheese and some rather bruised apples washed and cut up. The conversation at first was stilted but Emmeline was shrewd: she kept moving around, filling the wine cups from a great pewter jug one of the knights had brought.

'You look like your father,' Sir Philip Ferrers seized on a gap in the conversation. He toasted Richard with his cup.

'May God assoil him and give him rest,' Sir Walter Manning intoned piously.

'Why did you come?' Richard asked bluntly. 'My father died some sixteen years ago. This manor has lain derelict. I owe nothing to you. You certainly owe nothing to me, yet you came so quickly.'

Richard glanced where Barleycorn sat on an overturned keg. The master bowman had been strangely silent since his guests' arrival.

'Your messenger found us,' Sir John Bremner whispered. 'All of us, except Sir Philip, were at Grantham's manor house. It was easy for us to organise. The snow was falling thickly, we realised we had to leave quickly.'

'But that still does not answer my question,' Richard pressed. 'Why have you really come?'

The kitchen fell silent. No sound except the logs crackling in the hearth. From outside the creak of a barn door, somewhere high in the house a shutter rattled.

'What choice did we have?' Sir Henry Grantham muttered. 'For sixteen years your father's death and disgrace has hung like a sword above us. Don't you realise, Master Richard, there are many in the shire, as well as those at court, who never believed in your father's guilt?' He stared round at his companions. 'Let's be honest. On the night Lord and Lady Fitzalan were murdered, we were all here as well as Richard's father and mother. What is more,' he jabbed the air, his face now flushed with wine and anger, 'we had been summoned under suspicion of treason, of corresponding with the enemy.'

'Some of what you say is true,' Sir Walter Manning spoke up. 'We have all heard the secret gossip. No one has ever established whether those rumours of a traitor amongst us were true or not.'

'What was the evidence for such rumours?' Richard asked. 'After all, that must be the root cause of my father's troubles.'

Manning shrugged. 'Your father, together with Lord Fitzalan, was responsible for the defence of the Essex coast against French privateers. We played a part in that.' He spread his hands. 'Someone was informing the French, so the finger of suspicion was levelled at us.' He leaned across the table, hand out. 'But, Master Richard, now we have met, let me say I loved your father and honour his memory. I have spent sixteen years thinking about what had happened that night.' He spoke so forcefully tears brimmed in his eyes. 'I ask you, how do we know, God forbid, that Lord Fitzalan was not the traitor?'

'Or my father?' Richard added.

'Yes, yes.' Manning wiped his eye on the sleeve of his jerkin. 'No, don't take offence. I and my companions here have discussed this for long hours many a night. No proof was levelled against any of us and, I doubt, any exists now! We came tonight because of our oath to your father.'

Richard glanced round. Manning's four companions murmured in agreement.

'Then why was Fitzalan murdered?' Barleycorn spoke up from the corner of the table.

There was something about the tone of his voice, the way he turned his face sideways. Richard was convinced, whatever this master bowman said, he knew more about the mystery of Crokehurst Manor than he admitted. He'd crouched almost like a child listening attentively to every word. Gildas also, but more curious, eyes darting backwards and forwards. Buthlac pretended to be asleep: Emmeline sat like some lady in a stained-glass window, hands in her lap, now and again she would take a quick sip from her wine. Otherwise she kept still, like a good lawyer who was trying to sift the truth from what was being said.

Barleycorn's question remained unanswered for a while until Sir Lionel Beaumont scraped back his stool. His face looked even more haggard, his fish-like mouth kept opening and closing.

'I have to say something, Master Richard, and I must say it now.' He glanced at Emmeline. 'I suppose what you know was given you in a letter left with Master Hugo Coticol?'

'Yes.'

Richard's reply drew a sigh from Beaumont's companions.

'I thought you were his daughter,' Sir Lionel continued excitedly, pointing at Emmeline. 'Sharp as a needle he was, my lady. Pounce like a sweeping hawk he could. A good man, a sharp lawyer, he sometimes came to Crokehurst.' Sir Lionel turned to Richard. 'Now what we know, and perhaps your father didn't tell his lawyer, was that late in the day, just before the murders occurred, your father and the Lord Fitzalan had the most acrimonious quarrel.' He waved his hands quickly. 'No, no, I did not tell the sheriff this. Your father was damned enough without my statement. God forbid that I should add to his woes. Nevertheless, it is true. I was passing their chamber, your father was shouting.' He smiled grimly. 'A very rare event, for Sir Roger hardly ever raised his voice. But I remember the words well.' Sir Lionel closed his eyes. '"How can you blame me?" your father cried. "Only you and I, my lord, knew that information!" I didn't hear Lord Simon's reply. He was talking softly. Again your father exclaimed, "I take my oath upon the sacrament. Only you and I knew that information!"'

'But, Sir Lionel,' Emmeline intervened, 'how do we know you are telling the truth?'

'Because I was there,' Sir Philip Ferrers spoke up. 'I came up on to the gallery as well. Sir Lionel beckoned · e towards him. Sir Roger was beginning to curse. He kept repeating the same question. It was almost as if, well...' Sir Philip seemed more interested in the crumbs on his trancher. 'It was ε nost as if Lord Simon was pointing the finger of accusation at him rather than anyone else.'

'We did not mean to eavesdrop,' Sir Lionel kindly added to Richard. 'But then your father made to leave, so we hurried away along the gallery and up the stairs. Even so, your father must have left the chamber in a rage: he slammed the door with such force it sounded like a clap of thunder.'

'After that,' Sir John Bremner spoke up, 'he must have walked down to the lakeside.' He pulled a face. 'Apparently he was attacked and,' he spread his hands, 'the rest you know.'

'I know,' Richard retorted, 'that my father was later found, his clothes doused in blood and drink, in one of the stables. I know also that Lady Catherine was found with her throat slashed after being cruelly attacked and ravished.'

Richard glanced at Buthlac who was now popping morsels of cheese into his mouth and washing them down with gulps of wine. The hermit smirked, red-faced and bright-eyed, back at him.

'Lord Simon was found dead in his chamber, a dagger in his heart,' the hermit declared.

'That's not exactly true,' Sir Henry Grantham broke in. He turned those strange eyes, flat and lifeless, at Richard and scratched the shiny pate of his head. 'No one really knew what happened that night. It was I who went to Lord Simon's chamber. The door was unlocked, I opened it. The chamber was in darkness. I called Lord Simon's name. I was an early riser and he had asked me to rouse him as well. I went across the chamber and heard a groan from the far side of the bed. I took a tinder, lit a candle and found Lord Simon swamped in gore. He was dying. I immediately called for Sir Philip here and Sir Walter Manning. The dagger thrust was to Lord Simon's chest. It had narrowly missed his heart but there was a bloody froth on his lips. I picked him up, cradling him in my arms.' Grantham glanced away. 'His body was jerking. He was in a delirium. He muttered he was cold, very very cold and where was the Lady Catherine? He whispered, "Lord Roger, tell him, tell him the truth!" And then he said something which has always puzzled me: a quotation from the Book of Psalms.' Grantham paused to collect his thoughts. 'Lord Simon pointed towards the hearth, exclaiming, "There's nothing new under the sun." I asked him what the truth was, he said, "The eagle has the truth. There's nothing new under the sun." His body shook, he slipped into a swoon. A few minutes later I felt for the pulse in his neck.' He shook his head. 'There was none.'

'What did all that mean?' Emmeline asked.

'I don't know, I still don't. Lord Simon was feverish, in a delirium.'

'And then what happened?' Richard asked.

'We laid Lord Simon back on the floor and immediately became concerned for the Lady Catherine. I went to your father's room but there was no answer so we searched outside.'

'I went first,' Sir Philip Ferrers spoke up. 'God be my witness,' he whispered. 'I'll never forget what I saw. I went down the path through the woods towards the lake. I was calling for your father, then I glimpsed some colour, what I thought was a rag lying in the undergrowth. I pulled this aside. Lady Catherine was there, her throat slashed. We then searched for your father: he was in one of the small outhouses where the hay was kept, just sprawled there. The stench from the wine fumes was thick and rich. His robe was covered in blood. In his outstretched hand was a dagger, covered from tip to handle in blood. We roused him with buckets of water from the well. When he regained consciousness he didn't seem to know where he was and complained of violent pains in his head. We told him what had happened but he seemed unaware and asked for his wife the Lady Maria. We took him back to the manor house and told him what had happened then sent a messenger for the sheriff.'

'What could we do?' Grantham asked helplessly. 'When one of the King's most powerful courtiers, a royal favourite is murdered, his wife ravished, her throat cut whilst another of the King's henchmen is found covered in their blood?'

'Did anything else untoward happen?' Richard queried then paused. He sniffed the air and caught the smell of wood smoke, more acrid than that from the hearth.

'What's the matter?' Emmeline asked.

'Listen!'

He rose from the table and ran across to the shutters and opened them. It was still snowing, the sky was dark. He went out of the kitchen round to the front of the manor house. The others followed.

'Look!' Richard cried and pointed to the glow against the night sky. 'The bridge is burning!'

Chapter 4

Richard told Emmeline to stay with Buthlac. He led the rest, slipping and sliding on the snow-covered ground, eyes and faces stung by the whipped-up snow flakes, along the path down to the lakeside. As they drew closer, the smoke grew more intense and they could hear the crackle and roar of the fire. They burst out of the trees and stopped.

Not even during the campaigns in France had Richard seen such a fierce fire, like some hungry animal; the entire bridge was engulfed in flames which, despite the frozen lake and the falling snow, roared up into the night sky. Richard drew his dagger, just the feel of the steel in his hand gave him some comfort.

'That's no accident,' he shouted. 'But why should someone burn the bridge?'

'The outlaws,' Barleycorn said. 'Dogwort and Ratsbane, perhaps they have crossed?'

'Who?' Sir Walter Manning asked.

Barleycorn described his life-long feud with these outlaws, their meeting in Colchester and possible pursuit.

'I have heard of them,' Bremner replied. 'Their names constantly appear before the King's Justices.' The knight wiped the sweat from his face. 'But why burn the bridge?'

Richard remembered the knight pounding across the meadow, shield up, sword held high. Whilst the rest chattered and discussed the fire, he knew what had happened. The bridge had been set alight, not to stop anyone coming across to the island but to trap everyone who was on it.

'What about supplies?' Sir Walter Manning asked, rubbing his stomach. 'We can't bloody starve here! Perhaps...' His voice trailed off.

'Perhaps what?' Grantham snapped.

'Perhaps we shouldn't have come. Perhaps we could have met elsewhere.'

No one objected.

'Well, you are here now,' Richard spoke up. 'We are all here and, as for the supplies, the lake is freezing but, at the far end of the island, there is a causeway.' He stared up through the snow-covered trees.

'There's nothing we can do now,' he declared. 'It's best if we return and sleep.'

They returned to the kitchen. Richard told Emmeline what had happened. She had been warming posset in a bowl above the fire: the air was thick and rich with the smell of hot claret sprinkled with herbs.

'Take a cup before you retire,' she insisted. 'Everyone, it will warm your innards, keep your humours stable.' She spoke so sharply no one dared disagree. She then put the hot jug, a rag tied round the handle, back on the hearth and told Buthlac to keep an eye on it.

'The bridge is burnt,' she said thoughtfully, drying her hands on her dress, 'so we must all stay here till the truth is known. But having listened very carefully to what you all have said, one thing does puzzle me.'

'There speaks the lawyer's daughter,' Sir Lionel Beaumont declared patronisingly.

Emmeline made a mock curtsey towards him.

'Speak up, my lady,' Bremner sipped from his cup.

'Let us say,' she continued, 'causa disputandi – for the sake of argument – that the assassin had to kill Lord Fitzalan?'

'Why?' Manning asked.

'Because Lord Fitzalan was now hunting him, as was Richard's father?'

'I accept that,' Grantham replied.

'And Lord Fitzalan may have been getting close to the truth.' Emmeline smiled. 'That's why he had to die then?'

'Naturally,' Grantham drawled.

'But Lady Catherine's death was not really necessary?'

The five knights agreed. Richard watched this young woman, her eyes bright, body held stiffly; he could sense her excitement. He noticed how slim her waist was, the generous curves of her bodice, the long slender fingers clutching daintily at the folds of her dress and the proud tilt of her head. Despite his tiredness, Richard hid a smile. Sir Lionel was correct, if she wore a fur-tipped gown, Emmeline would be a lawyer before King's Bench.

'I don't mean to give offence,' she continued, 'but Lady Catherine must have had her own chamber, yes?'

'Aye,' Bremner replied. 'Otherwise her husband would have missed her?'

'Well,' Emmeline paused to collect her thoughts. 'We know that Lady Catherine must have retired for the night yet she is found fully clothed the following morning. Now, why would a lady, married to one of the most powerful men in Essex, leave her chamber in the early hours of the morning and go out along a lonely towpath? She was no fool. She knew about the dangers of the lurking outlaw or even some servant who had pretensions above himself.'

'What are you implying?' Grantham asked.

'To put it bluntly, the Lady Catherine must have gone out to meet someone.'

'I don't accept that,' Sir Walter Manning replied. 'Don't forget, my dear,' he added patronisingly, 'it was the height of summer, Crokehurst is a beautiful place. The Lady Catherine knew she was safe in Crokehurst Manor. She may have just been restless and gone for a walk.'

'Fully dressed?' Emmeline snapped. 'At that early hour?'

'I thought that as well,' Buthlac shouted gleefully.

Sir John Bremner lurched from his chair, much the worse for drink. He went over and stared down at the hermit.

'I remember you,' he whispered. 'I never forget a face.' He turned, grinning at his companions. 'Don't you remember the peasant, the filthy hermit Lord Roger always allowed into his hall? Ever listening he was at keyholes or under a windowsill.' He went to grasp Buthlac's jerkin. The hermit's hand went to his dagger.

'Careful, my lord,' he warned. 'I am not your man and these are not your estates. I am no peasant varlet to be threatened or bullied.'

'Leave him!' Ferrers ordered. He smiled at Buthlac. Bremner re-took his seat. 'What were you saying, man?' Ferrers asked.

'The same as this sharp-witted girl,' Buthlac replied. The hermit waved his hand airily. 'Remember as well: the stables were full of ostlers and servants, not to mention the retinue of my good lord here. Yet the Lady Catherine did not scream, shout or yell. She seemed to have offered her throat and body to the slaughterer without a murmur.'

Bremner half rose. 'I could clean your mouth with ash!' he grated. 'The Lady Catherine, God rest her, was of noble birth.'

'Then let me say it,' Emmeline offered. 'Is it possible that Lady Catherine went out to meet her lover? Someone here in the manor house? That person ravished and cut her throat before slipping back to murder her husband.' She paused before concluding, 'In other words, Lady Catherine's lover, murderer and the French spy in Essex were one and the same person. If he had only killed her husband, she would be left to point the finger, or even blackmail him.'

'Of course,' Richard breathed. 'The Lady Catherine was giving her lover the King's secrets, wittingly or unwittingly we don't know.'

'All things are possible,' Grantham retorted. 'Yet a royal sergeant of law might argue that perhaps your father was the Lady Catherine's lover.' He glimpsed the anger in Richard's eyes. 'Of course, I don't believe that. Your father had eyes for one woman and one woman only, the Lady Maria.' He glanced narrow-eyed at Emmeline. 'Our pretty, young lawyer here may have the truth of it. I remember when the Lord Fitzalan and his wife came here last. There was a coolness between them and one of my pages heard sharp words.' He raised his eyebrows. 'But,' he laughed, 'we are all married men and know that marriages made in heaven can turn out to be forged in hell.' He pulled a face. 'There might have been a lover but all this doesn't establish Lord Roger's innocence.'

'What happened to my father's papers?' Richard asked abruptly.

'Confusion broke out,' Sir Philip Ferrers replied. 'Your father asked me to look for certain things but all his manuscripts were destroyed or burnt.'

'Who by?'

'We don't know. You see, when a man falls from power, the sheriff and his posse arrive. All of Crokehurst was forfeit to the Crown. Of course, men have sticky fingers; most of the movables were taken away as general plunder.'

'And Lord Simon's papers?' Richard insisted, now intrigued by this. 'Surely some search was made for them?'

'Who said he had any papers?' Manning asked. 'None were found here.'

Richard studied each of the five knights: their faces showed this meeting was not turning out as they had hoped. The squire recalled the favourite phrase of Sir Gilbert Savage. 'If you intend to catch a dog by its tail, make sure it's not a wolf.' Richard closed his eyes: which was the wolf here? If only Sir Gilbert Savage was here now, he would advise him, ask the right questions.

'Everyone is growing tired,' Sir John Bremner said and made to rise.

'Savage,' Richard spoke up quickly, opening his eyes. 'You do recall my father's yeoman, Sir Gilbert?'

'Aye, your father's shadow in everything.'

'Why didn't he go looking for my father that night?' Richard asked.

The knights looked at each other.

'Well?' Richard persisted. 'Here we have a man utterly faithful to my father, who raised me as a child. My father disappears but there's no sign of Sir Gilbert.'

'The night the murder took place,' Ferrers retorted, 'Savage had left on some errand for your father. After the tragedy, your mother fled with you to Coticol's house but she was sick. The lawyer looked after you when she went to the nunnery.' Ferrers drained his cup. 'We never actually saw Savage again. He probably suspected one of us.'

'And afterwards?'

Ferrers extended his cup for Emmeline to refill.

'I heard,' he continued, 'a rumour that your father knighted him in his cell at Colchester Castle and that he took you into his care.' Ferrers smiled apologetically. 'It happened so quickly. One of us would have looked after you, raised you as our own but, by the time the dust was settled, Savage had disappeared. We heard rumours . . .'

'I even sent him letters,' Sir John Bremner interrupted. 'On behalf of us all, but I received no reply. Never once did he come into Essex.'

'Did you ever see him again?' Richard asked.

'No,' Grantham shook his head. 'He'd left your father by the time we visited him in the dungeons of Colchester Castle. Since then, as the others have said, we have seen neither hide nor hair of him.'

'So you visited my father in Colchester?' Richard asked. 'In his last letter to me, he said you took an oath to clear his memory.'

'What else did he say to you?' The knights looked uncomfortably at each other, shuffling their feet.

'We did what we could,' Ferrers declared quickly. 'We petitioned the King. But don't forget, Master Richard, in the eyes of the law, your father was a convicted murderer and traitor. His Grace the King and the entire court were furious. Nothing could be done.'

'And, when you saw my father just before his escape, he had nothing to say?'

'Or little to add,' Sir Lionel Beaumont replied. 'He protested his innocence. We told him what Lord Simon said before he died, about pointing to the hearth and saying, "The eagle has the truth. There's nothing new under the sun".'

'And what did my father say to that?'

'He became very sad and quiet. He got up, loaded with chains, and stared up at the light streaming through the cell window. Then he muttered something in a half-whisper: "I wish Lord Simon had told me." I asked him what he meant. All your father would reply was that "the Lord Fitzalan, after his quarrel with him, had promised to discuss something very important with him."' Sir Lionel fell silent and stared into the wine cup. 'After that we took the oath. We left and, on the following day, your father escaped. He was condemned in his absence: his corpse dragged from the Stour a few days later.'

'Why not tell him about the other corpse?' Buthlac broke in.

Everyone looked at the hermit where he sat in the corner of the hearth, grinning merrily like some mischievous gnome.

'Or have you forgotten?' Buthlac asked innocently.

'What do you mean?' Sir Walter demanded threateningly.

'Well, after all the excitement died down. When the sheriff's men had gone, the Lady Maria at the convent, the Lord Roger is in prison and the Lord Simon's body has been sheeted and sent for burial, old Buthlac discovered a corpse bobbing in the reeds near the causeway, naked as a worm he was.'

'That has nothing to do with this,' Grantham declared. 'It was probably the body of some stranger, some pedlar or traveller who had lost his way. Or,' he added meaningfully, 'some recluse who couldn't stop chattering.'

Buthlac rocked with laughter. 'I just thought I'd mention it,' he scoffed. 'Face all smashed in as if someone had hit him time and time again with a hammer. Just bobbing there like a leaf on a pond. So, old Buthlac drags him out and buries him down there near the causeway.' He dropped his voice to a whisper, eyes rounded and shining. 'If you go down there, when the mist rolls in before dawn or just after dusk, you knows, when the ghosts and demons walk, you'll see his shade there.' Buthlac's eyes slid away. 'But, there again, this place is full of ghosts.' He shivered. 'The island of ghosts,' he continued in a sepulchral voice. 'Pressing all around us they are: red-eyed, faces white, demanding vengeance and rest for their souls.'

'Shut up!' Ferrers snarled.

'It's true.' Gildas, who had been sitting, fascinated by the conversation, got to his feet, finger pointed. 'It is written in the Good Book how the souls of those sent into death unprepared, wander the earth looking for justice. Did not,' his voice rose, 'the witch of Endor in the Book of Samuel...?'

'Thank you,' Barleycorn said with finality.

Gildas opened his mouth to protest when they heard a heavy footfall in the gallery above.

'Some animal?' Emmeline whispered.

'Wearing boots?' Gildas scoffed. 'Listen!'

They all sat frozen, straining their ears but then, just when they were about to dismiss the noise as nothing, they heard the footsteps again. Slow and measured, as if someone was pacing up and down the gallery above them. Bremner sprang to his feet. Richard noticed how the sweat on his forehead was turning slightly black as the dye on his hair began to run. He fingered a tassel on his belt and nervously scratched at his brocaded jerkin, loosening the white shirt underneath.

'It's Lord Fitzalan,' he muttered.

'What do you mean?' Barleycorn asked.

'Listen! Listen!' Bremner's eyes were almost popping out of his head. 'Listen to the spurs!'

Again silence and the footfall, only this time they heard the jingle of spurs.

'Fitzalan always wore them,' Grantham whispered. 'Don't you remember?' He glanced fearfully at Richard. 'Your father always used to tease him about it.'

They all sat frozen: they heard the footsteps and the jingling of the spurs like some demonic bell. Barleycorn was the first to stir himself. He got up and lunged at the door, pulled it open, stumbled and fell. Richard told Emmeline to stay but she pulled a face and came after him. The five knights followed. Barleycorn was now at the foot of the stairs. He held a hand up. Richard stopped. He felt a freezing sensation down his back, his hair curling on the nape of his neck.

'For the love of God!' one of the knights hissed. 'What is it?'

Now doors up on the gallery were opening and shutting, crashing like claps of thunder through the derelict house.

'From all demons and spirits who walk by night,' Gildas at the back of the group intoned. 'From the Midnight Slayer, the Destroyer who walks at darkness!'

Barleycorn now had his bow ready, arrow notched to the string. Slowly he began to climb the stairs. Richard drew his dagger and followed. As they reached the first gallery, the noise stopped. Emmeline came up, her face white, her hands trembling slightly as she passed the candle to Richard. He took this and lit the sconce torches in the wall. The gallery flared into light. There must have been a crack in one of the shutters, the flames danced, making their shadows longer.

'Who's there?' Barleycorn shouted.

Silence.

'Who's there?' Richard repeated.

He was about to move on when he heard the laugh: long, low and chilling, as if something was in the shadows watching them all, chuckling at what it had seen. Barleycorn went further down the gallery. He opened the doors to the different chambers, pushing them back on their creaking, leather hinges. Followed by the rest, they reached the end of the gallery. Richard heaved a sigh of relief, ready to dismiss what he had seen and heard as some phantasm. Of course, deep down in his soul, he refused to accept this. He kept thinking of that charging knight, the iron-shod hooves pounding the ground. He recalled the words of some of the preachers he had avidly listened to as a boy: about how Satan stalked like a roaring lion seeking whom he may devour. Was Crokehurst full of demons? he wondered. Summoned up from hell by the dreadful events which had happened here?

He was about to tell Barleycorn and the rest to go back to the kitchen when, from the gallery above, came the horrid sound of those footsteps and the jingling of spurs. His body broke out in a sweat and, pushing Barleycorn aside, he raced like a greyhound up the stairs, shouting and yelling. Barleycorn and Ferrers followed. In the pitch darkness at the top, Richard crashed about, stumbling over bits and pieces of furniture lying there. He missed his footing but grabbed the wall. Ferrers, the guttering candle now in his hand, lit a torch. In the poor light of the flickering flames, Richard stared down at the gallery. It was cold, deathly cold, but desolate. He walked further down.

'Who's there?' he called. 'In the name of God!' He turned to speak to his companions and stepped back in fright at sight of some writing daubed on the white plaster walls. 'Quickly!' he urged. 'Bring torches!'

Gildas and Emmeline brought more from the lower gallery. They grouped round the wall and stared in horror at words written in blood, which was still streaking in small, fat drops.

'What does it say?' Barleycorn whispered.

Richard held the torch closer, spelling out each of the letters, forming them into words.

'Vengeance is mine, saith the Lord. I will repay.'

For a while Richard and his companions just stared at this macabre warning. Barleycorn touched the blood with the tip of his finger and tasted it gingerly.

'It is blood!' he said in astonishment. 'Lord save us! It really is blood!'

At Richard's insistence, they searched the gallery and the rest of the house but found no trace of any intruder. When they returned to the kitchen, Richard sensed the change in the atmosphere. The knights had lost their boisterous arrogance and he could tell from their faces that, perhaps, they regretted their oath. If the bridge hadn't been burnt, they may have even discussed the prospect of leaving. Nevertheless, the hour was late. They were tired after the wine they'd drunk and subdued by the ghostly happenings in the house. Each took their leave, Barleycorn offering to show them to their chambers. When he returned to the kitchen, Buthlac was fast asleep in a corner. Richard, Emmeline and Gildas were grouped round the dying fire, talking in whispers about the strange occurrences they had witnessed.

'What will happen now?' Barleycorn asked, taking a seat. He shook his head. 'All the evidence points to your father's guilt although there are cracks and rents in the accepted story.'

'Enough to cause suspicion,' Richard retorted. 'What did Lord Fitzalan mean? Those dying words of his? "Nothing new under the sun" and "The eagle has the truth"? And what was he pointing at? Why did he and my father quarrel? Why did Lady Catherine leave the house and die so silently out there in the woods?' He sighed and, picking up a twig from the hearth, he jabbed at a log in the fire. 'Do you think my father had his suspicions?'

'If he did,' Barleycorn replied, 'he kept them to himself. All his papers and manuscripts have gone, not a scrap of evidence or the slightest sign of where his suspicions lay.'

Richard glanced at Gildas. 'On your journey, travelling with the knights, did you glean anything?'

'I mentioned the prospect of some profit,' Gildas replied. 'But that only provoked laughter. The small, fat one, Manning, he guffawed so vigorously he almost fell off his horse. He said he was not returning to Crokehurst for any profit. The sheriff's men had plundered the house well, leaving no stone unturned and, what they missed, the royal searchers would have certainly found. No, I think they are here for a number of reasons: belief in your father's innocence; their oath to him not to mention any man who absented himself would incur suspicion.'

'Oh, they are worried all right.' Buthlac suddenly opened his eyes and sat forward on his makeshift bed. 'You tell them, Master. Tell them what I told you, about mysterious strangers visiting the island.'

Richard did, recounting all that had happened that morning; the knight, the meeting with Buthlac and the hermit's revelations.

'One of those men,' Buthlac declared, once Richard had finished, 'one of those knights is a murderer. But, Master Richard, how can we prove it?'

The squire rose and stretched.

'I don't know. I believe there are other people, forces on this island, that might show their hand and help us. We have enough food and drink, we are comfortable and warm. This is probably the first time all five knights have returned to where the murders took place. Someone's memory may be stirred. A scrap of information, certain words recalled, but only the devil knows how it's going to be done.'

He jumped at a knock on the door. Sir John Bremner, his cloak wrapped about him, walked into the kitchen. In his hand he held a small, calf-skin-bound book, the leather stained, its golden buckle broken.

'I'm sorry,' he murmured. 'I forgot to give you this.' He handed the book over.

Richard opened it: a Book of Hours. Once, years ago, it must have been a work of art but the illuminated pictures had faded, the inked words had lost their character, some pages were missing, others were torn and stained.

'Your father gave it to me,' Bremner declared. 'It's the only thing he took with him to Colchester prison.'

Richard opened the book, turning the pages carefully.

'I have studied it myself,' Bremner murmured. 'Believe me, Master Richard, there's nothing there. I am sorry,' he apologised. 'I should have given it to you earlier.' He turned and left the room.

For a while Richard just stood, leafing curiously through the book, fighting back the tears. This prayer book was the only possession he had of his father's. It was old, probably in the family for generations. He studied the binding, this had come away from the leather cover and, with a sinking heart, Richard realised that, if any secret message had been concealed there, he would never know. He looked inside the cover. Someone, probably his father, had drawn a family tree opposite a picture of an eagle, flying under the sun, wings outstretched, grasping an iron bar. He went back to his companions and showed them the picture.

'This must be my family escutcheon,' he remarked drily. 'I have seen it on stone hearths throughout the house.'

Buthlac, pulling back his greasy hair, leaned over and suddenly grasped the book.

'Yes, it is,' he said. 'I remember the tournament days. Your father had a great banner, a black eagle with a golden beak against a white background, a fiery sun above it, an iron bar in its talons. Brave sight! Brave sight!' he murmured. He shook Gildas who was falling asleep. 'Master, it's time we retired, tomorrow is another day.'

They all agreed. Barleycorn slipped out of the house, muttering he would be more comfortable in the stable away from ghosts. Buthlac and Gildas curled up like dogs but Richard felt restless and Emmeline, despite her paleness, also said that she was not yet ready for sleep. For a while they sat in front of the fire.

Emmeline grasped Richard's hand, stroking it gently.

'We are bound together, Richard,' she murmured. 'You know that, for better or worse.' She grinned shyly at him. 'My life and yours will never be the same. But don't worry.' She straightened up and turned her head as if listening for sounds. 'I believe you. The truth will come out.'

Richard stared into the fire; despite the problems which confronted him, he felt at peace: Emmeline was with him.

'Eagles and suns,' he remarked. 'Lord Fitzalan mentioned these as he lay dying and they both figure in the Greenele escutcheon.' He spread his hands out towards the fire. 'But what did he mean about the truth? Why the riddle?' He glanced at Emmeline. 'Now we have ghosts walking the house.'

She shivered and caught at his fingers.

'And the living are just as mysterious.' She nodded towards Buthlac and Gildas where they lay snoring as comfortable as pigs in a sty. 'We do not know who they are or where they came from and, if I understand correctly, Cuthbert Barleycorn is as much a mystery to you as he is to anyone. Whilst the five knights?' She shrugged prettily. 'Never forget,' she whispered as she released his hand, 'one or all of them could be involved in these murders. Lord and Lady Fitzalan were ferociously and skilfully killed as if they were no more than beasts in the slaughter house. Your father's reputation was destroyed, he, too, was a victim of this killer as was your mother.' She leaned over and kissed Richard on the cheek. 'What I am saying,' she whispered, 'is that one, or more of these men, have come not to discover the truth but to make sure it remains hidden for ever. To achieve it he, or they, will kill again and again without a moment's compunction.'

Words between the pilgrims

The franklin paused. He looked down at his feet, then rose and, crossing to a table, refilled his wine cup. Chaucer noticed that, as he passed the knight, he held his hand up: a secret sign that Sir Godfrey should hold his peace. The knight looked excited, face flushed, eyes shining. Throughout the tale, the knight had sat tense, only his eyes betraying him. As if he knew the story and would have loved to have intervened.

'I wonder,' Chaucer whispered to Mine Host sitting beside him. 'Just how many people here are part of this tale?'

'Aye,' the landlord replied. He glanced over at the franklin. 'Have you noticed the summoner? Earlier in the day he was drinking fit to burst but now he is as sober as any hanging judge.'

Chaucer glanced across the candle-lit taproom. The summoner had sat like a scholar in one of the Halls of Oxford, back straight, he too had been listening avidly to the tale. Never once had he farted, belched, made any obscene gesture or tried to interrupt the tale as was his custom. Instead he looked eager, sometimes secretive and sly.

Chaucer studied the summoner's ugly, wart-covered face. He

had already made his own private decision that, once he was back in London, he would make careful scrutiny about this summoner who travelled the lanes and byeways of the shires. Chaucer was certain that the summoner was more than he appeared; a man of secrets who might well be worth investigating.

'Are you part of the story?' The prioress, still carrying her lap dog, came over and smiled prettily down at the franklin.

He put his cup down on the floor and ran his fingers through his snowy-white beard.

'I suppose, my lady,' he replied. 'We are all part of everyone's story. Wait till the end.'

'I know who you are talking about.' She turned and smiled coyly round the room.

'What do you mean?' the franklin asked sharply.

'I stayed at a nunnery situated in rolling meadows outside Colchester, where there was a plaque in the church, a beautifully carved marble piece, just as you entered the Lady Chapel.' She closed her eyes, more for effect than just recalling lines. 'Yes, yes, that's what it said: "Of your mercy pray for the soul of my mother, Lady Maria Greenele, buried here in a pauper's grave, the victim of a terrible crime".'

'Stop!' The franklin held his hand up. His face suddenly hard, his eyes had lost that merry, carefree look. 'My lady,' he warned, 'your turn will come.' He turned abruptly to where the yellow-haired pardoner had stopped counting his pennies. He was now listening intently to their conversation. 'And the same goes for you, sir. You have been to Crokehurst?'

'Aye, I have,' the fellow replied in a screech of a voice. 'And strange are the tales they tell.'

'I, too, know Crokehurst,' the poor parson spoke up from where he sat nibbling at a piece of bread, quiet and as docile as a church mouse. 'I have heard of Crokehurst,' he repeated in a surprisingly strong voice. His eyes swept round the taproom.

'Years ago,' he smiled at the franklin. 'When I was younger, I was parson to the little church of St Cedd's, five or six leagues from the island. They told wondrous stories about it. About how it was haunted, how ghosts had thronged there and how...'

'Enough!' Mine Host interrupted. 'Sir.' He turned to the franklin. 'Continue your story.'

'One question,' the friar, sitting next to the wife of Bath, whose knee he had been trying to stroke, spoke up. 'One question,' he repeated in his bell-like voice, his berry-brown face boisterous with glee. 'Master franklin, you were telling us a story,' he shrugged and played with the cord round his waist, 'which may be more fact than fable. Now this mysterious, black knight, why didn't this young squire organise a search of the island?'

The franklin sipped from his goblet. 'Good Brother, if you ever travel to Crokehurst, you'll find it's no lump of clay in a mill pond but a place of thick woods, trees growing close together and all around them a tangle of bracken, not to mention deep snow in winter. So, let me continue my story. Richard was a good man, keen and sharp, and deeply enamoured of the Lady Emmeline. Now, this good parson here has mentioned ghosts and sprites but, it was also a place of grisly murder, as I will tell.'

PART III

Chapter 1

The squire and Emmeline rose early the next morning. Outside the snow had stopped falling but everything was now hidden under its thick white smoothness. Barleycorn was already cleaning the yard and he had the horses out, exercising them, their breath hanging like clouds in the frozen air. Gildas had built up a fire. Emmeline went off and returned to the kitchen. The knights came down, wryly admitting to thick heads after their late night of heavy drinking. In the morning light, the cheery bustle of the kitchen lightened the atmosphere.

'It's not your fault,' Sir Lionel spoke up, his mouth full of oatmeal, 'that the snow has fallen.' He glanced rather imperiously round at his companions. 'I'm glad I've come. For sixteen years I've wished to discharge my oath.' He smiled thinly. 'It's not as uncomfortable as going on pilgrimage or travelling to Outremer.'

The rest agreed, greedily eating the delicious oatmeal Emmeline had cooked: hot, thick and laced with nutmeg and honey.

'I don't believe in ghouls and goblins,' Grantham declared, licking his horn-spoon clean. 'Master Richard, what we should do is organise a search, go round this island. Whoever was in this house last night daubing messages on the wall, is flesh and blood. Not some ghost or demon spat up from hell.'

They all agreed and, once they had broken their fast, the kitchen cleaned and the fire dampened down, they went out into the morning air. In the full light of day the knights looked bleary-eyed and unshaven. Richard declared they should stay as a group and, with Buthlac leading, he led them back along the woodland paths towards the tournament field. This time, progress was a little slower. There were at least five inches of snow on the ground and this increased the eerie atmosphere of the island. The snow deadened sound and blinded the eye. Now and again they would jump as a pile of snow slipped from the branches, crashing to the ground below. Emmeline protested prettily and Richard was only too willing to act as the gallant squire, grasping her arm and helping her forwards. They followed the trackway, marked here and there by bird claw, rabbit print, the tracks of a badger or a hunting fox. The clouds began to break under a weak sun and gave the snow a silver sheen. Conversation was desultory. Sir Walter Manning asked again about supplies. Barleycorn pointed to the rabbit tracks.

'We'll have plenty of water,' he said. 'And we could withstand a siege for months, the wild life is plentiful.'

At last they reached the fringe of trees which marked the beginning of the great meadow. They all fell silent as Richard led them forward.

'It's magical,' Emmeline whispered, staring round at the white, glassy expanse. 'Who would have thought such a field existed?'

'I remember it well,' Sir John Bremner spoke up, leaning against a tree to catch his breath. He looked over his shoulder at his companions. 'Do you remember that tournament? Good Lord, Master Richard, what a sight it was. Pavilions, lists and standards flapping in the breeze. The war horses caparisoned in marvellous cloths, the shrill of trumpets, the ladies in their silks, knights in their finest armour.' Bremner's voice shook. 'All gone,' he whispered. 'All finished.'

'Your father used to have many tournaments here,' Ferrers added eagerly.

Richard nodded but he was more busy staring across the field. He remembered those foot-falls the night before. If someone had entered the house they might have crossed the field, either returning or going back, yet there were no footprints, nothing at all. He took a step forward. The wind whipped his hair, filling his face with snowflakes stirred up from the trees around him. He was about to urge the others to follow when, from the trees at the far end of the field, came the chilling, silver blast of a trumpet. Richard froze. His companions stared fearfully across the shimmering brightness. Again the trumpet blast, clearer, more powerful. From the line of trees on the other side of the meadow, at exactly the same spot Richard had seen him the day before, emerged the knight dressed in black armour, his great war horse snorting and shaking its head.

'The Lord and all his saints!' Grantham whispered.

'Kyrie Eleison!'

'Who can it be?'

'Who are you?' Richard shouted but his words just hung on the air.

The great war horse moved and the knight lifted his arm, his sword glinting in the weak sunlight; he pointed towards the group.

'Bring him down!' Ferrers exclaimed. 'Bring him down!'

Barleycorn, before Richard could stop him, was running across the field. The knight did not move. On the master bowman sped, bow at the ready, arrow notched.

'If he's a man,' Bremner muttered, 'he'll either retreat or charge. Barleycorn's arrows could pierce plate armour.'

Barleycorn was still running, drawing near to the knight.

Then he stopped and knelt, the snow rising up in flurries around him. Secretly Richard hoped that the knight would charge or withdraw but horse and rider stood stock-still. Barleycorn notched an arrow, the yew bow bent. He loosed: another arrow was notched even as the first skimmed through the air. Richard narrowed his eyes. The first arrow missed its target slightly but the second arrow took the knight full in the chest only to fall away. Another arrow followed, the same effect, as if Barleycorn was aiming at granite rock. Three, four more arrows followed, all with the same effect. The knight turned and, like a ghost, slipped back into the trees. Another arrow hit him in the back but with the same effect as the others. Barleycorn dropped his bow, drew his long Welsh stabbing knife and followed. Richard, shaking his arm free of Emmeline, ran across, the other knights lumbering behind him. The snow impeded their progress. Richard slipped, falling full length in the snow but he rose and struggled on. He reached the wood where Barleycorn, also breathless, crouched at the foot of a tree.

'No sign.' He shook his head, caught his breath then gestured round. 'Not a sign of him!'

Richard studied the ground. Any indentations of where horse and rider had once stood were now spoilt by Barleycorn and his own footprints. Although he could see tracks leading into the trees, these were not the ones he'd expect of a heavy war horse. No hoof print. No mark of a horse especially shod for war. Barleycorn collected the five arrows he had shot. All were broken, the arrow heads snapped off.

'I can't believe it.' He thrust the arrows into Richard's hand. 'I've brought down French knights wearing the best armour in Europe, yet these have no effect. It was like aiming at stone.'

Richard turned round as his companions joined him. Across the field Emmeline lifted her hand and waved. All five knights stared at the arrows in Richard's hand.

'He was no phantasm!' Manning snapped. 'Yet those arrows

should have brought him down.' He walked through the line of trees. 'God knows where he's gone or where he hides.' He spun round. 'Can't we search the island?'

'It would be like chasing a will-o'-the-wisp.' Bremner spoke from the back. 'Do you really think we'd catch him?'

They followed the pathway which wound round towards the lake. The day had now lost some of its brightness. Richard was puzzled. He didn't believe that the knight was some ghost or ghoul but what did he want? How could he have withstood Barleycorn's arrows? He wished he was alone with Emmeline: she was a sharp and an astute observer. They reached the edge of the lake and stared out across its frozen stillness. So engrossed in his own thoughts, Richard hardly bothered at the exclamations of his companions. He looked up and followed Barleycorn's pointed finger. The far shore was clear but, from where he stood, he could see where the snow had been broken by both foot and horse.

'Someone's been down!' Buthlac cried.

'The knight?' Bremner asked.

'No, no,' Barleycorn replied. 'I would guess thirty, forty men, some on foot, others on horse. Sometime just before dawn.'

'Who could they be?' Sir Philip Ferrers' broad, craggy face was now a mask of concern. 'Master Richard, are you bringing a force here?'

The squire just shook his head. For a while they stood and stared at the hooves and footprints which swept down from the brow of the hill to the edge of the lake.

'Well, who ever they are,' Ferrers declared. 'There's no bridge.'

'There is a ford,' Barleycorn observed. He grasped Buthlac by the shoulder. 'And, if I and my friend here can cross we'll find out who this force is and where it comes from.'

Before Richard could object, Barleycorn and Buthlac were already hurrying away along the shore line, Buthlac excitedly crying he knew where the ford would be. Richard, now worried about Emmeline, allowed them to go. They went back across the meadow. Behind them the knights whispered in hushed tones. Richard kept his thoughts to himself. He now believed that his journey to this island had been arranged as had the presence of the five knights. Someone else was on the island, intent on seeing justice done. Of course, nothing in life runs to order. Richard secretly believed Dogwort, Ratsbane and their coven had arrived and were also a force to be reckoned with. The outlaws had probably followed them from Colchester, intent on finishing their quarrel with Barleycorn once and for all.

Emmeline, her face pink from the cold, sat, her cloak wrapped around her, resting on a boulder.

'I thought you'd disappeared,' she cried, getting to her feet. She grasped Richard's arm but the squire warned her with his eyes to keep silent.

'It's best if we return to the hall,' he declared. He forced a smile. 'God knows I'm starving, my stomach thinks my throat's been cut.'

They returned to the manor house. Tired by their long walk in the snow, the knights sat round the fire, laughing and joking as they shared a huge bowl of rabbit stew and some of the bread they had brought. Richard kept to himself, sitting at the table, ears straining, waiting for Barleycorn to return. The knights finished their meal. Gildas, who had been left to guard the manor while they were gone, said there were fires now lit in every chamber so the knights decided to play a game of chess to while away the time. Ferrers had apparently emerged as their spokesman and, after he had praised Emmeline for her cooking, came across and stood over Richard.

'We can stay three more days,' he declared, staring down at him. 'Master Richard, we took an oath to your father that if we could help we would. However, the snow has fallen. We have our own families and farms to care for. We will tell you what we can, offer what ever assistance we're able to but then we must go.' He smiled and nodded over his shoulder at his companions. 'Our journey here has woken memories, both good and bad.'

He was about to continue when Sir Lionel Beaumont came over, licking his fingers.

'I heard what you said, Ferrers.' He sat on a stool half-way down the table. 'And, going out to that field this morning.' He tapped the side of his head. 'It made me think.'

His companions must have overheard him because all fell silent.

'Now at mid-summer,' Sir Lionel continued, his eyes closed, 'when your father summoned us here, it wasn't all trouble and woe. There was a tournament.' He looked over his shoulder. 'You all remember, don't you? Two days before the murders happened, I remember it so clearly.' He opened his eyes. 'Your father broke his lance against Lord Fitzalan. We then all ran a course. Afterwards, in the evening, there was feasting and drinking. Now I noticed Lord Fitzalan seemed rather concerned, distant from his wife.'

'Do you know why?' Richard asked.

'Well, we all wore our lady's favours. Lord Simon was cross that his wife had given her colours to someone else. And do you know,' he tapped his chin, 'I think someone else was wearing them but, for the life of me, I can't remember who.' He got up from the table. 'But, if I do, I'll tell you!'

He and his companions then left the room.

The knights were hardly gone when Buthlac and Barleycorn threw open the door and almost fell into the kitchen. They were red-faced, breathing heavily, their boots and leggings soaked wet from the snow. Emmeline stared in alarm as the master bowman and the charlatan pushed their way to the front of the fire, peeling off their gloves, stretching out their frozen fingers.

139

'What did you find?' Richard asked.

'There's been horse and foot,' Barleycorn replied hoarsely. 'But the snow is fairly deep and we couldn't follow.'

'And then there's the corpse,' Buthlac added.

'We followed the tracks,' Barleycorn explained, 'up to the brow of the hill. Before us nothing but a white expanse and the signs that horses and men had come that way and then retreated. However, lying in the snow was a man's corpse. He had been stripped of every item of clothing, his throat cut and left there.'

'He was an oldish man,' Buthlac interrupted. 'Very little hair, unshaven cheeks.'

'Could it have been the outlaws?' Emmeline asked. 'Did they meet some poor pedlar, kill him, strip his body and pass on?'

Barleycorn rose to his feet. He unhitched his cloak, then put his quiver and bow in a corner.

'It's Dogwort and Ratsbane,' he declared. 'They followed us here and it would not be hard. After all, three men and a young lady travelling through the frozen countryside would have been seen.'

'And the corpse?' Gildas asked.

'Oh, that's Dogwort and Ratsbane's work,' Barleycorn replied. 'I don't think it was some innocent pedlar. Probably one of their own men had fallen sick. They do the same in the forest, cut the poor bastard's throat and leave him. They show no mercy, not even to their own.'

Richard shivered and looked at the leaping flames. He closed his eyes and tried to hide his panic. He was in his father's house, with the power to unlock the mysteries of the past and clear his father's name. However, because of Barleycorn, an outlaw band was pursuing them across the frozen wastes of Essex, bent on vengeance.

'Why?' he asked, opening his eyes. 'Why, Barleycorn?'

'I've told you, Master Richard,' the bowman replied. 'I have killed their kith and kin and, when this business is over, I intend to kill more. They, in their turn, want my head. Kill or be killed,' he whispered. 'There is no escape.'

'Will they attack?' Gildas asked anxiously. 'Perhaps they'll go away and leave us alone?'

Barleycorn caught and held Richard's gaze. 'They have gone back for more men,' he declared. 'Food and better arms. They'll know we are here, they could have even burnt the bridge. They know I am trapped. They'll cross the lake, even if they have to sprout wings.'

'And we just wait for them to do so?' Gildas asked impatiently.

'No,' Barleycorn replied. 'They are looking for the ford. By the tracks in the snow, I think they have found it. I think we've got one, perhaps two days' grace. But then they'll return, cross and scour the island for us.' He breathed in deeply. 'I am sorry, Master.'

'You could go out and meet them,' Gildas observed sardonically.

'No,' Richard snapped, grasping Barleycorn's arm. 'Cuthbert is my friend and my companion. If he dies, I die with him.'

Emmeline nodded in agreement.

'You don't know these men,' Richard continued. 'Barleycorn rescued me from a band in the forest. They'll remember my face. If Barleycorn went out to meet them, they'd simply cut his throat and still cross to the island. They'd be looking for treasure.' He glanced quickly at Emmeline. 'And anything else they can lay their hands on. They'll show no mercy and give no quarter.' He picked up the posset jug warming in the ingle-nook and began to refill the cups. 'But, don't forget they'll be in for a surprise. They do not know about the knights or how well armed we are. We'll set up a watch near the ford and, if they come, we'll be waiting. Now,' Richard beckoned his companions to sit round the table, 'you've all heard,' he continued as they took their seats, 'what each person has said.' He paused. 'There is no doubt in my mind that the assassin is back in Crokehurst. Yet we know very little.' He glanced at the charlatan. 'You've a quick eye and a quick mind.'

Gildas pulled a face. 'I sees what I sees.'

'And what do you see?' Richard asked.

'Well,' Gildas replied, preening himself, 'the real key to this mystery is not the traitor but Lady Catherine Fitzalan. We have two pieces of information about her which could lead to a solution. First, why did she go along that lonely path at such an early hour? And why didn't she resist or struggle against her attacker? Secondly, which knight was wearing her favour at the tournament? What I am saying, Master Richard, is that many a wife has betrayed her husband. What happens if Lady Catherine, also wittingly or unwittingly, revealed confidential information to her lover?'

'Who is?' Emmeline interrupted.

'One of the five knights,' Gildas replied, 'who realised Lord Simon was suspicious and decided to act. He killed the Lady Catherine and Lord Simon, then ensured your father carried the blame.'

'I agree,' Barleycorn interrupted and pulled a face. 'It's the only sensible explanation we have, except, of course, Lord Simon's dying words. What was he pointing at? And what did he mean by the phrases: "There's nothing new under the sun" and "The eagle has the truth"?'

'I don't agree.' Buthlac jumped up and down on his stool excitedly. 'I don't agree at all. It could be someone else. I told you, master, how in the last sixteen years, a mysterious stranger has visited the island.'

'Fiddlesticks!' Gildas trumpeted. 'We have only got your word for it.' He jabbed a finger at Buthlac who, for some reason, he seemed to detest. 'We haven't yet investigated what you were doing at the time.'

A fight would have broken out if Emmeline had not intervened. She rapped the table, glaring at both men so imperiously, their shouts faded to mumbled words and they sat like two chastened schoolboys.

'You'll make friends,' Emmeline insisted. 'Go on, clasp each other's hands. There's been enough violence.'

Both men obeyed her instructions.

'Buthlac, you were saying?' Richard quietly asked.

'Well, strangers have come here. Now we have these eerie walkings in the galleries above as well as this knight in black armour. What happens if he's the killer? What happens if he is trying to drive us off? Keeps us away from Crokehurst? He must know a great deal about this mystery yet he is as elusive as a will-o'-the-wisp.'

Above him, Richard heard the murmur of the knights' voices as they argued over their game.

'Buthlac is not lying,' he said slowly. 'After my father's death, apparently someone took a great interest in this island. He came back looking for something here in the manor house. But what it was?' Richard shook his head. 'God only knows.' He rose to his feet. 'We have eaten and drunk enough. Let's search this place from garret to cellar.'

The others agreed to search the cellars before going to hunt for fresh meat. Richard and Emmeline climbed the stairs to the top of the house. It was much colder here, the freezing air seeping through cracks between the shutters. The garrets and attics were empty, but for dust and cobwebs and scuttling mice and rats. There were tawdry, pathetic scraps of a former existence; a bent candle snuffer, a broken quill, scraps of leather, worthless items which the plunderers had ignored. Richard recalled those ghostly footsteps of the night before and looked for secret entrances or passageways but he could find no trace of any. Emmeline, wrapped in a cloak which covered her from chin to toe, searched like some child playing a game of

Hide and Seek. They reached the gallery and entered the room where Lord Simon Fitzalan had been murdered.

'Do you think he was killed before his wife or afterwards?' Emmeline asked.

Richard didn't answer: he stared round the desolate chamber. The empty, gaunt window seat, the shuttered window, the blackened beams, the carved stone fireplace, all illuminated by the thick, yellow tallow candles he and Emmeline carried.

'What is there?' he muttered. 'Lord Simon died here whispering: "Nothing new under the sun. The eagle has the truth." And what was he pointing at?' Richard went out into the gallery where Buthlac and Gildas were busy arguing about ghosts and sprites. 'Give my compliments to the knights,' Richard called. 'Ask them to come here.'

Buthlac hurried off. The five knights arrived, thronging into the chamber; all carried wine cups. Richard ignored Emmeline's grin, for Sir Henry Grantham was finding it difficult to walk. He was cheery and mellow but the others grumbled about the cold and having to leave their game.

'Where was Lord Simon lying?' Richard asked, 'when you found him?'

Ferrers thrust his cup into the bowman's hand.

'The body was here.' He pointed to where Emmeline was standing. 'The bed was nearby and he was on the floor, feet towards the fireplace. I picked him up,' Sir Lionel declared. 'I cradled him in my arms.' And, without being invited, he sat on the floor, glanced at Richard then put his finger out. 'Yes, that's it. I held his back, he was dying: the blood was pouring out of his mouth. There was a horrid, bubbling wound in his chest. He pointed and whispered: "There's nothing new under the sun. The eagle has the truth." Then he fell back.'

'And the Lady Catherine?' Emmeline interrupted. 'When she was found? Was the blood dry?'

'It had congealed,' Manning replied. 'But, yes, my lady, to

answer your question.' He smiled. 'I catch the drift of your meaning, Lady Catherine must have been killed first. Lord Simon was in his bed linen, the murderer must have struck just before dawn.'

Richard thanked them. The knights, shrugging their shoulders and talking amongst themselves, shuffled out of the chamber and back to their game. Richard closed the door. He grasped Emmeline by the shoulder and kissed her on her cold cheeks.

'The lawyer's daughter,' he teased.

She stepped back. 'So we have Lady Catherine probably being killed in the woods and the murderer coming back here to murder her husband.'

Richard pointed at the floor. 'The only thing which could have been facing Lord Simon,' he said, 'was the fireplace.'

'Could there have been something else?' Emmeline observed. 'A table or chair?'

Richard shook his head. He crouched down and studied the carvings on the hearth. The fireplace was considerably old, the stone intricately sculptured: writhing snakes decorated either side but the broad cross-piece had the Greenele arms. A sun above an eagle, wings extended, it carried an iron rod between its claws. Richard was sure Lord Simon was referring to this in his dying breath, but why? The squire sat with his back to the hearth and stared up at Emmeline.

'Let us say, fairest lady,' he teased, 'that I have come in here to kill you. I wound you mortally in the chest. I flee, leaving you dying on the floor. Let's say Barleycorn and Gildas break in. What would you do? I mean, in your dying moments?'

'Say I loved you,' Emmeline replied innocently but looked directly at him.

All Richard could do was gape and nervously run his fingers through his hair. He was about to get up.

'But, there again,' she teased. 'I might only be lying.'

Richard sat back and glowered at her.

'Minx amongst minxes, answer the question.'

'I'd say your name. Tell those who came to help that Richard Greenele had wounded me mortally.' She came and sat beside him and looped her arm through his. 'I understand what you are saying,' she added and, without any affectation, leaned her cheek against his shoulder.

Richard didn't know what to do. If he was honest, his knowledge of any young lady was meagre to say the least. Fleeting friendships with serving girls and tavern wenches on his travels. He felt embarrassed at Emmeline's innocent directness yet wary of her sharp mind and tart observations.

'We have a mystery,' he stammered. 'Here is Lord Simon in his bed chamber, asleep in bed. Let us say the door had been locked yet he opens it. Someone comes in, stabs him in the chest then leaves just as abruptly. Now why should a fighting man like Lord Simon do that? Surely he'd query a knock on the door? And he certainly wouldn't allow a stranger so close?'

Emmeline lifted her head and stared up at the ceiling.

'Yes, yes,' she breathed. 'So it was not a stranger but someone he knew: one of the knights or your father. However, if his killer was one of the knights, then surely he would have gasped out his name?' She squeezed Richard's arm. 'Try and put yourself in his place,' she whispered.

Richard did, imagining Lord Simon opening the door, allowing someone in, perhaps not paying full attention, feeling a tap on his shoulder, he'd turn and the dagger was thrust into his chest.

'It's a servant!' he exclaimed. 'I'm sure that's who it was or someone pretending to be one. Lord Simon is in bed. He's had a poor night's sleep. He's worried about who could be the traitor. He's had an argument with my father and a disagreement with his wife. He hears a knock on the door. He goes and unlocks it and, like around any great lord, servants come and go, so he pays no more attention to them than a dog does its fleas. The man has brought something in, a jug on a tray. Lord Simon turns away. Perhaps he heard a sound or fingertips on his shoulder. He whirls round and the dagger is embedded in his chest,' he paused.

'The assassin flees,' Emmeline continued. 'Lord Simon lies on the floor, too weak to cry for help. However, in those last moments before his death, he realises he has been tricked. His mind is confused, he is delirious. The knights come in, Lord Simon utters his message and breathes his last.' Emmeline got up and grasped Richard's hand, pulling him up too.

'So, we know how he died,' he agreed. 'But not who did it. Come on, let's continue our search.'

They went from room to room but they could discover nothing. Gaunt, stark, ruined chambers greeted them. Richard was pleased Emmeline was with him, her constant chattering and flirtatious teasing kept the demons at bay. They entered Sir Lionel's room to find the knights had fashioned a table out of a beer cask. A fire roared in the hearth, jugs and wine cups stood around. All five men were gossiping, chattering about the news of the shire whilst watching Manning and Bremner move pieces on a chess board. They hardly made any comment when Richard came into the room, not even showing Emmeline the courtesy of rising. Richard explained what they were doing. Bremner muttered something in reply and, when Richard and Emmeline left, the door slammed shut behind them.

'They won't stay long, you know,' Emmeline declared as they walked to the top of the stairs. 'The assassin will soon realise we know very little. He will want to go whilst the others will believe they have discharged their vow and scuttle back to their comfortable manor houses.'

'How can I make them stay?'

'You can mention the snow,' Emmeline pulled at his sleeve. 'If I were you,' she whispered, looking over her shoulder to make sure no one else was in the gallery, 'I'd tell them the truth. I mean about the outlaws.'

They returned to the kitchen. Emmeline went to build up a fire. She had cleaned the small oven, built into the wall next to the fire and announced she would try to bake some bread. Of Buthlac, Gildas and Barleycorn there was no sign. Richard went to the door and opened it. A blast of cold wind made him flinch. The snow in the cobbled yard had turned to a dirty slush and now this was freezing as the afternoon drew on. Beyond the yard he could see the snow lie thick whilst, above, the sky was beginning to darken. Barleycorn and Buthlac with Gildas trotting behind, suddenly rounded a corner. Barleycorn stopped and lifted up the bird he'd killed whilst, on a pole slung across Gildas' shoulders, hung four rabbits.

'We'll not go hungry,' Richard waved them forward. 'Quail or pheasant pie, not to mention more rabbit stew.'

The three men came into the kitchen, stamping their feet, laying the carcasses on the table. Buthlac drew his knife, saying he'd gut and clean them for cooking.

'Did you find anything?' Richard asked as Gildas warmed his fingers before the fire, loudly praising Barleycorn's skill with the bow.

'Nothing,' Gildas replied. He lifted his head and looked mournfully at Richard. 'But it is true what the Good Book says: "Their halls shall be deserted and in their rooms the owl shall raise its young".'

'We found nothing, Master Richard,' Barleycorn looked up. 'And, before you ask, we visited the ford. There's no sign of the outlaw band.'

Richard thanked them and, his stomach slightly queasy, decided he could not stay in the kitchen whilst the dead birds and rabbits were gutted. He walked out into the yard and across into the makeshift stable where Bayard was standing patiently, head down, eyes half-closed.

'Are you sleepy?' Richard asked. 'If it wasn't so cold I'd take you out for a ride. And what a gallop it would be.'

The horse snickered with pleasure, nodding its head as it nuzzled Richard's chest.

'I'll get you something.'

Richard went out of the stable door. He glanced up at the manor house; the windows were like eyeless sockets, others were covered by shutters. He saw a sudden movement to his right, high on the third floor. His heart skipped a beat. He was sure he had seen it. A face, only a blur, a few seconds before the shutter was pulled over.

Chapter 2

On his return to the house, Richard did not voice his suspicions that somewhere in the manor an elusive stranger was watching and listening to them. He kept his fears to himself and helped Emmeline prepare the evening meal. Darkness fell early. Barleycorn said he would watch during the night lest the outlaws returned. He took some food in a linen cloth, a tinder flint and candle and said he would make himself comfortable. Buthlac offered to accompany him, as did Gildas, but the master bowman refused.

'You'd best stay here,' he declared.

And, without any fuss, he collected his cloak, bow and quiver of arrows and slipped out into the cobbled yard. Through a gap in the shutters, Richard watched him go and wondered why Barleycorn had really left. To watch the ford? To plot? Or to meet that stranger, the one he had been talking to that night outside the tavern on the Epping road? Emmeline came up behind him and put her small, warm hand over his.

'You are uneasy, Richard.'

'I can't trust anyone,' he said in a half-whisper, then grinned. 'Except you.'

She nipped his skin playfully. 'Doesn't that include Barleycorn?' she asked.

'Yes, yes, it does but I can't understand how we met. How quickly he agreed to accompany me here. And this dispute with the outlaws? Surely such a man would end the feud by fleeing to some other part of the kingdom? And, finally, why join me here on a barren, deserted, snowswept island?'

'I am wondering about Buthlac,' Emmeline looked over her shoulder to where the hermit and Gildas sat by the fire arguing noisily over who should work the makeshift spit.

'Gildas I can trust,' Richard observed. 'But Buthlac is an enigma. Why did he stay here for so many years?'

'I believe he's telling the truth,' Emmeline replied. 'On the night Lord Simon and his wife were killed, he may well have been snoring like a pig after drinking too much. But what did he do afterwards? I mean, the sheriff's men arrived, your father was arrested and the other knights left. Would not Buthlac have gone searching? Wouldn't he comb this house from top to bottom for anything he might need? Not only food and drink but the odd trinket? Moreover,' she added, 'your father was supposedly very kind to him. Wouldn't Buthlac search for some sort of proof of his innocence? Didn't he find anything amiss?'

Richard recalled Buthlac's cottage with its nooks and crannies: he secretly promised himself that, if the opportunity presented itself, he would search there. Emmeline was about to continue when the door to the kitchen crashed open and the five knights came in. By their hard-set faces Richard knew what was coming. He made them welcome as they sat round the table. The conversation was desultory. All pretending to be interested in what Emmeline was cooking. Sir Lionel Beaumont, hands clasped together, stared round, under lowering brows at his companions. He pulled his thin face even longer, his sad eyes studying Richard. He coughed and cleared his throat. Ferrers, however, impatiently drew his dagger and beat the pommel on the table.

'Master Richard, Master Richard,' he began. 'Many years ago your father was wrongfully arrested for murder.' Ferrers put the dagger down and spread his hands, fingers splayed. 'We do not dispute that. Nor do we deny that we all took an oath in Colchester gaol that, if the opportunity ever presented itself, we would do all within our power to clear your father's name. But,' he ran thickset fingers through his greying hair, 'we have now purged ourselves of our oath so, what more can we do? We have no new information. In the last sixteen years we have discovered nothing new and you must accept that.'

'Here we are,' Sir Walter Manning spoke up, 'in a ruined manor house on a snow-covered island. Winter is drawing in. Advent will begin and Yuletide will soon be here. Master Richard, we have estates and families. We intend to leave tomorrow.'

'Even me,' Sir Lionel remarked. He closed his eyes. 'I saw something, I learnt something on the day of the tournament here.' He opened his eyes. 'But I can't remember, it's so long ago: so much has happened.' He blinked and glanced round. 'I don't like being here. I don't want to be here,' he added querulously. 'I want to go home.'

'You can't!' Richard's reply was like a snarl.

All five knights looked at him in surprise.

'You can't go home!' Richard insisted. 'You gave my father your oath: that means more than coming to meet me at a deserted house. These matters have hardly begun. Sir Lionel himself admits that returning here has awoken memories. Who knows, as the days pass, such images may become clearer.'

Sir Philip Ferrers' face broke into a false smile. 'Master

Richard, you can say what you like but you can't stop us. If we wish to go then, we shall, and that is the end of the matter.'

'Oh, go if you want!' Emmeline came to the tablet wiping her hands on a rag: her face looked unusually severe. 'Go,' she said harshly, 'and you'll die!'

'This is ridiculous.' Bremner pushed back the beer barrel he was sitting on. 'Will more murder be committed? Are you going to stop us, young lady? Will that mysterious master bowman take us out of the saddle?'

'The bridge is burnt,' Gildas called across. 'You can't leave.'

'We can go by the ford,' Sir Henry Grantham retorted. 'If we are careful ...'

'And if you do get across it,' Richard declared, 'the outlaws will be waiting for you.'

'Outlaws!' Beaumont screeched, head up, neck tight like that of a chicken. 'Outlaws? What outlaws?'

As Emmeline went back to the fire, Richard pithily described the depredations of Ratsbane and Dogwort: how he was certain they had the island under close scrutiny.

'But they wouldn't attack us,' Manning scoffed. 'Five, well-armed knights?'

'Five, well-armed knights,' Richard retorted, 'who are dismounted, leading their horses through the snow, wearing costly clothes, carrying good arms, leading sound horseflesh each with its own harness. What sort of challenge would that be for three score outlaws also well armed, hiding in the trees? They'll cut you down one by one just for the plunder as well as to ensure that, when they cross to the island, there'll be no witnesses to talk to the sheriff.'

'They'll not let you leave,' Buthlac added. 'They'll kill you.'

'If you have studied the heart of the wrong doer,' Gildas intoned, coming across to stand beside Richard. 'If you have

154

looked at the malice in their souls,' he continued, 'and regard them as the prophet did the dogs of Bashan, the priests of Belial, you'll recognise their wickedness for what it is. Cunning and sly, they have set traps.'

'What on earth are you babbling about?' Ferrers growled.

Gildas smiled and sketched a blessing in his direction.

'In my wanderings, sir, I have lived and walked with many strange men. I've immersed myself in the doings of the human soul . . .'

'Shut up!' Beaumont screeched. 'For the love of God, either shut up or speak honestly!'

His hand fell to his dagger but Gildas drew his out in the twinkling of an eye and pressed the point into the table-top. At the same time he clasped Richard's shoulder.

'The squire saved my life. I am, therefore, until the debt is paid, his man in peace and war. As you were his father's.'

Richard glanced round at the knights, pleased to see that some of them were shamed.

'You can go,' he added quietly. 'But, don't you realise, the outlaw band will attack? If not for plunder or to massacre any witnesses, they'll probably recognise you as great men of the shire. They may even think you are going for help.'

Walter Manning nodded in agreement.

'These outlaws,' Richard continued, 'are well away from their forest. True, the snow lies on the ground: pathways and trackways are blocked. However, they would not like to be caught out in open countryside by any sheriff's men you might send back.'

Beaumont opened his mouth to speak but Manning rapped the table with his knuckles.

'I know what you are going to say, Sir Lionel,' he spoke hastily. 'But I did take an oath and, on reflection, to leave so quickly is a coward's act. The outlaws will attack. They would not let us pass.' He turned and grasped Sir Lionel's shoulder.

'And you, friend,' he urged. 'What is it you think you saw or heard that day?'

Sir Lionel just shook his head.

'Well,' Gildas snapped, leaning on his dagger. 'Will you go or stay?'

One by one the knights gave their word they would stay at least another week.

'But, on the first Sunday of Advent,' Sir Walter Manning spoke up, 'we will leave. By then my vow will be complete. Perhaps the weather will have broken. If the outlaws have not attacked by then, it means that they have withdrawn back into the forest.'

Richard was about to thank them when he heard a footfall on the gallery above.

'Hush!' He raised his hand.

Emmeline, a basting spoon in her hand, stared fearfully at him.

'Nothing but the wind,' Bremner scoffed.

As if in answer the footfall grew more heavy and they heard the jingle of spurs. Emmeline dropped the spoon. Gildas lifted his dagger, staring up at the ceiling, his sallow face even paler. Beaumont whimpered but then Ferrers, springing up, drew his dagger and dashed to the door. Richard followed, racing up the stairs behind Ferrers. He reached the top: the gallery was cloaked in darkness.

'Don't go down!' Richard seized Ferrers' arm. 'One of you, quickly!' he called down the stairs. 'Bring a torch!'

Buthlac, hobbling as fast as he could, came up, a sconce torch flickering greedily in each hand. These were passed up to Richard and Ferrers. They went along the ice-cold gallery. The flames of the torches danced in the icy draughts seeping in through the open windows or between the shutters. Richard glanced to his right, fresh red marks were daubed on the wall.

'Here!' he whispered. 'Look!'

Ferrers came back as the others joined them. Slowly, laboriously Richard made out the message.

'Haceldema,' it read, 'the field of blood. Prepare the great meadow for a tournament. The hour of vengeance is close.'

Richard looked at his companions, their faces ghostly in the flickering torch light.

'Haceldema is the Field of Blood,' Gildas murmured. 'The Potter's Field of the gospels which the chief priest bought from the silver they'd paid Judas to betray Christ.'

Ferrers, muttering under his breath, went along the gallery studying the walls but there were no further messages. He stared up at the ceiling.

'God forgive me for saying this, Master Richard, I am tempted to ask you all to leave then I'll burn this house from garret to cellar just to see what the flames drive out.'

'And what happens if it is a ghost?' Sir Lionel muttered. His words were not mocked by his companions.

'What does it mean?' Bremner urged. 'How can we get the meadow ready for a tournament in the middle of winter when it is covered by snow?'

They walked back towards the top of the stairs. Richard turned as he heard a floorboard creak.

'Who's there?' he called.

The rest, half-way down the stairs, froze and looked back.

'Who's there?' Richard called again.

'Could it be an outlaw?' Grantham muttered. He came up, his bald head and smooth face lined with sweat.

As if in answer, Richard heard the gallery creak and something came bouncing towards them along the floorboards. At first Richard thought it was a ball, a child's plaything but, as it rolled towards him, he saw it was a piece of canvas with blood seeping through. He drew back in horror.

'The Lord and all his Saints protect us!' Bremner whispered, crossing himself.

157

There was a crashing on the stairs: Gildas, his courage failing him, fled back to the safety and warmth of the kitchen, Buthlac hobbling quickly behind him.

Richard found he couldn't move. His legs were like iron plates, his arms tense as he gripped the sconce torch. He could only stand, horror-struck. Behind him, on the stairs, none of the knights dare move.

'What is it?' Manning whispered.

This time Richard did scream as another bundle came rolling down the gallery towards him. This time faster, more direct, a grisly, bloody parcel as if it possessed a life of its own, bouncing towards him, hitting a wall then rolling across to stop at his feet. Richard had to act. He grasped the torch and, screaming and yelling at the top of his voice, threw himself down the corridor. In his fear he was ready to fight what ever dark force threatened at the other end of the gallery. Yet, when he got there, nothing. Only a shutter opening and closing above the narrow stairs leading up to the top gallery. All was quiet except for the scrabbling of some rat. Richard squatted in the window seat, not caring how he held the torch until he realised it was beginning to scorch the floorboards. He looked back from where he had come. The knights had regained their courage. Ferrers was holding a torch up whilst Manning and Bremner cut at the canvas cloth. Like a man in a trance, Richard retraced his steps. There were muttered curses. Beaumont, a hand to his mouth, clattered down the stairs. Richard stared down at the decapitated heads lying together, like those of two pigs he had seen on a butcher's stall in York: eyes half-closed, the neck a ragged remnant of jagged flesh, blood trickled out of the corner of the mouth, staining the greying skin of the unshaven, vicious face.

'Lord, have mercy on us!'

Richard crouched down, determined to keep his courage: in a

way he felt grateful. During that long walk down the gallery he had prayed, fought against the terrible panic that one of the heads might be Barleycorn's.

'Go down to the kitchen!' he ordered. 'Get some old sacking!'

Ferrers was only too pleased to hurry away.

'And don't tell Emmeline!' Richard called after him.

The knight returned, fighting to keep back his nausea as Richard picked up the severed heads and placed them like rotting apples into the sacking. He grasped the piece of twine Ferrers offered, tied the neck of the sack, picked it up and walked down the stairs. He went out of a side door into the crisp coldness of the night. The snow lay like a gleaming cloth, hiding everything. Above him, the stars twinkled like jewels on a black cushion. The wind was low, cold and biting. It whipped at his face and his hair. Richard heard a sound behind him. Gildas, carrying a torch, its flame fighting valiantly against the wind, joined him. They both silently walked down to the line of trees.

'What shall we do with them?' Gildas murmured. 'The ground will be rock hard.'

They reached the trees. Richard buried the heads in the snow, packing it around them. He glanced up at the charlatan.

'Tomorrow, Gildas, take a mattock from the stables. You'll find one there. Dig a hole and put them in.'

'Who are they?' Gildas whispered. 'How did they die?'

Richard looked back at the manor house, a dark, sinister mass against the night sky. Above him the wind sighed through the trees, rustling the branches. Richard shivered, not so much because of the cold but, for the first time ever, he began to regret coming to Crokehurst Manor.

'Do you think Demons lurk here?' Gildas asked. 'What happens, Master, if the house is haunted? A killing place for Christian souls? Once,' Gildas continued, 'I met a man who had been in houses so evil, it became a gateway into the pit of hell. Devils, and those spirits which wish us ill, could enter our world and wreak terrible acts on the souls and bodies of men. I . . .' Gildas broke off at the sound of strident shrieks from the manor.

Richard kicked some more snow over where he had buried the heads, turned and ran back. Gildas followed, slithering and slipping on the close-packed snow. They went through the small door which Gildas slammed behind him, along the passageway and into the kitchen. Everyone stood grouped round Barleycorn who leaned against the wall gasping for breath.

'In God's name, what's happening?' Richard shouldered his way through. 'Cuthbert, you look as if you have seen a ghost!'

'You'd best come with me,' the master bowman replied. 'And anyone else who has a strong stomach.'

'What's happening?' Emmeline cried. 'More blood daubed on the walls! Severed heads rolling like stones down the gallery!' She came over. 'Richard, where have you been?'

He grasped her hands, they were cold.

'Stay by the fire,' he ordered. He looked at the knights. 'Two of you should stay with her. The rest, if you've got the stomach, come with me.'

Ferrers told Beaumont and Bremner to stay. Buthlac also remained: crouching in the ingle-nook like some little hob-goblin. The rest followed Richard and Cuthbert out into the night. They stumbled out of the yard and along the frozen trackway down to the great meadow. Just before the trees thinned, Cuthbert told them to stop.

'I have never seen the like of this,' he whispered. He pointed ahead, holding up the torch and indicating where the trackway turned. 'You will see them there.'

Gingerly they followed him. The forest on either side of them loomed black and silent. The only sound being sparks from their spluttering torches. They turned the corner. At first Richard couldn't believe the grisly sight: a tangle of arms and legs, at least three corpses lying in the snow. He stopped. Barleycorn went on, holding up the torch. Richard and the rest saw it: another severed head fixed on an ash pole.

'St Michael and all his Angels!' Manning breathed. 'What is this?'

Richard studied the severed head, the bearded face, sunken cheeks, half-closed eyes and blood-caked lips. The headless corpses were clothed in nothing more than a collection of rags held together by pieces of cord but the boots were of good quality as were the baldrics, belts and weapons they carried.

'I went down to the ford,' Barleycorn explained, turning his back on the grisly sight. 'For a while I watched then grew sleepy. I awoke, suddenly nervous. I am sure no one had crossed the ford yet, I was certain there were people in the woods around me. I decided to return to the house, as I did, I came upon this.' He grasped Richard's arm. 'Emmeline mentioned something had happened in the house?'

Richard snatched the torch from him.

'Let's go back,' he ordered. 'We're vulnerable out here in the open.'

They all walked back to the manor house, a little faster than when they had come. Once inside Emmeline served them hot posset, the wine strong, the crushed herbs giving the kitchen a fragrant summery smell. Richard wrapped his numb fingers around the cup.

'Whoever cut those heads off,' he began, 'means us no harm.'

'Nonsense!' Ferrers snapped. 'Footsteps in the gallery, blood-red writing daubed on the walls. Severed heads rolling down to our feet. Decapitated corpses in the forest!'

Richard shook his head. 'Cuthbert, Gildas.' He looked round. 'You must go back to the ford and guard it well.' He held up his hand for silence. 'What I think happened is this. Sometime today, probably early in the evening, Dogwort and Ratsbane sent a scouting party across the ford to establish our

strength. The mysterious knight ambushed them and took their
heads. Can you imagine it? The three wolfheads stumbling
about in the dark against a skilled, fully armed knight. They
could offer little defence. One sweep of the sword, it would be
like a farmer cutting ears of corn.'

'But why bring their heads here?' Gildas asked.

'I don't know,' Richard replied.

He winked reassuringly at Emmeline and recalled that his old
friend and patron Gilbert Savage had taught him well. He
remembered how, years ago, when they had been in the Forest
of Dean travelling to Gloucester, they had been attacked by a
group of footpads. He and Gilbert had tracked them down,
catching them by the bank of a strong rushing stream. The
knight had killed them as effortlessly as a fox would a group of
trapped chickens. Richard's hand went to his mouth: some other
memory stirred but he couldn't place it.

'Master,' Gildas interrupted his thoughts. 'If this mysterious
knight killed the outlaws, then why bring two of their heads back
here?'

'I am sorry,' Richard broke free from his reverie. 'This knight,
and I believe he's no phantom, sees one of us or, perhaps all, as
his enemy. He has business with us and does not want any
outside interference. The outlaw scouts were killed as a warning
to the rest of their coven.' Richard lifted his cup and sipped from
it. 'This same knight is also trying to frighten, as well as impress,
us with his skill, speed and ability to move round the island.'

'So, what do we do?' Ferrers snarled. 'Sit here and wait for
him to take our heads as well? I'd leave the island,' he
continued, 'but there's our vow and I accept what you say,
Master Richard. If we stay together we have more protection.'
He flung his hand out at Gildas and Barleycorn. 'But couldn't
we send one of these for help? They could cross the ford . . .'

'And that's one man fewer,' Richard replied. 'It would take
days to reach Colchester or Chelmsford. The plague is raging in

the towns, winter is here. It might be weeks before some official
or one of your powerful friends organises a force to relieve us.'

The rest of the knights agreed with Richard except Beaumont:
he sat like a child with his finger to his lips, eyes half-closed, lost
in his own thoughts.

'Sir Lionel,' Richard called out. 'Are you well?'

The man shook his head. 'I was just thinking,' he murmured,
'the writing on the wall to prepare the field for a tournament. So
different,' Beaumont whispered, 'from that tourney so many
years ago at the height of summer. I do remember something,'
he continued. 'Lady Catherine Fitzalan under the trees. Her
husband remonstrating with her. She was holding the colours of
some knight in her hand,' he shook his head. 'If I could only
remember. Yes, if I could remember...'

'Perhaps tomorrow?' Emmeline added kindly. She rose.
'Richard, we should sleep. Tomorrow morning God knows what
dangers we might face. Master Barleycorn, Gildas, let me
prepare you something to eat.'

Gildas looked as if he was about to object. His sallow face and
quick, darting eyes betrayed his fear but Barleycorn slapped him
on the shoulder.

'Come on, charlatan,' he declared, getting to his feet. 'You
are safer with me out under the trees near the lakeside.'

'What happens if there are more outlaws?' Gildas protested.

'I doubt it,' Barleycorn retorted. 'Ratsbane and Dogwort will
wait for their scouts to return. When they don't they'll show
their hand.'

They collected their possessions. Emmeline busied herself,
filling a water pannikin with wine and wrapping some of the
dried meat in strips of linen. The knights, red-faced and sleepy
after the hot posset, also made their farewells whilst Buthlac
curled up like a mouse near the fire. A short while later,
Barleycorn and Gildas slipped into the night, leaving Richard
and Emmeline alone. They sat, hand in hand, in front of the fire

watching the logs spit and crackle in the heat. Now and again Buthlac would stir in his sleep and mutter. All became quiet, the occasional footfall from a chamber above, but not the sinister clinking and awesome sounds they had heard before.

'Who could this knight be?' Emmeline asked abruptly. 'I mean, all the people involved in your father's tragedy can be accounted for.' She drew her breath in. 'Unless of course,' she pointed at the sleeping hermit. 'Remember what he said? How a naked, faceless corpse had been found in the lake. Perhaps there were more murders?' She grasped Richard's hand more tightly. 'Promise me,' she pleaded, 'promise me that we will do what we can but then leave. Richard, there's another life we can follow.' She swallowed hard. 'If we stay here,' she whispered, 'we might all die.'

Words between the pilgrims

The franklin paused in his story and stared round at his silent companions.

'Blood and Vengeance,' the pardoner spoke up, combing his flaxen hair with his long, skeletal fingers. 'Blood and fire,' he said, winking at the franklin. 'Sir, you tell a strange tale.'

'He tells the truth,' the knight observed tartly.

All heads turned towards him.

'What do you mean?' the wife of Bath cried.

The knight just shrugged and looked away.

'This tale of haunted footsteps,' the good wife continued, 'mysterious black knights, severed heads rolling down moon-lit galleries, decapitated corpses in snow-filled forests.' She looked at the franklin. 'Does Crokehurst Island exist?'

The parson sprang to his feet, his saintly face alive with excitement.

'Yes it does! Yes it does!' he shouted. 'I remember now. There's a tumulus on it.'

'What's that?' The miller snorted, so drunk he was finding it hard to hold the bagpipes which seemed to jerk around in his hands as if they had a life of their own.

'A tumulus,' the Oxford scholar replied, 'is a burial mound!' He looked narrow-eyed at the poor parson and wondered how a priest so shabbily dressed, so profoundly innocent of the affairs of the world, could know such a word.

'Aye, that's what I was saying,' the parson declared. 'A mass grave. Once, when I was in Essex, a brother priest gave me lodgings. He was a chantry priest, singing Masses for the repose of the souls of the departed. On Lammas Night, he said he had to rise early to say three Masses for all the slain; all those who lay buried on Crokehurst Island.' He glanced sideways at the franklin. He had just got up and walked towards the buttery, declaring that speaking so much gave him an appetite.

'You, sir!' the parson called out.

The franklin turned, stroking the end of his beard. He stood in the shadows as if trying to hide his face from the priest.

'Were you on that terrible island?' the parson asked, coming forward.

'I merely tell a story,' the franklin replied and, spinning on his heel, went through into the buttery.

'What do you think?' Mine Host whispered to Geoffrey Chaucer.

'I don't know,' Chaucer replied. 'I have sat here, wondering whether this is fact or fable. The knight knows something. Moreover, when I was working in the Customs, levying the tolls and dues, I heard a strange story. How the King himself went to Crokehurst. Oh, not on a royal progress but, secretly: I am sure Sir Godfrey went with him.'

In the buttery the franklin had persuaded a sleeping scullion to take down a leg of ham hanging from its hook beneath the rafters. He was now cutting off strips which he neatly laid on a pewter plate. He heard the door open behind him and pushed another coin towards the heavy-eyed lay brother.

'Find me some cheese,' he said, 'and some of that onion sauce.'

The lay brother pocketed the coin, muttered something about all Christians being in bed but he tottered off to the store room.

'I thought you'd come,' the franklin declared, not bothering to look up. 'It's been many years now.'

'Who are you?' the summoner asked, leaning forward, pushing his wart-covered face close to the franklin's.

The franklin smiled but held the knife by the handle, its ugly tip only an inch away from the summoner's protuberant belly.

'I gave you a life once,' the franklin muttered. 'Don't force me to take it away!'

The summoner stepped back. 'Many good men died that day,' he replied. 'My companions, men who had reared me.'

'They were demons,' the franklin retorted. 'They were Godless and died Godless.'

He paused as the lay brother came shuffling back, carrying what he had asked for. The franklin lifted the plate but kept the knife in his hand.

'Let's return,' he said softly. 'Let's go back to Crokehurst and the blood which was spilt there.'

PART IV

Chapter 1

Richard and Emmeline stayed up a little longer, sifting through what they had learnt. Outside the wind rose, rattling at the house as it moaned through the trees. A shutter high in the kitchen wall flew open, forced back by the buffeting wind. Richard got up, closed it and looked out at the snow: the swirling flakes were already covering the slush in the yard.

'I hope Barleycorn is safe,' he murmured. 'And that the outlaws leave us alone.'

'Can you trust him?' Emmeline called out: her face now had a translucent paleness, emphasising her high cheekbones and those marvellous eyes.

Richard wanted to kiss her, hold her in his arms, yet he knew this was neither the time nor the place.

'I trust him,' he stammered a reply.

Emmeline caught the catch in his voice.

'Where does he come from?' she insisted. 'Why is he helping you, Richard, a complete stranger?'

'He's not as strange as you think.' Buthlac stirred and lifted his head.

'What do you mean, hermit?' Richard asked.

'What I say.'

The hermit rubbed his eyes. Richard wondered if he had really been asleep or had he been listening to everything they'd said? Buthlac rubbed his finger along his nose.

'Over the years different people have come to this island. Oh, they slip in like ghostly shadows but old Buthlac, he is not as stupid as people think. When I saw him with you, "Oh, says I, that face looks familiar."'

Richard crouched beside the makeshift bed, wrinkling his nose at the hermit's foul stench.

'You should wash more often,' Richard teased. 'Cleanliness is no bar to sanctity.'

'When spring comes,' Buthlac's eyes shifted. 'When spring comes, old Buthlac will wash and change in preparation for Easter.'

'But you have seen Barleycorn before?' Richard insisted.

'Oh yes, I am sure I have but where, I can't be certain.'

Emmeline got up and came across to join them.

'And what about you, Buthlac?' she asked quietly. 'What have you got to hide?'

The hermit's face blanched: he shifted uncomfortably on his bed of straw.

'Why do you say that, Mistress?' His eyes would not meet hers.

'Well,' she half knelt beside Richard, 'here's old Buthlac the hermit: sixteen years ago Richard's father falls from power and grace. The Sheriff's people came swarming across and the house was plundered. Didn't you join them? Didn't you see if there was some little tidbit or juicy morsel left for Buthlac?'

'I never came here,' the old hermit retorted. 'Not once.'

'You are lying,' Richard grasped the hermit's wrist. 'Buthlac,' he pleaded. 'You know why we are all here. Soon, the snows will go and these knights with them. When that happens,' the squire clasped his hands together, 'the door shuts tight on my father's memory, his honour and any hope of justice. How will you answer to God for that?'

Buthlac picked at a piece of straw. Emmeline leaned over and kissed him on the cheek. The old hermit's head came up, eyes shining.

'Why did you do that?' he asked, combing his straggly beard with dirty fingers. 'No damsel has done that to Buthlac, not for many a year. And the last one who did. Well,' he grinned in a display of broken teeth, 'she was paid to. Ah well, God helps those who help themselves.'

Richard thought he was about to lie down but, instead, Buthlac sat back, undid his moleskin jacket and pulled out a small pouch. He undid the dirty cord at the top and emptied the contents into his hand: a silver piece. He picked it up.

'After Yuletide,' Buthlac grinned, 'I shall journey to buy some cheese.' He shook the sack again and a small ring, the metal turned green, fell onto the straw. Buthlac picked it up and held it before Richard's eyes.

'Why do you show me that?' the squire asked.

Buthlac turned the ring, pointing to the empty socket where a jewel or some other insignia had once rested.

'Believe it or not, Master Richard. I did not come back here to plunder your father's possessions. However, after they removed the Lady Catherine's body from the undergrowth, I went back there to hunt. People who fall, well, they lose things; a necklace, a brooch, maybe a few coins.'

'And you found this?' Richard asked, his disappointment evident.

'Oh yes, Master. But listen awhile. Look at the ring.' Buthlac thrust it into Richard's hands. 'Tell me what you think!'

The squire looked down at the clasp shaped in the form of a triangle.

'It's a ring,' he said. 'The metal is brass or copper. The clasp contained a jewel or some other precious stone but that's gone now. Perhaps it belonged to Lady Catherine?'

'Slip it on your finger,' the hermit invited.

Richard did so and was surprised at how loose the ring was.

'It didn't belong to her,' Buthlac added slyly.

Richard glanced up.

'It must have belonged to the killer,' Buthlac declared.

Richard took the ring off and held it up. 'Of course,' he breathed. 'It's an insignia ring and the clasp here would not hold a jewel but the arms or escutcheon of its wearer.' Richard grasped Buthlac's arm so tightly the hermit winced and drew away.

Emmeline rose, clapping her hands in excitement. The squire glanced up, warning her with his eyes to keep her voice down.

'When I found it,' Buthlac continued, 'it was lying under some leaves. The metal was clearer, it's turned green over the years. Really I should polish it.' He leaned back against the wall. 'At first I thought it was Lady Catherine's and had fallen off in the struggle but, when I put it on my finger, I realised it must be a man's. Now, if that had been lost by someone else they would have organised a search.'

'Instead,' Emmeline intervened, 'it must be Lady Catherine's assassin. Oh, where?' she exclaimed. 'Where is the emblem it once bore?'

Buthlac spread his hands. 'Mistress, as the angels are my witnesses, I have gone back to that place but found nothing. Somewhere,' he pointed in the direction of the door, 'out there in the soil or under some rotting vegetation lies the evidence, Master Richard, of who really did kill the Lady Catherine.'

'And you have told no one of this?' Richard asked.

Buthlac shook his head. 'Of course not, sir. To do so would be my death warrant. I didn't tell you at first. I had to be sure.' He pointed at the ring. 'I think that's the assassin's ring: that's what he comes back to the island for.'

'Is there anything else?' Emmeline pleaded.

The hermit shook his head. 'My lady, there's nothing. If I had the insignia I would give it to you.'

And, without a by-your-leave, Buthlac lay down upon his bedding and pulled his cloak over his head.

'You can keep the ring,' he muttered. 'Use it for whatever you want. I wish you luck.'

For a while Richard crouched in front of the fire, moving the charred logs, banking the flames. His eyes grew heavy and he found himself falling in and out of sleep. He heard a sound behind him and saw that Emmeline had already prepared herself for bed: her gown and cloak neatly folded, she now lay on a bed of straw, her face to the wall, the blankets pulled so high only her curly hair was showing. Richard extinguished the candle and sat down. He took off his boots and, for a while, lay on his own bed staring into the darkness. Above and around him the house creaked and groaned, buffeted by a strong wind. Richard closed his eyes and slept, his mind drifting into a nightmare. He was in the centre of that field, staring across into the trees. The black knight was also there bestride his great war horse, lance at the ready. Nevertheless, Richard was not frightened of him. He kept glancing across the snow at the figures slipping in and out of the trees. The dream became more confused, there was a crash and Richard's eyes flew open. He seized his war belt and crouched in the darkness. The fire had died to a few smouldering cinders. Buthlac was snoring like a hog, Emmeline's sleep had not been disturbed. Richard just sat but he heard nothing else, so he returned to sleep.

He was awakened the next morning by Emmeline building up the fire, helped by Buthlac; they were both trying to get a large bowl of oatmeal to hang on the makeshift steel bar above the fire. Buthlac smiled as Richard, his face creased in sleep, stumbled to his feet and staggered out of the door into the yard to relieve himself. He was almost blinded by the light, the snow lay like a great sheet covering everything. Nevertheless, the sky was clear and the snow caught the sun and dazzled in its rays. The wind had dropped, the air was cold but fresh. Richard answered nature's call, did up his points and, picking up snow, washed his hands. He then went into the stables to check on Bayard and the other horses. Barleycorn had done a good job. All the cracks and vents had been sealed: the stables were snug and sweet-smelling. Bayard lay contentedly in his stable, raising his head and snickering with pleasure. Richard crouched and stroked him on the muzzle, checking his eyes and neck to ensure all was well.

He returned to the kitchen. The knights, except Beaumont, had also risen: some had already washed and shaved.

'The weather's changed,' Manning exclaimed, going to the window. 'What do we do now, Master Richard? We can hardly sit round the fire like a gaggle of old crones?'

'There's wood to be cut,' Emmeline called out. 'Then brought in here to be dried.'

'The horses need exercising,' Grantham added. He joined Manning at the door, staring out over the snow. 'How thick do you think the snow lies?' he asked.

'A few inches.' Ferrers, his face shaved, hair oiled, looked as if he was back in his own solar rather than taking refuge in a gaunt, half-ruined manor house.

'We could go to the tournament field,' Grantham suggested excitedly. 'We have our arms! A little exercise for us wouldn't go amiss.' For a while they discussed this till Emmeline called them to the table and served ladles of hot, spicy oatmeal and stoups of watered ale.

'Where's Beaumont?' Manning asked, licking his horn spoon clean. 'It's unlike him. He always follows his belly.'

Richard ignored them and stared towards the door. Outside it looked so peaceful, the sunshine, the hard-packed snow, this warm kitchen. He felt uneasy and wondered how Barleycorn and Gildas were faring. Surely he should relieve them?

'I am going to get Beaumont,' Grantham declared and, getting to his feet, stumped off.

Richard remembered the severed heads. He called Buthlac over, gave him a coin and told him what he wanted done.

'Of course! Of course!' The hermit smacked his lips and gripped the coin. 'I have buried dead before, Master. Years ago, on the Scottish march, I served with the Percies. Dug a great ditch I did. Put all the corpses in. Me and others who tried to desert.'

He hobbled off and was hardly out of the door when Grantham burst into the kitchen.

'I can't wake him!' he shouted. 'Beaumont, he's . . .'

Richard and the rest followed him up the stairs on to the first gallery. Beaumont's chamber had been one of the best. The door still hung on its leather hinges and Richard remembered how, the day before, he had noticed the handle and lock were still undamaged. For a while he and the others pounded on the door, first with their fists and then the pommel of their daggers. There was no answer. Richard stood back, his gaze going to that macabre warning still scrawled on the wall. In the daylight he could also see the marks of the blood where the heads had rolled towards him the previous night. Was the house haunted, he wondered? Had some terrible power which had killed those two outlaws and daubed the warning on the wall, struck again? Was it responsible for the terrible silence in Sir Lionel's chamber? He glanced up; the others were staring at him.

'Break the door down!' he ordered.

For a while there was confusion as they looked for something to use. Ferrers remembered a stump of log lying in the courtyard. This was brought up and they began to pound on the door. The lintel shook, decaying plaster crumbled away but the door held fast. Grasping the wet log, they brought it swinging backwards and forwards, smashing the handle until at last the lock began to give way. Richard was about to stop them, advise they should concentrate on the hinges when at last there was a snap. The lock weakened, a few more blows and it swung open.

Richard was first into the room. It smelt musty and stale, the windows were shuttered. He glanced round, his eyes growing accustomed to the gloom. He glimpsed the overturned kegs and barrels which the knights had used after their games the previous day. Ferrers opened the window, the light poured in, making Sir Lionel's corpse slouched against the wall even more gruesome. He lay, sprawled, one arm resting on a stool, his face turned away. Richard went across and pulled him by the shoulder: the corpse flopped over. Richard saw the great wound in the man's chest, the blood had soaked the front of his gown and formed a great sticky pool beneath him.

'Pull him away!' he ordered.

The other knights, swearing and cursing under their breath, lifted the blood-sodden corpse.

'Look at the wall!' Grantham shouted.

Richard did so and saw the strange shape.

'He tried to write something,' Manning declared.

Richard stood back.

'He tried to form a letter,' Manning went on. 'Look.'

Richard went over to the corpse. He tried not to look at Beaumont's face, the half-open eyes, the blood-soaked mouth and sallow skin. He grasped the dead man's right hand and studied the index finger: it was caked with blood and plaster.

'Beaumont tried to write,' he murmured. 'In those few seconds before dying he tried to scrawl the name of his killer.'

'It looks like an M,' Grantham boomed, tracing the outline of the bloody mark.

'I think it is,' Bremner agreed.

All eyes turned to Walter Manning but the little knight stood his ground, lips tight, chin forward.

'I am no murderer,' he grated. 'Beaumont was my friend. Why should I kill him?' He went across and tapped the bloody marks. 'I agree, it could be an M, or a B, or even an F.'

The others just looked at him. Manning's hand fell to the hilt of his dagger. He half drew it.

'Any man who calls me a murderer,' he threatened, 'will answer to me.'

'There's no proof,' Richard intervened quickly, alarmed at the growing tension in the room.

Grantham drew in his breath sharply. 'Master Richard is right,' he snapped. 'A simple mark on the wall is no proof.' He went towards the door. 'Look, the bolts were still drawn, the windows were shuttered. How did the assassin get in and, above all, how did he get out?'

Richard went across and stared down. He tried to visualise the door as he had seen it last. The rusting lock still worked and there was a bolt, a crude affair, which had slipped into the clasp on the lintel. Richard glanced across at the window. He remembered bursting into the room but the shutters were closed: the makeshift bar pulled down so how had the assassin entered the room and then left? And why hadn't Sir Lionel Beaumont cried out? He was a knight, a warrior; he could have resisted yet everything was in place.

'There must be a secret passage,' Ferrers declared. 'There has to be.'

Sir Lionel's body was covered with a blanket then the room was searched. Floorboards were prised up: the shutters examined, the walls tapped, even the ceiling was scrutinised. No passage or secret aperture was found. Only one thing was amiss: when they examined the bolt on the door, Richard saw it had been cleaned and smeared with oil. He called the others over.

'Why is this?' he asked.

'Perhaps Sir Lionel did it himself?' Emmeline suggested.

She, too, had come up from the kitchen. Richard was

surprised at her calm demeanour at the news of Beaumont's death.

'It's quite possible,' she repeated. 'If Sir Lionel wanted to make himself more secure and drew the bolt across. He could have taken some fat or oil from the kitchen and...' She shrugged.

'Yet the mystery remains,' Ferrers declared. 'Sir Lionel, God rest him, could be peevish and sharp, worried about this or that. Yet he was a fighting man. Why didn't he resist? Shout for help?' Ferrers stuck his thumbs in his belt. 'I can understand someone coming into the room at Sir Lionel's invitation, the door being bolted behind him. But how did the assassin get out?'

'I heard nothing amiss,' Grantham spoke up. 'I have the chamber next door and I slept like a baby.'

Richard walked to the window and looked down at the front of the manor. It gave him a good view of the ring of trees and the pathway leading down to the lake.

'Didn't you hear anything?' he asked over his shoulder. 'Anything at all?'

A chorus of denials greeted his words. Suspicious glances were once again thrown at Manning and Richard noticed how the rest of the knights had distanced themselves from him. He looked quickly at their hands: Ferrers and Manning wore no ring but Bremner and Grantham did.

'Sir Henry,' he asked, walking across to where Grantham stood beside Emmeline. 'You have a signet ring on your finger. May I have a look?'

The man shrugged in surprise, took it off and handed it over.

'What's so important about a ring?' Ferrers asked sharply.

Richard studied Grantham's ring carefully. A circlet of copper with a small insignia shaped in the form of a shield bearing Grantham's arms: a black lion rampant on a white background with a gold star in each of the corners.

'I just wondered.' He took the rusty ring Buthlac had given

him out of his wallet. 'Last night,' he continued, 'Buthlac gave me this: the insignia is lost but it was found in the undergrowth just where Lady Catherine Fitzalan's corpse was discovered.' He slipped it on his finger. 'It's a man's ring, not hers. Probably owned by the assassin.'

The room fell silent.

'I've never worn them or those,' Manning declared defiantly. He splayed out fleshy fingers. 'I cannot abide rings on my fingers.' He undid the top of his jerkin and pulled out a gold chain on which a small brooch hung. 'This is my insignia.'

'No one said it was yours,' Bremner added slyly. 'But, Master Richard, are you saying one of us dropped that ring?'

'No, no, he's not,' Emmeline intervened quickly. 'And it's pointless pointing the finger of accusation at each other.' She smiled at Sir Walter. 'Those marks on the wall, they could be anything. How do we know Sir Lionel tried to name his attacker?'

'What do you mean?' Grantham said crossly. 'My lady, look at Sir Lionel's fingers, they're stained with plaster and blood.'

Emmeline walked across to the corpse, knelt down and pulled back the blanket. She raised Sir Lionel's right hand and studied the index finger. She then picked up his left hand.

'There are no marks here,' she said in a half-whisper.

'Why should there be?' Manning asked, then his jaw fell: he smiled and, going across, he grasped Emmeline's hand and raised her to her feet, kissing her fingers as if she was a queen.

'Sir Lionel couldn't have made those marks,' Emmeline beamed triumphantly around. 'For God's sake, you clever knights, use your noddles. Tell them, Sir Walter!'

'Beaumont was left-handed,' Manning declared. 'We all remember that. Even in a joust he carried his lance differently from us.'

'The assassin did it,' Emmeline went on, 'he took Sir Lionel's hand, dipped it in his blood and daubed those marks on the wall. And, if you look at them, they could be anything, an M, a B, a G. It was done to cause confusion. And, what's more,' Emmeline walked across to the corpse. 'Why was Sir Lionel killed here?' She pointed across the room. 'There's no sign of disarray so he wasn't retreating before his killer.' She beckoned Richard over. 'Master squire?'

Richard, bemused, joined Emmeline, her eyes dancing with mischief.

'Now, master squire, you come into this room to kill me. Why here? Up against the wall?'

Richard stared at her.

'Draw your dagger,' she urged.

Richard did so.

'Now,' Emmeline continued, 'here we are beside the wall. You have thrust your dagger at me. What circumstances would prompt that?'

'You invited me over,' Richard grinned back.

'But why?'

'Either to eavesdrop,' Richard replied, 'or to look for something.' He re-sheathed his dagger. 'Yes, that's it.' He glanced back at the knights. 'Somebody whom Sir Lionel knew and trusted, came in here. Sir Lionel would have lit the candle. The assassin takes him out of the light into the darkness, not to hear what is going on in the next room but something else. They were looking for a secret passageway,' Richard paused. 'Maybe that's the answer. Sir Lionel's visitor was probably wondering how these messages could be scrawled on the wall outside. He uses it as a ruse. Sir Lionel goes across, perhaps they were examining this wall or the floorboards beneath. The assassin drew his dagger and strikes.'

'But how did the assassin leave?' Grantham asked. 'And yet bolt the door from the inside?'

'I don't know,' Richard replied. 'More importantly, the Lady

Emmeline and I were in the kitchen with Buthlac all night.' He paused, his words hung like a noose in the air.

'So, you are saying it was one of us?' Ferrers edged his way forward. 'Master Richard, with all due respect, everyone fell asleep, yourself included. You or Lady Emmeline or Buthlac could have come upstairs as easily as we to knock at Sir Lionel's door.'

'And we mustn't forget the other two,' Manning declared. 'Barleycorn and Gildas. This is a sprawling manor, Master Richard, with unshuttered windows. Perhaps there are secret entrances.'

Richard was about to reply when he heard a pounding on the stairs and Gildas burst into the room. His boots and leggings were soaked, his face cut from overhanging branches. For a while he just crouched, gasping for breath. He didn't even bother to enquire about the corpse half-covered by a blanket.

'Where's Barleycorn?' Richard shook Gildas' shoulder. 'What's happened?'

'The outlaws,' Gildas gasped 'They've come. They tried to cross the ford. They suddenly appeared, moving quickly on foot. Barleycorn killed some with his arrows and they fell back. But he thinks they'll attack again.'

'We'd best arm,' Ferrers exclaimed. 'Mistress Emmeline, you should stay here.'

'Take bows,' Richard cried. 'Arbalests, long bows, whatever you have brought!'

'The horses,' Gildas said. 'Barleycorn said to bring the horses.'

'They'll slow you down,' Emmeline grasped Richard's hand. 'Go!' She urged. 'Take the rest. Gildas and I will bring the horses down. At least to the edge of the great meadow.'

They all hurried off, each to his own chamber. Richard went down to the kitchen. He put his war belt on, sword, dagger and a long Welsh stabbing dirk. He then picked up an arbalest and a quiver of bolts and went out into the stable yard. Emmeline and Gildas were already clumsily trying to harness and saddle the horses. The rest of the knights joined them. No suspicions now, all intent on facing the common danger. Sir Walter Manning was dressed in a chain mail shirt. Bremner and Grantham had brought their helmets; steel conicals with broad nose-guards. All were armed with sword and dagger. Ferrers carried a long bow, the rest had crossbows. Slipping and sliding over the snow, they made their way out of the manor courtyard through the woods. At first they moved as quickly as they could but Bremner shouted out and they paused, gasping for breath.

'We should be careful,' he warned, gesturing across the snow-covered meadow. 'If the outlaws have returned or if they've captured or killed Barleycorn, they could be waiting to catch us out in the open.'

'Then I'll act as scout,' Richard offered. He paused at sounds from behind them.

'That's the Lady Emmeline,' Bremner said. 'She and that wretch are bringing up the horses.'

'Sir John,' Richard replied, 'Gildas is no wretch and, before this day is done, you might be glad of his presence.'

'And when this day is done!' Bremner snapped, his face more fierce under the iron helm. 'I'll have to think again, Master Richard. I am tired of this godforsaken island. I do not want to die here!'

Richard made no reply but turned and began to run as fast as he could across the meadow. The snow was not as deep as he had expected, high as his mid-calf but quite firm. Now and again he paused and stared at the trees before him or glanced across to where the black knight had appeared but there was nothing. At last he reached the edge of the trees. He could hear nothing so he followed the beaten path down to the lakeside. He stopped and crouched behind a bush. He could see the ford and the long line of stones stretching to the distant shore. He moved to get a better view and saw at least three corpses sprawled out on the frozen lake. Each lay on his back, a feathered arrow in his chest. Their blood was already freezing in great puddles around them.

Silently Richard slipped further along the path. He left the trees and stepped out to the open ground before the lake. He whistled under his breath. More corpses lay, each taken by an arrow, most of them were clothyards but he also recognised Gildas' handiwork. One corpse lay nearer the shore, a crossbow bolt had smashed straight into his face. On the far shore he could see the trampled snow where the outlaws must have gathered. Looking to the left and right he could see no sign of Barleycorn: he was about to open his mouth to shout when he felt a presence behind him. He whirled around. Barleycorn stood, leaning on his long bow.

'Cuthbert, I thought you had been taken.' Richard came forward and clasped the man's outstretched hand.

The master bowman nodded at the corpses. 'Scum of the earth,' he replied. 'They came charging across, slipping and slithering. A child of ten couldn't have missed.' His face grew grave as he pointed across the lake. 'They've withdrawn beyond the brow of that hill,' he declared. 'They'll be back.'

'What happened?' Richard asked. He stared at the bowman's unshaven face and red-rimmed eyes.

'Gildas and I were amongst the trees. We had slept comfortable enough. We had trapped a rabbit, skinned it and were roasting it. I admit we were tired. I heard a sound and I looked across the lake: Dogwort and Ratsbane seemed to have sprung from the snow. They were moving quietly down the hill towards the ford.' Barleycorn rubbed his eyes. 'They came on so quickly, not a shout or a yell. Well, not until I started to loose.' He glanced over Richard's shoulder.

The squire whirled round. The brow of the hill was no longer deserted. A long line of men, carrying bundles of bushwood before them, were moving silently down towards the ford.

Chapter 2

Richard and Barleycorn retreated into the woods as the line of outlaws slithered silently down the snow-covered hill to the edge of the lake. Richard watched and shivered. Even when he stood at Poitiers and watched the French phalanxes advance in all their glory, trumpets blaring, banners snapping in the breeze, he had not felt so afraid as of this silent, threatening line of men moving down to the water's edge. They advanced with purpose; narrowing his eyes, Richard could see they were armed to the teeth. All carried sword and dagger, some had arbalests, a few had long bows. They were dressed garishly in animal skins. One had deer antlers on his head: another had a cap made out of fox's fur, others of badger or otter. A few had leather masks hiding their faces, others wore helmets with broad nose-guards which gave them a fearful, nightmarish look. They never spoke and even their horses were muzzled. Richard was about to speak but the master bowman shook his head. Richard counted and reckoned there must be at least three score. Suddenly another group came over the hill, four or five men in lincoln green. Two others, dressed in bearskin and mounted on nimble, sure-footed garrons, followed behind.

'Ratsbane and Dogwort!' Barleycorn hissed. 'Oh, at last, they've come to the dance!'

The outlaws stopped on the edge of the lake. One of the mounted leaders, holding a ragged standard, gestured forward. Apparently they knew where the ford was: a strip of water where the river bottom rose and great flat stones formed a footbridge across. The line of outlaws gingerly made their way over. Barleycorn tapped the small arbalest Richard had brought.

'On my mark,' he whispered.

The squire watched those ghastly figures slipping and slithering towards the shore. Barleycorn notched an arrow to his bow, moving silently back to get a better aim. Richard crouched and cranked the arbalest, slipping the bolt into the groove. Bringing it up, he sighted it on one outlaw slightly ahead of the rest.

'Loose!' Barleycorn shouted.

The line of outlaws stopped. Richard pulled the lever even as Barleycorn's bow began to hum. The outlaw he had aimed at suddenly stepped back, arms out, his sword falling on the ice. Two more did a little dance as Barleycorn's arrows took them in the chest and throat. Pools of blood began to wash over the ice. The outlaws stopped. Richard heard a voice shout; cursing and yelling, the outlaws continued. Richard brought his arbalest up, feverishly putting another bolt in, silently admiring Barleycorn's consummate skill: for every bolt he loosed, Barleycorn fired four arrows leaving twitching, blood-soaked corpses on the ice. They must have downed eight or nine but the line of outlaws drew nearer. Barleycorn hissed they should fall back. The outlaw leaders must have seen this and cheered their men on, even as Richard and Barleycorn retreated quickly back along the snow-covered path. The outlaws followed. Now and again

Richard would stop, arrows were loosed. They heard cries and screams but now the outlaws not only had the protection of the wooden faggots they held before them, but also made good use of the trees and undergrowth. Barleycorn kept looking to his right and left.

'They mustn't outflank us!' he hissed. 'If they do, we are trapped!'

He loosed one more arrow and began to run, beckoning at Richard to follow him. They had the advantage of surprise and the outlaws were fearful that they might be led into a trap. Barleycorn and Richard were half-way across the great meadow, the snow flying in flurries on either side of them before they heard the strident sound of a hunting horn and the triumphant cries of their pursuers.

Richard ran, the sweat coursing down his body. Now and again he would look round but the outlaws were still out of sight. In the line of trees ahead of him, he glimpsed Buthlac, Gildas and the knights waiting and, behind them, Emmeline holding the horses. The meadow stretched before him: the deep snow hindered his progress. On one occasion he fell on his hands and knees, coughing and retching: Barleycorn grasped him by the arm, pulled him up and pushed him on. At last they were in the trees and Richard immediately sank to the ground fighting for breath. There were curses and groans from the knights directed as much against Richard as the outlaws. However, by the time the squire had regained his breath and got to his feet, the knights were already preparing for battle, Buthlac and Gildas with them, all armed with bows and arrows. Richard staggered over to Emmeline who stood pale-faced but determined. Bayard nuzzled at her neck but already his ears were flat back against his head. Now and again he would lift his head and whinny as if he could sense the coming battle.

'Take a horse!' Richard urged, grasping Emmeline's hand. 'Go back to the manor house!'

Emmeline, her eyes wide, shook her head.

'If you die,' she whispered, clasping one of his fingers. 'If you die, what is the use, Richard?' She forced a smile. 'I can handle a bow and a sword. I prefer to die here. Please! Not burnt alive in the manor house or captured to be abused, raped and have my throat cut.' She stamped her foot and pointed to the arbalest swung over the saddle horn. 'I am not going.' She leaned forward and kissed Richard full on the lips. 'If you make me go, I'll never kiss you again!'

'Never?' Richard exclaimed.

'Well,' Emmeline pouted prettily, 'not for a long time.'

Richard turned. The outlaws were now appearing on the other side of the meadow.

'Do what you have to,' he retorted and hurried off to join the rest.

'Why don't we ride them down?' Manning suggested. 'A good charge will send them back.'

'Aye and they'll pull you down one by one,' Barleycorn replied. 'There's too many of them.'

'Can they outflank us?' Bremner asked.

'They could try,' Buthlac joked. 'They'd soon get lost in the woods. No,' he hawked and spat. 'They'll come across.'

'May the Lord of Battles be with us!' Gildas intoned. 'May he go before us. May a thousand fall on our right hand and ten thousand on our left. May you go back,' he stood up, shouting across the meadow. 'May you go back to the pit from which you came!' he yelled. 'May the Lord of Hosts smite you hip and thigh...'

An arrow zipped through the air and Gildas fell flat on his face.

'That's the shortest prayer I've heard!' Buthlac joked.

'Together!' Barleycorn shouted. 'Everyone, loose with me!'

The knights did not object. They were all seasoned veterans and had seen the power of the long bow on the battlefields of

188

France. They crouched silently, Emmeline beside Richard, one long silent line, bows and arbalests at the ready. The outlaws, nonplussed by the great meadow, paused but then they began to cross.

'Oh, thank God!' Barleycorn whispered. 'Bunched together like sheep. I hope Gildas prays to the Lord of Hosts that they don't scatter.'

Slowly the outlaw band came on. About thirty to forty of their number. They advanced in three lines. Richard's heart sank as they began to fan out but then Barleycorn suddenly leapt forward, running into the meadow. He notched an arrow to his bow even as he held one in his mouth. He knelt, taking aim, oblivious to the catcalls and arrows of the outlaws which whirred all around him. Barleycorn loosed. An outlaw on the far left of the band staggered back, clutching at the arrow which had caught him full in the mouth. Barleycorn abruptly turned and loosed at a man on the far right of the band, taking him in the stomach. The master bowman then ran back into the trees as Richard laughed at what he had done: the outlaws now fearful of Barleycorn's skill, bunched closer together as if this would protect them from his deadly aim. One of the knights hissed that they should loose but Barleycorn shook his head.

'When it comes to the bow,' he whispered hoarsely, 'trust me.'

The outlaws came on. They could not see their assailants and, as they drew closer, apparently hoped that Richard and his band had retreated back to the manor house.

'Don't forget,' the squire murmured. 'They still don't know how many we are.'

The line of outlaws drew closer. Richard could make out individual faces: he quietly murmured a prayer that these men, as savage and wild as the skins they wore, would not gain the upper hand. He glanced at Emmeline. The woman caught the strange look in his eyes and nodded. There was no need to speak. The agreement was made. If they faced defeat and no escape was possible, Richard would kill her, rather than let her fall into the hands of these wolfsheads. The squire breathed in deeply.

'When? When?' he gasped.

Barleycorn brought up his bow, arrow notched.

'Draw!' he ordered. 'Aim for the centre!'

The knights obeyed, Bremner pulling back the great long bow he had brought. Others followed suit. Gildas couldn't stop trembling and kept muttering prayers to himself.

'Aim!' Barleycorn shouted.

Richard steadied the crossbow. He drew in his breath.

'Loose!' Barleycorn roared.

The air hummed with their arrows. Some missed their mark but others had a deadly effect. Six or seven outlaws dropped screaming; the arrows, fired so close, ripping flesh and muscle, spilling blood out into the snow. The other outlaws, surprised, stood stock-still.

'Loose!' Barleycorn shouted.

Another even more deadly hail. The outlaws tried to rush forward.

'Loose!' Barleycorn cried.

This time the outlaws broke and fled.

'Advance!' Barleycorn bellowed. 'But keep in line with me!'

Richard told Emmeline to stay as he advanced with the rest. One last volley, more outlaws fell whilst the rest, learning from bitter experience, broke and fled in different directions across the meadow. For a while Barleycorn held his line, still making sure the enemy were retreating before drawing his dagger, the rest following suit and moving amongst the fallen outlaws. Some had died quickly. Others moaned and cursed, writhing in pain, scrabbling at the snow as if trying to draw back the pools of blood gushing out from wounds in neck, chest and stomach. Richard muttered his excuses and went back to see if all was well with Emmeline. He took her by the shoulder.

'Don't look,' he said. 'Go back to the horses.'

'Why?'

She struggled to look over his shoulder. Then she saw Ferrers, his sword held like an axe chop at a wounded outlaw's neck. She turned and abruptly fled. Richard wanted to go back but the fury of battle had left him. His companions, however, moved like the angels of death, slitting throats, collecting arms until Barleycorn shouted that the enemy were re-grouping and they retreated back into the trees. Barleycorn and the knights looked grim. Buthlac wore a self-satisfied smile whilst Gildas, disappearing into the wood, had been promptly sick.

'Was that necessary?' Emmeline asked, coming back amongst them.

'What else could we do?' Ferrers jibed. 'Pour oil on their wounds, bind them up and send them back?' He dropped the pile of weapons he was carrying. 'We did them a mercy,' he declared. 'A swift death is more than they deserved.'

The rest of the group agreed even as Gildas returned, wiping his mouth on the back of his hand. Nevertheless, the excitement of battle had faded from the group. Richard stared out at the bodies lying grotesquely on the snow, limbs twisted in different positions. The sun glinted on the bloody pools and Richard had to quickly look away: it seemed as if the whole meadow was soaked in blood.

'They are coming,' Barleycorn growled. 'This time they know how many there are of us. Even Dogwort and Ratsbane won't be so stupid a second time.'

He was proved right. There must have been about two score of the outlaws. The entire force strung out in one long line, gaps between each of them. On horses behind them, rode their two leaders. This time they moved more slowly.

'If we let them come too close,' Grantham snapped, 'they'll outflank us. They may even get back to the manor.'

Richard glanced at Barleycorn and glimpsed the look of desperation in the bowman's eyes.

'What can we do?' he hissed.

'Wait and fall back,' the bowman urged. 'Perhaps retreat into the stable yard.'

The outlaws came on then they stopped. Emmeline came up and whispered in Richard's ear.

'I know why Beaumont died!'

Richard looked up in surprise.

'The meadow,' she whispered. 'Don't you remember, Richard? The tournament your father held here? And the words between Lord Simon and the Lady Catherine? How the baron's wife wore the colours of a certain knight? Beaumont must have remembered. That's why he was killed.'

'Well, it's too late now,' the squire replied.

'We left his room so quickly,' Emmeline continued. 'On the table in a corner, I saw an inkhorn, quill and scraps of parchment. I wonder what he was writing?'

The squire grinned at her and tweaked her cheek.

'Ever the lawyer's daughter,' he retorted. He nodded towards the line of outlaws. 'If the Lord delivers us from them, we might find out.'

'Prepare your bows!' Barleycorn shouted as the outlaws fanned out even further and walked slowly towards them, urged on by their leaders riding up and down behind them.

'As soon as they are within range,' Barleycorn ordered. 'Choose your target and loose!'

Once again the bowman ran forward, arrow notched. He chose his targets and two of the outlaws fell. This seemed to break the rest and, as Barleycorn ran back, the outlaws pursued. Richard and the rest now fired but their arrows fell short. Only three or four of the outlaws fell. The rest were charging on when, through the air came the lucid, sweet sound of a horn. The outlaws stopped, looking round in fear. Their leaders urged their horses towards the trees from where the sound had come. The meadow fell silent. No sound except the heavy breathing of men intent on war. The outlaw leaders were just about to turn back and urge their followers on when the knight in black armour burst out of the trees, shield up, sword in his hand, his great war horse pawing the ground and snorting loudly. The outlaws did not know what to do. Were there other men in the trees? Should they go on against the deadly arrows of Barleycorn or turn to face this new danger? The knight lifted his sword, dug his spurs in and moved into a gallop.

'Like the fury of the Lord!' Gildas intoned. 'The Anger of God!'

His companions stood dumbfounded as this terrible figure, sword glinting in the sunlight, crashed into one of the outlaw leaders sending horse and rider tumbling, his sword falling and rising in a bloody, cutting arc. Barleycorn was the first to break from his reverie.

'Now!' he screamed. 'Now mount your horses!'

Richard and the rest ran back. He grasped Emmeline by the arm.

'Go back!' he whispered. 'Go back to the manor house. Lock yourself in but search Beaumont's chamber.'

He kissed her full on the lips then sprang into the saddle. He and the knights clustered together. Manning waved his sword and, despite the thick snow, they broke into a canter, Barleycorn, Buthlac and Gildas running behind him. The mysterious knight was already wreaking bloody havoc: like a farmer with a threshing flail, he struck to the right and left. Once again the meadow became littered with wound-gaping bodies. In his wild charge Richard saw a severed head, an arm, a hand. The snow had turned a bloody crimson and the air dinned with the screams of men.

When Richard and his companions joined the knight, all heart went out of the outlaws. They threw down their arms and tried to surrender only to be cut down. Others followed their leader in headlong flight across the bloody meadow. Now and again a group of outlaws stopped and turned, forming themselves into a knot but the horsemen simply rode through them. The outlaws reached the woodland path. Here Richard found it hard to keep his mount steady. An outlaw turned, lifting his sword but Bayard flailed out, his hooves catching the man a crushing blow on his head. At last he was through, down to the lakeside. As he broke from the trees Richard found the icy causeway had been blocked. Someone had pushed a burning mound of faggots across the ice. It was too thick to melt immediately but already cracks were appearing. Water was seeping through whilst dancing flames blocked any further retreat. Two outlaws, desperate enough, tried to make the crossing. One was hit by an arrow, the other stumbled and fell into the flames. His screams were terrible until Barleycorn loosed an arrow into him. Richard glanced around: the mysterious knight had disappeared. The outlaws were trapped by the lakeside and the knights were not inclined to show any mercy. The outlaws were being cut down like sheaves of corn. At last Richard could stomach it no longer.

'Stop! Stop!' he screamed.

He wrenched a sword from Manning's hand, disgusted by the blood-lust in the man's eyes. Bremner, Grantham and, finally Ferrers, reined in their horses, slumped in their saddles grasping swords soaked in blood. The outlaws, no more than ten or eleven now, grouped round their leader who had also dismounted, pulling off the bearskin from his head. The wolfsheads crouched, hands extended in a gesture of peace. Richard dismounted and walked over to them. He looked down at the leader and, though sickened by the bloodshed, the squire was repelled by the evil in the man's narrow, thin face. Like a weasel, Richard thought: cruel mouth, hard small eyes in his unshaven face.

'Mercy,' the man whispered, his eyes sliding to Barleycorn and Richard caught the hatred blazing there.

The squire pushed the man away and stared at his companions. He glimpsed Buthlac slip back into the woods, that long Welsh stabbing dirk in his hand and realised there would be no wounded.

'Kill them!' Ferrers demanded. 'Kill them all!'

Richard stared round the group. Never had he seen such a band of depraved evil men. He shuddered at what would have happened if the victory had been theirs. Only one face moved him to compassion. An ugly, pimply-faced boy, no more than twelve years, hiding behind the leader.

'They should all die!' Bremner shouted. He looked round, 'And where has our mysterious saviour gone?'

Richard shrugged and glanced back towards the meadow. He remembered how the knight had charged, his absolute control over his horse, the scything cuts of his sword. It stirred memories but Richard was too tired and the knights were thronging round him.

'Master Richard.'

Manning stood before him, legs apart. He pointed with his thumb over his shoulder to where the outlaws crouched, herded together. The knight stopped to cough as smoke billowing from the fire on the ice swept in across the island.

'What Manning is going to say,' Ferrers, leaning on his sword at the back of the group, spoke up. 'Is that we are all Justices of the Peace in this county. We carry the King's commission. These men are outlaws, wolfsheads.' He came forward, forcing his way through the group. 'Which means that they can be killed on sight.'

'It's true,' Grantham looked shamefacedly at Richard. 'We have to execute them.'

Richard glanced away.

'We don't need your authority,' Ferrers warned. 'But, as a courtesy, we are telling you what should be done.'

His words created moans of despair amongst the outlaws. The leader now got to his feet. He would have moved forward but Barleycorn's dagger was at his neck.

'Then damn you all!' he shouted. 'I'll not beg for life!' He grasped the young boy, the lad had red spiky hair, a wart-covered face, popping eyes and slobbering mouth. 'The boy shouldn't die.' He turned to Barleycorn. 'Kill me but spare my son.'

Barleycorn looked quickly at Richard and nodded. The squire turned away, closing his eyes. He knew the knights were right. They had the law on their side, that's why outlaws were called wolfsheads. They could be killed on sight. And what could he do? If he resisted he'd be over-ruled. One outlaw with thick, matted hair, his face almost hidden by moustache and beard, staggered forward. He threw himself down at Ferrers' feet, clawing at his boots and tugging at the hem of his cloak. He jabbered in a tongue neither Richard nor the rest could understand. Ferrers kicked him away but again the man caught at his cloak. This time the voice was harsher more strident then, before Richard and the others could act, Ferrers had drawn his sword and, in one cutting arc, sliced the man's throat from ear to ear. The outlaw knelt, gurgling on his own blood, eyes staring up at his killer and then, tilting sideways, crashed on to the snow. Ferrers leaned down and cleaned his knife on the man's leather jacket. He looked up, a smile on his harsh face.

'He claimed to be one of my tenants,' he rasped. 'And begged for mercy.'

'His speech?' Barleycorn asked. 'What tongue was that?'

'He came from the Fens,' the outlaw leader declared. He hawked and spat at the outlaw's corpse. 'He really believed he might obtain mercy.'

Richard stepped over the fallen man and studied the outlaw group. His gaze moved from one depraved face to another.

'There'll be no hangings,' he called over his shoulder. 'Let it be done quickly! Gildas, go and get Buthlac. If any man here wishes to be shriven...' Richard leaned across and grasped the boy still cowering behind his father. 'No child will die.' He pushed the boy out of the way. 'Go on, lad,' he urged.

'I'll take care of him,' Barleycorn offered: he re-sheathed his dagger. 'I have hunted these men and they have hunted me. Yet I see no joy in their deaths.'

Sir Henry Grantham stepped forward and held his sword up.

'I, Sir Henry Grantham,' he shouted, his voice ringing like a death knell. 'King's Commissioner and Justice of the Peace in this shire, do, by the power given to me, condemn you to death for divers crimes against the Crown and the People! Sentence is to be carried out immediately!'

He stepped back. Bremner and Manning dragged forward a piece of wood. They all waited until Buthlac returned. The hermit moved amongst the outlaws who sat devoid of any resistance: a few prayed, some cried but most followed their leader's arrogant example, He was hustled along and made to kneel down, Bremner raised his sword and in one terrible cut took his head clean from his shoulders. The horses, stirred by the smell of blood, became restless. Gildas led them away as the second outlaw was hustled forward for execution. Richard closed his eyes, crossed himself and, leading Bayard by the reins, walked back up towards the meadow. Barleycorn and the boy were waiting for him. The bowman gestured at the corpses which now littered the snow.

'Master Richard,' he grasped the boy by the collar. 'We must send a messenger across the lake. These corpses have to be buried.' He nodded back towards the shore where the executions continued to be carried out. 'We must get confirmation of what we have done.'

The squire didn't answer him: he just stared round at the great blotches of blood staining the meadow and glanced up at the cruel, yellow-beaked ravens now circling, waiting to feast on the carrion below.

'Do you think this island is cursed?' he asked.

Barleycorn just shrugged. 'Ratsbane and Dogwort were not invited here,' he replied. 'They came and received their just deserts.'

'And the knight?' Richard asked.

'He was here in the meadow when the killing was taking place,' Barleycorn replied. 'when the outlaws broke and ran towards the ford, he disappeared. It was probably he who lit the fire.'

The squire looked down at the boy. He d never seen a child so ugly and yet so frightened. His pitted face was covered with tears: he began to shake so much, Richard took off his cloak and wrapped it round him.

'Take the boy back,' he urged. 'Put some wine and food into his belly.'

Barleycorn grasped the boy's shoulder. 'We should kill him, Master,' he caught the look in Richard's eyes. 'Yes, I am hard,' he replied. 'Hard and cruel. Yet, if they had taken me, there would have been no quick death.' He blinked and looked up at the sky. 'I was sweet on a girl once,' he continued. 'Golden hair she had, her skin was nut-brown. Aye, a high rich laugh and lips which were meant for kissing. Her father was a wood cutter: they had a house in a small clearing just north of Epping. One fine day Ratsbane and Dogwort paid them a visit. I was away in another part of the county.' The bowman gnawed at his lips. 'I found the girl's corpse, naked, deep in the woods. She must have taken days to die.' He shoved the boy away in front of him. 'So I have no mercy. When that young girl died, so did all my compassion.' He was about to say something else but then caught himself. 'We all need to eat and drink,' he murmured then strode off across the meadow, his long bow slung over his shoulder, one hand on the boy now wrapped in Richard's cloak.

The squire stared across at the trees. He wanted to mount Bayard and search every inch of the island until he found that knight. He stirred as he heard the sound of voices and laughter on the path behind him. Richard realised that the executions must be finished, so he mounted Bayard, dug in his spurs and, looking neither to left nor right, followed Barleycorn back to the manor.

Words between the pilgrims

The franklin paused in his tale. For a while, he just sat rocking himself quietly in his chair.

'By all that's true!' Mine Host got up to stretch his limbs. 'I've heard of bloody fights but none so terrible as what happened on Crokehurst Island.'

The franklin smiled thinly. He pointed across at the hour candle on the mantelpiece above the hearth.

'The hour is growing late,' he declared. 'Perhaps I should leave the rest of my story until tomorrow night.'

'Oh no!' his fellow pilgrims chorused.

'You must finish it now!' the wife of Bath cried.

'It would be wrong not to,' the shipman shouted.

The franklin walked towards the door. 'Let me give my throat a rest. The night is calm and cool. I'd like to take the breezes for a while.' They all agreed to this, Mine Host heading straight for the kitchen to look for more wine, ale and victuals.

'To replenish,' he declared, 'their good cheer after such a bloody tale.'

The franklin ignored them. He went out of the door and into the small yard of the priory. Flickering cresset torches bathed the cobbles in light. The franklin sat on a small, stone bench before a small garden full of sweet-smelling flowers. He loosened his tunic, stretching his neck to catch the cool night breeze. Around him, in the different windows of the priory, candlelight flickered. Straining his ears, the franklin caught the faint chanting of the monks at their night office. He closed his eyes and smelt the flowers. He would be glad when this pilgrimage was done. Every three years he made it in fulfilment of his solemn vow. He heard a sound on the cobbles and put his hand to the hilt of his dagger. A man coughed. The franklin relaxed and looked over his shoulder at the knight standing there.

'A pleasant evening, Sir Godfrey?'

The knight came and sat down beside him and pointed to the flower bed.

'Nothing smells so sweet on an April evening,' he murmured softly. 'Their fragrance always calms me.' He glanced sideways at the franklin. 'A fragrance most welcome to those used to the stink of battle!'

'Why have you really come, Sir Godfrey?' the franklin asked.

'To see who you really are,' the knight looked at him squarely. 'I went to Crokehurst,' he continued. 'The King sent me north with a troop of royal sergeants. We hired labourers and dug the great grave pit our good priest mentioned. I arrived at the end of your tale.'

'Well, now you know I speak the truth.'

'And the killer?' the knight asked. 'The assassin?'

The franklin pressed a finger against the knight's lips.

'Sir Godfrey, you finished your tale about the dreadful Strigoi, but the story really goes on, does it not?'

The knight nodded.

'And so does mine,' the franklin added. 'And it's not done

yet.' He heard the door to the refectory quietly open and close. 'I think someone else wishes to have words with me.'

The knight hitched his sword belt up and returned to the refectory. The franklin turned back and stared at the flowers though this time he drew his dagger, turning it deftly so the blade slipped up his sleeve. The summoner came and sat beside him.

'So, you recognised yourself?' the franklin asked.

The summoner's wart-covered face looked even more dreadful in the flickering torchlight.

'Of course,' he replied. 'Not a day passes, Master franklin, that I do not think of that terrible day on Crokehurst Island.'

'Then you should thank God that you were spared,' the franklin said. 'That compassion was shown to an ugly, snivelling boy, his face all covered in warts.'

The summoner picked at a dirty fingernail.

'I also know the end of your story. Isn't it strange? When I first met you, with your florid face and snowy white beard, your silk purse and velvet clothes, I thought there goes a capon waiting to be plucked.'

The franklin laughed softly. 'I know,' he retorted. 'You tried to steal my purse.'

'And you did not try to stop me.'

The franklin stood up, plucked the dagger from his sleeve and pushed it back into its sheath. He glanced down at the summoner: his eyes were no longer merry.

'If you'd taken it,' he grated, 'you'd not be here to listen to the end of my tale!'

And, spinning on his heel, the franklin walked back to the refectory.

PART V

Chapter 1

By the time Richard returned to the old manor house, Emmeline had built up the fire and prepared cups of posset. Barleycorn had thrust the outlaw brat into a corner and lay down upon some sacking, his body twitching as he slipped in and out of sleep. Richard studied the prisoner who gazed owlishly back: the squire felt a pang at the mixture of misery and cunning in that small, ugly face. He could hardly speak to Emmeline as the aftermath of the battle, combined with the heat and the posset, took their effect. He felt hot, his limbs heavy as if in a dream and he became acutely aware of how he was surrounded by death. Beaumont's bloody corpse stiffening upstairs whilst, outside in the snow, lay the cadavers of the outlaws with their mangled wounds and their headless torsos drenching the lakeside. He heard the cries of jubilation from the returning knights and put his head in his hands. They burst into the kitchen, faces flushed, their weapons and clothing still bearing the bloody marks of battle. Cloaks were doffed and sword belts loosened. The kitchen rang with the cries of triumph and declamation as each man vied, especially in the presence of Emmeline, to describe their feats upon the battle field.

Buthlac and Gildas squatted like dogs watching the noble ones. They, too, looked sickened by the bloodshed. The outlaw boy huddled in a corner, whimpering quietly. Grantham went across to give him another shake and frighten him even further. Barleycorn abruptly sat up, drawing his dagger, and Sir Henry withdrew. Ferrers sat at the head of the table: he took off his gauntlets and carefully placed them down.

'A great victory, Master Richard. Your father would have been pleased.' He indicated with his hand to the rest, 'We shall wait, one day,' he continued, 'the weather will grow milder: we will count the slain then leave.'

Richard glanced at Barleycorn but the archer lowered his head. Gildas and Buthlac still looked frightened. Emmeline had her back to him, stirring the cooking pot under the growing flames of the fire.

'You have no objection?' Manning asked, taking a seat beside Ferrers.

Richard just shook his head. He felt exhausted, tired and weary of Crokehurst and all its bloody mystery.

'And what about Sir Lionel,' Emmeline declared, not bothering to turn. 'How will you explain his murder to his kith and kin?'

'We shall sheet his body,' Bremner replied. 'And take it back to his manor. After that my companions and I will draw up a report for the King.'

'And is that how your oath to Richard's father will be resolved?' Emmeline continued. 'With all the questions still unanswered?' She got up, her face flushed from the heat of the fire. 'You are forgetting one thing,' she said quietly. 'Oh yes, Dogwort and Ratsbane and all their followers are dead. But that knight still remains.' She turned back to the fire, speaking over her shoulder. 'He may not let you leave.'

Richard sipped from his cup. He was tired, determined not to be drawn into an argument. He got up and lay down on his bed of sacking. He wrapped his cloak around him, turned his face to the wall and fell into a deep sleep. Now and again he drifted in and out of this. The knights were still talking loudly amongst themselves. Emmeline was also asleep: of Buthlac, Gildas and Barleycorn there was no sign. Richard wanted to get up but felt so heavy with sleep he found he could not move He slipped back into nightmares of frozen fields, full of stiffening, headless corpses and a knight in black galloping silently towards him. He slept on and was roughly awakened to find Emmeline bending over him, her fingers to her lips.

The kitchen was now dark except for the glow of a tallow candle and the flickering flames of the fire.

'Come with me,' she urged. 'Quietly now. The rest have all retired.'

She led him out of the kitchen into the cold, draughty passage, up the stairs and along the gallery where so many dreadful events had occurred. At the stairs at the far end Emmeline paused. She crouched down and began to pull at part of the staircase. Richard, still half-asleep, watched in surprise.

'What is the...?'

Emmeline waved at him to keep silent. He would have helped but she knocked his arm away.

'I can't find the secret clasp,' she muttered. 'But they do slide.'

As she spoke Richard heard a click like a twig breaking and both the step and its wooden side came away. Others followed. Emmeline took the candle she had brought from the kitchen and pushed it into the draughty black hole. Richard peered in: he saw red brick and a rope ladder attached to it.

'I don't believe in ghosts,' Emmeline whispered. 'When I first arrived here, I noticed the wall at this end is thicker whilst the second storey juts out more than it should. Moreover, if you go outside,' she exclaimed, her eyes bright with excitement, 'you'll notice there's no window in the side wall.' She lifted the candle and pointed to the gap. 'This appears to be a shaft running from top to bottom of this side of the house. I discovered it this afternoon when you were all gone.' She grinned. 'As I said, I don't believe in ghosts: this is how our mysterious walker made his presence felt.'

'Where does it lead to?' Richard asked.

'Oh, by St Michael and all his Angels!' Emmeline replied. 'I wear a dress and petticoats, Master squire, or have you not noticed?'

Richard smiled. He carefully climbed into the hole, grasping the rungs of the ladder. The shaft was dark, icy cold and the sweat froze on his body. Emmeline held the candle out and he went down, moving slowly, testing every rung. At last he reached the bottom where a small passage ran off to his right. He found the stonework surprisingly hot. He studied the bricks and saw a crack of light. He edged across and looked through the gap: as his eyes became accustomed to the light, Richard realised he was looking into the kitchen, still faintly illuminated by the dying embers of the fire. He climbed quickly back. When he reached the top, he leaned against the rungs, wiping the sweat from his face.

'The kitchen's below,' he whispered. 'I can feel the fire from the hearth. Once upon a time this was probably some huge chimney stack.'

'And at the bottom?' Emmeline whispered back.

'A narrow passageway.' Richard replied. 'Probably leading to some entrance in the house. There's a vent in the wall. Anyone who climbed down could hear everything that was said.' He pointed further up the shaft. 'That is subtly contrived; the smoke from the fire must be taken up by a different route.' He looked up into the darkness. 'I wonder if Father knew this was here?'

'And this was how our ghost moved around?' Emmeline asked anxiously.

'I don't know,' Richard replied. 'But it's time we found out.'

This time he climbed upwards until his head reached wooden floorboards. He scrabbled around, found a catch, pulled back the bolt and pushed down the small trapdoor. He poked his head through this but all he could feel was a rush of cold air through the musty darkness. Richard had neither tinder nor candle so he closed the trapdoor and climbed down and back through the aperture into the gallery.

'There must be some sort of loft or garret,' he explained as he helped Emmeline replace the false steps into their grooves.

Once this was done, they walked quietly down the gallery.

'It's a wonder no one heard us,' Richard whispered.

'Bearing in mind what they drank,' Emmeline replied tartly, 'and the exertions of the day, I doubt if Gabriel's horn could rouse our brave knights!'

They returned to the kitchen. Richard glimpsed Buthlac sleeping in a corner.

'Where's Gildas and Barleycorn?' he asked.

'They took the outlaw boy out to the stables,' Emmeline replied. 'They said they preferred to sleep there and keep the boy well guarded. He could slit our throats whilst we sleep!' Emmeline pulled two battered casks up to the fire. 'I have something to show you.' She opened the leather pouch on a belt round her waist and took out scraps of parchment. 'When I returned here, I went immediately to Beaumont's room.'

'What did you find?'

'Nothing,' Emmeline answered. She held her hand up. 'Oh, I have no doubt that Beaumont had been writing something but his killer was not stupid, he took it with him.' Emmeline brushed the scraps of parchment. 'I also examined the door,' she continued. 'The murderer came in and went out that way. Now the bolt was not only newly greased but the clasp which held the bolt had been repositioned, So, if you slammed the door from the outside, the bolt would slide into the clasp, locking it behind you.'

Richard rubbed his eyes and stared at her.

'It's quite easily done,' Emmeline explained. 'You prise the bolt and clasp loose with a dagger, reposition them and hammer the nails back in again. The bolt is greased as is the catch, give the door a slam and the bolt slides home.'

'Are you saying Sir Lionel would have done that?' he asked.

'Of course not,' she snapped. 'But the assassin did. Tomorrow, go round the house and find a door with a bolt and clasp. If you move then grease them, the same can be done: the assassin did the same knowing he was going to visit Sir Lionel.' She shrugged prettily. 'Then he could blame it on the spectre, the ghost or whatever ghoul inhabits this house. What I think happened is that the assassin knocked on Sir Lionel's door and was admitted. Beaumont had been sitting at his table, perhaps writing down his thoughts. The assassin talks, lulls Beaumont's suspicions: he claims there is some secret passageway round the house. Beaumont follows him across the chamber into the shadows, the assassin draws his dagger...'

'Of course,' Richard interrupted. 'Beaumont would have died quickly by choking on his own blood. The assassin daubs some blood and plaster on his fingers, then leaves, slamming the door behind him.' He held his hand up. 'And that's the sound which disturbed me from my sleep last night.' He grasped the scraps of parchment. 'But there's nothing written here.'

'The assassin removed those on top,' Emmeline replied. 'But,' she took the scraps of parchment back and held them up against the fire, 'you can make out the faint outline on those underneath.'

Richard knelt, took a piece and held it up against the glowing fire. The parchment was thin and cheap. He held it closer and made out the faint drawing of an eagle, its wings stretched and in its claws a bar of iron.

'My father's coat of arms!' he exclaimed. 'What did Beaumont mean by drawing this?'

'Look at the bar of iron,' Emmeline insisted. 'See how it's scored time and time again.'

Richard sat back in his chair. 'What was Beaumont thinking about?'

'Something had jogged his memory,' Emmeline retorted. 'About that tournament years ago: the one your father held in the great meadow where the Lady Catherine wore another knight's colours. I think Beaumont remembered whose colours they were.'

'But, according to this,' Richard replied, 'it would seem the Lady Catherine wore my father's. Which only proves,' he added bitterly, 'the accepted story: that my father and the Lady Catherine had an illicit affair and that he killed her and the Lord Simon in a fit of rage.' He tapped the parchment. 'And yet I know that to be a lie.'

'It's strange,' Emmeline declared, her hands stretched out to catch the warmth from the fire. 'When the Lord Simon died, he pointed across the room and whispered something about "the eagle has the truth" and "nothing new under the sun". Don't forget, Richard, he was dying, his brain was confused. Now, while I waited for you to return this afternoon, I went up and visited the chamber where Lord Simon's corpse was found. On the hearth are your coat of arms. Remember it: a sun, the eagle beneath and, in its talons, a bar of iron. Now the phrase, "nothing new under the sun" could refer to your father's emblem: it bore a sun.'

'As it does an eagle and a bar of iron,' Richard added. He glanced across where Buthlac snored peacefully: the squire wondered if the hermit was really asleep or just pretending to be.

'What are you thinking?' Emmeline asked.

'I am trying to recall the insignia of the different knights. Manning's is a lion; Ferrers' is a ship with silver stars.'

'Bremner's is a hawk,' Emmeline said, 'carrying a sun in its claws. Whilst Grantham's,' she tilted her head back, 'Grantham's is a bear holding a ragged staff against a sable field.' She shook her head. 'There's nothing there.'

She started as the door behind her crashed open: Barleycorn burst in, pieces of straw clung to his hair and beard, his clothes were all dishevelled.

'The brat!' he exclaimed. 'The outlaw boy, he has gone. I had him tied.' He walked towards the fireplace. 'But he gnawed through the rope like a dog.' Barleycorn went back and closed the door behind him. 'Master Richard, shall I pursue him?'

The squire shook his head. 'God knows where he is in this darkness,' he commented. 'And if he can make his way back to the ford any pursuit would be useless.' He clapped Barleycorn on the shoulder and brought him closer to the fire. 'Anyway, I am glad he has gone. One less problem for us to address. I am sure if our good knights had their way, they would have taken his head as they did the rest.'

Barleycorn squatted down in front of the hearth. Buthlac, disturbed by the noise and inrush of cold air, also awoke and sat up, rubbing his face and muttering about Christian souls unable to sleep.

'He was certainly frightened,' Barleycorn declared, stretching his fingers out to the fire.

'Did he say anything?' Richard asked.

'He cursed, snarled and spat at me and called the knights every filthy name he knew. Especially Ferrers, killing that outlaw so cold-bloodedly.'

'Will he survive?' Emmeline asked. 'I mean, the boy?'

'Oh, he'll reach the lakeside,' Cuthbert replied wearily. 'And find his way across the ford.' He glanced at Richard, his eyes red-rimmed with exhaustion. 'Master, we've got to send for help. The island is like a battlefield. Corpses need to be buried: pits should be dug and Masses sung.' He gazed round the room. 'If this place wasn't haunted then it must be now!'

'I'll go,' Buthlac volunteered from where he crouched in the corner. He got up and came forward, tapping the master bowman on the shoulder. 'Barleycorn is correct, Master. We need help.'

'Sooner than you think,' Emmeline intervened. 'The knights now believe their vow to your father is fulfilled. They are intent on leaving.'

A short, sharp discussion followed until Richard reluctantly agreed to Buthlac taking a staff, sword and small crossbow and some food.

'Colchester must now be open,' Buthlac remarked. 'Perhaps the sheriff and his comitatus will come.' Cloaked and hooded he walked towards the door. He turned, a smile on his strained, twisted face. 'Don't worry.' He tapped his leg. 'My hobbling gait won't stop me, though it will be strange to be off this island.'

Then he was gone into the darkness, slamming the door behind him.

Everyone else returned to their beds but Richard, refreshed after his sleep, sat on a stool staring into the dying embers of the fire. Now and again Emmeline would stir restlessly in her sleep and he'd smile as she called out his name The squire closed his eyes. He had always been taught to pray for the dead but now he prayed to them: to his mother Maria, summoning up her ghost.

'Please,' Richard whispered. 'Please, for the love of God, help find your murderer!'

A log spluttered and crackled in the heat. Richard's eyes flew open. He picked up the parchment from Beaumont's chamber, and studied the faint outline in the fading firelight. He recalled the other pieces of information he had collected, fighting hard against the despondency which threatened to overwhelm him.

The ring Buthlac had found: Lady Catherine Fitzalan dying out there on the path; Lord Simon, delirious in his chamber. Richard closed his eyes. Lord Simon had been pointing at an eagle, wings outstretched, carrying an iron bar.

Richard got to his feet. He looked at the scrap of paper and wondered why his family had a coat of arms but no motto? After all, they were becoming more and more common. He pulled a face. Perhaps he should compose one? He knew a little dog Latin: 'Aquila sub sole', 'The eagle under the sun'? Or 'Aquila fertur ferrum', 'The eagle carries an iron bar'? Richard paused, his stomach clenched in excitement.

'It can't be!' he whispered. 'No, no, it can't be!'

He sat down on the stool and applied the conclusion he had just reached to everything he had learnt. Outside a bird screeched in the night and Richard jumped at a hand on his shoulder. He stared up at Emmeline's sleep-laden face.

'Richard, you must sleep.' She leaned down and kissed him tenderly on his hair.

'I know the assassin,' he said quietly and grasped her hand. 'Emmeline, I know the truth and I think I can prove it.'

'Who?' She gasped.

Richard put a finger to his lips. 'Be discreet now. The walls have ears,' he murmured. 'We know that to our cost.' He got up and opened the door: the sky was beginning to lighten, the clouds had now disappeared. 'It's going to be a fine day,' he declared. 'The snow's stopped falling. It will melt even quicker when the sun rises.'

He staggered forward as Emmeline pushed him.

'Tell me,' she hissed.

'Prepare a good breakfast, woman,' he teased back. 'Summon our companions and I'll at least whisper his name.'

An hour later Emmeline had transformed the kitchen. She still looked tired but her hair was purposefully tied back. She had built up the fire, filling their makeshift cauldron with oatmeal and laying out on a platter what was left of their precious cheese and smoked bacon. Pewter jugs were filled with ale. Barleycorn came in from the stables. He must have caught their mood: he looked at Richard quizzically but the squire refused to be drawn. Gildas also came in, loudly moaning how his arms weighed as heavy as iron after his exertions of the previous day. He then went and sulked in a corner as Barleycorn began to tease him.

The knights came down, still full of their victory the previous day: they didn't seem to care about the outlaw boy's escape.

'Well, we're going as well,' Grantham trumpeted, polishing his bald pate with his hand. 'We've fulfilled our vow, Master Richard.' He pointed to the half-open door where the morning sunlight was streaming through. 'A thaw has begun. Home and hearth calls.'

'So it does,' Richard said, sitting down on a stool at the end of the table. 'And yesterday, sirs, you fought valiantly. Sir Walter, talking of valiant fights, if a knight wears a lady's favour at a tournament, where does he carry it?'

'Usually where no one else can see it,' the knight scoffed back. 'After all, her husband might object.'

'No, seriously,' Richard asked.

Ferrers pointed to his right side. 'Here, in the gap between the corselet and the armlet. Usually a piece of silk or cloth the lady has worn.'

'The rules of the tournament,' Sir John Bremner intervened, 'say the knight should place the colours there just before he charges.'

'And so who knows?'

'Ah! That's all the mystery,' Grantham barked. 'The lady and her knight do. The favour must always be worn in the actual passage of arms.'

'Very good, very good.' Richard popped a piece of bread into his mouth. He glanced quickly at Barleycorn and caught the excitement in the master bowman's eyes. 'And on the day of the great tournament,' he continued quietly, 'which of you fought against Baron Simon Fitzalan?'

Manning choked on his beer. Ferrers sat up straight in his chair. Bremner and Grantham gazed open-mouthed as they realised the implications of what Richard had said.

'It was done by lot,' Manning replied quickly. 'Aye, Grantham fought against your father.'

Richard held his hand up. 'Did my father fight against Baron Fitzalan?'

'No, no, it was...' Grantham put his face in his hands.

'Each man had two opponents, that's right! For example, my opponents were Bremner and Manning.'

'And Fitzalan?'

'Sir Lionel Beaumont,' Grantham replied slowly: then he turned and pointed towards Ferrers. 'And you, Sir Philip!'

'So,' Richard intervened quickly. 'If Baron Fitzalan's wife was intriguing with a knight: that knight would have worn her colours?'

'Yes, yes, that's true!'

'What are you saying?' Ferrers snarled.

'Sir Lionel Beaumont's dead,' Richard answered quietly. 'Foully murdered. But you, Sir Philip, also fought against Baron Simon. Were you wearing his wife's colours? Did he glimpse them as you broke lances in the lists?'

'This is foolish!' Ferrers growled, kicking back his stool.

'Is it?' Richard continued. 'Remember Baron Simon's dying words. He said "nothing new under the sun": he was referring to the ancient sin of adultery. He died pointing to the fireplace where my father's coat of arms were depicted. Everyone thought he was in a delirium or indicating something which has now vanished: he was, in fact, pointing to the eagle carrying the iron bar. The word "to carry" in Latin is *"ferre"*, the word for iron is *"ferrum"*. Your name is Ferrers.'

'Stupidity!' Ferrers snapped. 'Absolute stupidity! I loved the Lord Simon.'

The other knights protested. Manning even drew his knife but Barleycorn, who'd abruptly left, now returned, an arrow strung to his bow.

'Everyone will remain seated,' the bowman ordered. He looked at Richard, his eyes gleaming with excitement. 'We will continue.'

'I call you an assassin,' Richard declared, pointing down the table at Ferrers. 'I call you a traitor and a foul-hearted murderer. You, Sir Philip Ferrers, were a knight in my father's retinue. You own land in Essex and undoubtedly some of it runs along the Essex coast.'

'That's true,' Sir John Bremner murmured. 'He has a small manor outside Walton-on-Naze.'

'You'd go to the port,' Richard continued, 'and small harbours where, I am sure, some French merchant first made the approach. Baron Simon was a member of the King's war council. The coast of Essex is exposed and vulnerable and the French would like to know about levies, the fortification of castles, which towns were vulnerable and which were not. You took French gold and, at the same time, paid court to the Lady Catherine Fitzalan. She was no great beauty, her husband was often absent and you crept like a cat into his cradle. The French knew our secrets because his wife told you or, the poor woman, not fully aware of your evil intent, would not object if you saw certain papers and memoranda.'

Ferrers made to rise but Barleycorn, standing behind him, pricked his neck with the tip of his arrow.

'Soon,' Richard continued remorselessly, 'it became apparent that there was a traitor in the camp. But who? Baron Simon was the King's own companion. Suspicion fell on my father but Baron Simon rejected it. Instead, in that golden summer so many years ago, Fitzalan and my father decided to hold a council

217

of their knights: a tournament also took place.' Richard paused and sipped from the battered goblet. 'I suppose,' Richard continued, 'the Lady Catherine was now becoming insistent. It's one thing to play cat's cradle in her bower when her husband is absent but, at the tournament, she insisted that you wear her colours. You did so, quite unobtrusively.'

'Of course,' Sir Walter broke in excitedly, 'Ferrers would only wear those colours just before the feat of arms.'

'But why?' Sir Henry spoke up. 'That would be too dangerous!'

Richard shook his head. 'Ferrers had no choice. If he didn't wear them, Lady Catherine, who would be watching intently, might create a scene and arouse her husband's suspicions. In the end, Ferrers was running no great risk: a piece of cloth is a piece of cloth.'

'But Fitzalan saw it,' Bremner interrupted.

'Yes he did.' Richard stared down at Ferrers, his face like stone, his eyes staring at some point above Richard's head.

'It would only be a matter of seconds,' Richard continued, 'As the two knights galloped down the lists on that bright summer's day, Lord Simon glimpsed a flash of colour. He recognised the cloth as belonging to his wife.'

'If that's the case,' Ferrers snapped, 'why didn't Lord Simon approach me? Make an issue of it in public? He was a gentleman, a knight.'

'And make a mockery of himself?' Richard interrupted. 'Proclaim to all of Essex, not to mention the kingdom, that one of his knights had made him a cuckold? And what proof did he really have? Lady Catherine would hotly deny it, as would Ferrers.' Richard stared at the other knights. 'If you were in Lord Simon's situation, would you make such an accusation which you couldn't prove? Even if Ferrers admitted to wearing the favour, it still doesn't prove adultery. Lord Simon would only portray himself as a figure of fun, the jealous husband.'

'But Lord Simon,' Gildas spoke up from the bottom of the table where he had been watching, eyes bright with excitement, 'would he suspect that Ferrers was also the traitor?'

'What proof would he have of that?' Richard retorted. 'Can you imagine Lord Simon accusing Ferrers? Sir Philip is a wily man. He would immediately use his possible adulterous liaison with the Lady Catherine as his defence, how Lord Simon was jealous and wished to destroy him.'

'But your father,' Barleycorn asked, 'he must have had his suspicions?'

'Perhaps he did.' Richard shook his head. 'However, knowing the little I do of Lord Fitzalan, I doubt if he even wanted my father to know that he had been made a cuckold.' Richard sipped from the goblet. 'Lord Simon began to brood, to despair, to talk of "nothing new under the sun". He might have suspected Ferrers had used the Lady Catherine to obtain secret information but what proof did he have?'

'And your father?' Grantham asked.

'Perhaps Fitzalan raised Ferrers as a possible traitor but my father dismissed it: I believe Buthlac may have even overheard him doing exactly that.'

'So why the murders?'

'I don't really know,' Richard replied. 'However, I suspect that, though Lord Simon couldn't accuse Sir Philip in public, he could take issue with his wife in private. Ferrers became alarmed. After all, if Lord Simon interrogated his wife and took counsel with my father they might act more secretly, perhaps have Ferrers arrested and taken to London.' Richard ran his fingers across the top of the table: as he did so, he prayed silently to the ghosts of his parents not to desert him at this, his hour of need. 'What ever, perhaps the Lady Catherine became insistent? I think it was she who stirred the evil in Sir Philip's soul, insisting that he meet her on that lonely path leading down to the lakeside. Sir Philip,' Richard paused, his hand over his purse as he prepared the lie which he hoped would trap the murderer, 'I think Sir Philip went out to meet Lady Catherine and killed her. He then hurried back into the manor house. Remember, it was still dark, just before dawn. He crept along the gallery and tapped on Lord Simon's door. Fitzalan let him in. Sir Philip told some lie, whispered in the darkness, and drew near. A quick stab, Lord Simon went down and then Ferrers went to the stable where he dragged my father after knocking him unconscious. He smeared him with blood from the dagger, poured wine over his clothes and returned to his own chamber.' Richard sipped from his cup. 'The scene is now set for the most bloody of murders with my father as the scapegoat.'

He would have continued but Ferrers banged his fists on the table.

'Lie upon lie!' he roared. 'You have no proof!'

'Oh, yes I have,' Richard replied quietly and, opening the neck of his purse, he drew out the ring but kept it tightly in his fist. 'Sir Philip Ferrers, I have all the proof I need!'

Chapter 2

Richard drew the ring out of his purse. He slipped it on to his own finger, ensuring the clasp was turned away from Ferrers.

'What's that?' Sir Philip made play not to have seen it before.

'Why, your ring,' Richard retorted. 'You remember, Sir Philip, you used to wear one bearing your coat of arms. The night you met Lady Catherine you made love to her in the undergrowth then slashed her throat: she didn't expect her paramour to kill her. During the murder your ring rolled off your finger: you often came back here looking for it but all the time Buthlac had it. Which is why,' Richard added, 'the hermit has now left the island: he fears your wrath.'

'You are lying!' Ferrers snarled. 'There's no insignia, it's lost!'

'How do you know that?' Emmeline intervened. 'We have the ring so how do you know what's really missing?'

Ferrers just glared back.

'You are the assassin, Sir Philip,' Richard accused. 'You killed the Lady Catherine and stabbed her husband to death.'

'I never wore a ring!' Ferrers shouted, red spots of anger high on his cheeks.

'Yes you did,' Manning interrupted coolly. 'I remember, Sir Philip, you wore an insignia ring.'

'Well, if I did, I never lost it. I never went to meet the Lady Catherine.'

'Lady Catherine left her own message,' Richard lied. 'Which Buthlac also found: a letter...'

'She never wrote...' Ferrers closed his eyes, his head slumped.

'What were you going to say?' Manning asked. 'That she never wrote letters to you, Sir Philip? How would you know that?'

'You were close,' Grantham spoke up. He snapped his fingers excitedly. 'That's right: now and again I used to catch the love-lorn glances.'

Richard sensed the mood of the knights change: they drew away from Ferrers as if he was a leper.

'You are a killer,' Richard jabbed his finger down the table. 'You are responsible for the dreadful murders here. You blamed my father.'

'But why did he kill Beaumont?' Manning asked.

'I think Beaumont had his own suspicions,' Richard replied. 'Remember, he, too, was thinking about that tournament so many years ago. He remembered something and, in his chamber that night, sat down and began to brood. Don't forget, he was there when Baron Fitzalan died. Beaumont remembered Lord Simon's dying words: "nothing new under the sun" and "the eagle has the truth". Sir Lionel also recalled the insignia on the fire hearth and, like me, solved the riddle of the eagle carrying the iron.' Richard drew from his wallet one of the scraps of parchment Emmeline had taken from Beaumont's chamber. 'That was why Sir Lionel kept scoring with his quill, the iron bar the eagle carries. Now,' the squire continued, 'Ferrers became alarmed and so plotted another murder. You may recall the day you spent in Beaumont's room playing games, whiling away the

222

time? Ferrers must have seen the clasp on the door. He realised how, if the bolt was moved and carefully oiled, it would slide into the clasp when the door was slammed shut. Ferrers made sure it did. On the night Beaumont died, Ferrers went along to Sir Lionel's chamber full of some madcap theory about secret passages. He would take Beaumont out of the light, over to the wall as if looking for some concealed compartment.' Richard shrugged. 'The rest was easy. Ferrers drew his knife and killed Beaumont. He then took the scraps of parchment Sir Lionel was poring over and slammed the door shut.' Richard smiled bleakly. 'If anyone heard that they might think it was a spectre or a ghost and be most reluctant to investigate.'

The squire glanced down the table. Ferrers was lost in his own thoughts. Richard slipped the ring off his own finger and put it back in his wallet, glad that no one had asked to examine it more carefully.

'Finally, we come to the outlaws' attack: when we took prisoners, one of them recognised Ferrers here and ran jabbering at him. According to the outlaw leader this man was from the fens, probably a smuggler: he spoke in his own strange dialect. I wonder if he was reminding Sir Philip of what he used to do, years ago when Sir Philip used him and others to attract the attention of French ships at sea. The man was not begging for mercy, he was trying to blackmail him: that's why Ferrers killed him out of hand.'

Ferrers raised his head. 'Show me the ring.' His hand went out. 'Show me the ring bearing my arms. Show me any further evidence you have.'

Richard shook his head.

Ferrers studied him intently, eyes narrowed, his rat-trap mouth firmly clenched. Richard's heart sank. In reality, he had very little evidence to present before the King's Justices. Ferrers, sly and cunning, was aware of this. Ferrers' hand went beneath the table and he drew his gauntlets from his belt.

'I am a knight,' he said. 'Before God I swear my innocence!'

He threw one of the gauntlets down the table in Richard's direction but, before the squire could pick it up, Barleycorn moved swiftly, sweeping the heavy leather glove on to the floor.

'You can't do that!' Bremner declared. 'Sir Philip here may be an assassin and a traitor but, he has called on God and challenged his accuser to mortal combat.' He glanced pathetically at Richard. 'Our squire here is of noble birth. We can attest to that: if he does not accept Sir Philip's challenge, he must tell that to the Justices and it will weigh heavily against his accusations.'

Richard, keeping his voice steady, held out his hand.

'Cuthbert, give me the gauntlet.'

'He'll kill you,' the master bowman replied. 'He's an accomplished lance. He'll kill you and walk away scot free.'

Richard knew Barleycorn was correct but kept his hand extended.

'Please.'

Barleycorn shook his head and stood away: an arrow notched, the bow pulled back. Ferrers stared at the arrow aimed directly at his heart.

'Are you going to murder me?' he sneered. 'Kill me in cold blood?'

'You called on God,' Barleycorn replied quietly.

'So?'

'You called on God,' Barleycorn repeated. 'Then let God answer.' He glanced at Richard. 'Master, let us go down to the great meadow.' He looked at the hour candle burning between two stones just under the window. 'I promise you,' he continued. 'If you come down to the great meadow, the gauntlet will be taken up.'

Bremner was about to object but Manning held his hand out.

'There are other mysteries here,' he said. 'Other secrets and riddles. If Master Greenele accepts the challenge, we are knights, we can be the witnesses. The "Lutte à Outrance", the fight to the death, must take place in the great meadow so, we might as well go there.'

Emmeline sprang to her feet as if trying to hide her anxiety by putting some food in a linen cloth. She picked up a wineskin as well as an arbalest, placing three bolts into a small sack. Ferrers pushed back his stool and made to go towards the door but Manning caught his arm.

'I think it's best, Sir Philip,' he remarked quietly, 'if Bremner and I escort you: Grantham can go with the young squire.'

They paused for a while to collect their war belts and cloaks. Gildas had already gone ahead: for a few moments they stood in the stable yard as both Ferrers' horse and Bayard, tossing their heads and prancing with excitement, were taken from their stalls to be saddled. At last all was ready. Emmeline sidled up beside Richard and pinched his arm.

'I shall pray for you,' she whispered into his ear. 'God will not forsake you.'

They moved off in silence. Barleycorn, an arrow still strung to his bow, took up the rear. Richard, trying to keep Bayard quiet, wondered what the master bowman intended and fought to calm the tingle of excitement in his belly. Ferrers moved ahead of him, also leading his horse. The knight moved with a purposeful gait, never once turning to the left or right, or even glancing over his shoulder at his prospective opponent. The sun was growing strong: the air was no longer icy cold and a deep thaw had set in. Snow fell crashing from the branches, making the birds wheel and turn noisily in the sky above them. Emmeline refused any offer of help and managed to keep her footing on the slush-covered trackway. At last they reached the great meadow. Corpses, twisted in grotesque positions, lay in puddles of congealed blood. Richard felt his stomach lurch as Gildas, a

225

silent spectator of this drama, pointed out the tracks of foxes and other wild creatures leading in and out of the trees. Even the air seemed to have the iron tang of blood.

'A place of slaughter!' Grantham intoned.

'It's as good a place as any,' Ferrers tossed the reins of his horse at Manning and started strapping on his metal breastplate.

'On horse or on foot, Master Greenele?'

'It should be on horseback,' Manning declared. 'Sword against sword. God will decide.'

'God has yet to intervene,' Barleycorn spoke up.

He walked into the meadow and, putting his hunting horn to his lips, blew three, long haunting blasts. The master bowman stood, as if listening for an answer.

'For whom are you waiting?' Ferrers taunted. 'The Angel Gabriel?'

Barleycorn stood, head slightly cocked. Once again he blew three long blasts. Richard felt his blood tingle: he watched the line of trees near the end of the meadow. Suddenly, on the breeze, came the answering blast of a horn, loud and triumphant. Richard gripped Bayard's reins. He glanced quickly at Ferrers and noticed how the man had paled. Barleycorn was still staring intently across the meadow. Richard caught the faint sound of harness and the knight, dressed from head to toe in black armour, burst from the trees and bore down on Barleycorn. The master bowman did not move. With superb skill, the knight turned his horse, bringing it to rest within yards of Barleycorn and lifted his visor. Everyone strained their eyes but the knight had his back to them. He handed his lance to Barleycorn and listened intently to the bowman, then his hand came out. He grasped the gauntlet Barleycorn gave him, brought the visor of his helmet down and cantered towards Richard and his party. The knights half drew their swords but then the stranger stopped, raising one gauntleted hand in the sign of peace. He took off his helmet, pulling back the chain mail coif beneath. Richard's heart lurched. He had to bite back the scream on his lips as he stared at the stern but now cleanshaven face of his own mentor and lord, Sir Gilbert Savage.

'It can't be!' Grantham staggered forward and grasped the reins of the knight's horse. He looked up then sank to his knees. 'My Lord Roger!' he whispered.

Richard stood open-mouthed. The knight carefully dismounted: he thrust his helmet into Grantham's hand and came towards Richard. He embraced him tightly, giving him a kiss on either cheek. He stepped back.

'I owe you all,' he declared harshly, 'an apology and an explanation.' Tears brimmed in his eyes. 'To my son and, above all, to good, true knights whose reputation I have suspected for many a year.'

He smiled at Gildas then bowed in the direction of Emmeline. He seemed as if he didn't want to meet Richard's eyes, as if he was fighting back tears. Instead he swung on his heel, walked up to Ferrers and, bringing back the gauntlet, gave the knight a resounding blow across his cheek. Ferrers took it unflinchingly.

'I call you a coward, a caitiff, a traitor and a murderer!' he shouted. 'It is I who take up your gauntlet, Sir Philip Ferrers. I call on God,' he raised his voice, 'his Mother Mary and all the court of heaven to prove my innocence upon your body.' He then seized Ferrers' face in his hands. 'Why?' he whispered hoarsely. 'In God's name, Philip, why? I gave you everything: lands, money, preferment?'

Ferrers stared unblinkingly back.

'Why?' Lord Roger pleaded. 'Before one of us die, at least tell me why?'

'You've changed, my lord.' Ferrers bowed mockingly. He touched Lord Roger's face. 'You've changed,' he repeated. 'Your hair was once black and flowing. Your beard and moustache rich and well oiled.'

'You forced me to change,' Lord Roger retorted. 'You drove

me out into the wilderness. Made me nothing more than a wolfshead.'

'And I thought you were dead,' Ferrers sneered. 'Oh, I have heard stories about your heir, going hither and thither with some strange companion but I never guessed it was you.'

'I kept well away from Essex,' Lord Roger replied, 'and if I happened to meet anyone who might recognise me, I hid. I cropped my hair and shaved my beard. The years took care of the rest.'

Ferrers looked up at the sky. 'It will be to the death,' he murmured.

'To the death,' Lord Roger replied. 'No quarter given, no quarter asked.'

'By sword and horse?'

'By sword and horse.'

'And if I win?' Ferrers lowered his head. 'If I win, what then?'

Lord Roger held his sword up by the crosspiece.

'I, Lord Roger Greenele of Crokehurst manor, do solemnly swear on my eternal soul that, if vanquished in battle by Sir Philip Ferrers, he may walk away a free man.' The knight lowered his sword. 'Why?' he rasped.

'I shall confess nothing,' Ferrers blustered, aware of how the rest were watching.

Even the horses were silent and Richard had forgotten about the snow, the cold, the sunshine, even the corpses rotting in the great meadow.

'I shall confess nothing,' Ferrers repeated. 'But I am glad we fight, Lord Roger. I have always hated you. You, with your manners, your easy ways, full of courtly piety.' Ferrers sneered. 'I used to watch you and Baron Simon walk arm in arm then hear how the King would make you sit by him at table and carve your meat. Everywhere you went, people stretched out to you.'

'I refused you nothing,' Lord Roger interrupted.

'Can't you see?' Ferrers retorted. 'Generosity is a dangerous virtue, my lord? No one likes to be a dog waiting for the crumbs from the table.'

'You were no dog,' Lord Roger replied. 'And why Baron Simon?'

'A chivalrous fool,' Ferrers sneered. 'Him with his dumpy, fat wife: the way he would dote on your counsel,' he hawked and spat in the slush.

Lord Roger stepped back.

'Then, it is as you say, to the death. Barleycorn?'

The master bowman came running over.

'If either of us try to flee the field, kill him.' Lord Roger turned. 'Sir Henry Grantham, Sir Walter Manning, you will be the marshals.' He pulled a face. 'Though there will be few rules to this combat!'

Ferrers was already swinging himself into the saddle, checking the reins, making sure his sword and dagger moved easily in the scabbard. He pulled his hood up and put on his heavy jousting helm with a broad nose-guard. Lord Roger took off his armour, stacking it at his son's feet. He looked up, now his eyes were clear, almost laughing.

'I'll have no advantage,' he murmured. 'If I die, they are yours.'

'And, if you die,' Barleycorn came up beside him, 'I'll kill Ferrers.'

'You can't!' Lord Roger rasped back.

'With all due respect,' Barleycorn winked wickedly. 'You won't be in a position to object!'

Lord Roger mounted his horse and rode off to the far end of the field. Richard turned as Bayard reared in excitement, ears back, nostrils flared. Emmeline came over, a wizened apple in her hand. Bayard stilled and plucked it from her fingers. Emmeline stroked the horse's neck.

'Richard,' she stared round-eyed at the squire. 'So much

mystery! The man you wandered the kingdom with was, after all, your real father.'

Richard shrugged. 'My lady, on reflection he was that, in everything but name.' He peered across the snow. 'But the young can have shallow hearts, inclined to take for granted what is so generously given.'

'Will he win?' Emmeline asked anxiously.

'I don't know.' The squire turned to Bremner. 'Sir Philip is a warrior?'

'He's an accomplished fighter,' the knight answered grimly. 'A born horseman and a most skilled swordsman, he's fighting for his life,' he broke off as Manning raised his voice.

Richard anxiously watched both knights ready themselves for the charge. They raised their swords, turning sideways, fighting hard to control their horses which, in spite of the slush and snow, were pawing the ground, their breath rising in small clouds on the cold morning air. They seemed to wait for an age: Richard was aware of the black trees round the meadow; the cawing of the ravens; Emmeline standing motionless beside him. Even Bayard had fallen quiet. Manning and Grantham were now walking away from the line of the charge. Both stopped, turned and held their hands up. The two warriors readied themselves. Again a burst of cawing from the rooks. Richard glanced at the corpses from the previous day's conflict and wondered whether their shades would linger to watch this bloody fight. So many questions teemed in his mind. He felt numb. He still couldn't fit the pieces together to form a picture. All he was aware of was that he had lost his father, found him again only to face the possibility of losing him for ever.

'Now!' Manning screamed: his hand fell.

Both knights tightened their reins, their horses began to walk slowly forward, then into a trot. Barleycorn ran forward, an arrow notched to his bow. Both knights were now charging, their horses' hooves drumming the ground, brilliant flashes of sunlight from their helmets and raised swords. Richard held his breath. They met with a tremendous crash, the horses slipping and skittering on the snow-covered ground yet both men remained firmly in the saddle. They hacked at each other, ducking and swerving, using all their power, their horses and their swords to bring their opponent down.

The first few blows were fast and furious but both men grew tired. They drew off, calming their horses, gripping their swords, and again they met in a shrill clash of steel, each trying to circle, to get the advantage over the other. Lord Roger fought like a man possessed but Ferrers was the silent, cold-hearted killer. Richard had to admire the skill and ease with which he moved his horse, swinging blows at his opponent's head. Once or twice Richard turned away as Ferrers, seeing an opening, struck at Lord Roger's neck: the knight would move just in time and, before he could deliver any counter-parry, Ferrers had moved away. The horses, neighing and lashing out at each other with sharpened hooves, were also part of the mêlée. Abruptly, Lord Roger moved his horse, a sharp, quick flurry of snow round its hooves, and sent it crashing into Ferrers, whose horse skittered away, its legs buckling. Ferrers fought hard to keep his seat but, realising it was useless, cleared his feet from the stirrups and jumped off. His horse, terrified and exhausted, pounded away into the sanctuary of the trees. Ferrers stood, sword extended.

'Oh no!' Emmeline murmured. 'Chivalrous but foolish!'

Lord Roger too was now dismounting, refusing to take advantage of his opponent. Ferrers didn't even wait for his horse to clear but came in at a run, swinging blows at Lord Roger's head. The knight moved swiftly away from Ferrers' cutting blows.

For a while both knights rested, sucking the air in greedily, then they closed again. Swords clashing high or low in parry and counter-parry. Ferrers stood back. He brought his sword up for a killing blow aimed at Lord Roger's head. The latter moved away, the blow missed but then Lord Roger retaliated, quick as a striking viper. His sword scythed the air, flashing in the sunlight. It took Ferrers' head off. Emmeline screamed. Richard glanced away as the head bounced through the slush. The torso remained upstanding, the blood spurting out like a fountain before it too crashed to the earth. Lord Roger dug the tip of his sword into the snow and knelt down, his lips moving soundlessly in prayer. Then he got up and staggered forward into his son's arms. The squire stood, holding his father, feeling the furious beating of his heart, his hot breath on his cheeks.

'I am sorry,' Lord Roger whispered. 'God be my witness, son, I am sorry for what I have done.'

'It's over,' Richard declared. 'It's finished now. You've been vindicated in the eyes of God and lawful witnesses.'

Lord Roger stood away, smiling.

'I wish your mother was here,' he said, the tears brimming in his eyes. 'I wish she could see the baby she always wanted, grow into the man she always wished you to be. As we travelled round the kingdom,' he continued, 'sometimes at night I used to stand over you, I'd stare at you for hours, wishing I could tell you the truth but that would have been too dangerous. I taught you everything I knew.' Lord Roger smiled. 'Before we left England,' he said, 'as the troop mustered at Dover, I think someone recognised me. One of the knights from the royal household. Barleycorn and I decided it was time to act.'

'Barleycorn?' Richard exclaimed and stared over where the bowman stood grinning at him.

'Indeed, Barleycorn has been with me from the start,' Lord Roger waved his hand. 'But I'll tell you about that later.'

'So it was you who met him on the Epping road?'

'Oh yes, from the moment you left Poitiers I shadowed you. When you landed in Dover, Barleycorn was there, watching.'

Richard grinned and ran his fingers through his hair.

'I thought I wasn't alone but, at Poitiers?'

Lord Roger shrugged. 'It was easier than you think. The field was awash with blood. Darkness was falling. As we passed through the village, I bought a pig's bladder filled with blood.' He grinned. 'The rest was, as you saw: a dark, wet ditch well away from marauding French. Once you had gone, I waited for a while and followed.'

Richard picked his father's helmet up from the ground and stared at where Ferrers' head and torso were lying.

'So, you planned all this?'

'Are we going to freeze out here all day?' Grantham shouted.

'Sir Philip Ferrers?' Manning asked. 'What shall we do with his remains?'

'Whatever you like!' Lord Roger snapped. 'As for me, I'm finished!'

He went back to gather the reins of his horse.

'Leave the dead to bury the dead,' he said, quoting the scriptures. 'I saw Buthlac leave. The sheriff's men will be here. They can dig the grave pits.'

Emmeline came over and shyly took Richard's hand.

'It's finished,' she whispered, her eyes bright with excitement. She stared across the field. 'Do you remember the gospels, Richard? The field which the chief priest bought with the money Judas returned? What was it called?'

'Haceldema, the field of blood,' Richard replied.

'Aye,' she murmured. 'Well, this is a field of blood, Richard: a place of retribution and vengeance. When I first saw it I thought it was a field of dreams.' She stared across to where Lord Roger stood surrounded by his knights, accepting their congratulations. 'It's a place of nightmare,' she added. She shivered and pulled her cloak tightly round her shoulders. 'Come on, Richard, there's nothing a warm fire and hot cups of posset won't do to warm our bodies: your father has a great deal to tell us.'

They walked back along the trackway, leading the horses. Bayard was strangely quiet as if the violence had drained his energy and spirit. Richard felt weary: his legs heavy, a bitter taste in his stomach and the back of his throat. He realised his father's struggle had been so violent, he'd bit his lips to the quick. He dabbed at the blood and wondered what would happen now. Would his father go to London to sue for a pardon? They reached the manor house: Lord Roger striding into the stable yard, leading his horse as if he had never left. Gildas and Barleycorn took the horses in to unsaddle and wipe them down whilst the rest went into the kitchen. Richard helped Emmeline build up the fire and hung a makeshift bowl of posset above it. His father took his rightful place at the top of the table, his knights crowding round, badgering him with questions. Lord Roger heard them out, just nodding or grunting in answer. The squire came and sat beside him.

'It was you, wasn't it?' Richard began. 'You were in the house all the time?'

Lord Roger's face creased into a smile. 'Of course,' he whispered. He stared across where Emmeline stood, leaning against the hearth, looking down at the roaring flames. 'Your mother used to stand there like that,' he observed quietly and stared round at the clutter and the dirt. 'But it was different then. The walls were lime-washed, the pots and pans used to glow like gold, the air was always fragrant with newly baked bread and freshly roasted meat. Maids and scullions...' He wiped his eyes on the back of his hand and grasped Richard's wrists. 'You won't remember but you used to sit and play with a toy horse I made. I thought it was my Eden.' He shook his head. 'Never once did I think the Serpent would ever enter.'

He paused to smile his thanks as Emmeline brought across a tray of pewter cups and a collection of rags to hold them. Lord Roger took his and sipped it carefully, wrinkling his nose at the smell of herbs.

'But, yes, it was me. Crokehurst has a warren of secret passageways.'

'I found the one behind the hearth,' Richard declared.

His father smiled. 'Oh and there are more than that; in the cellars, in the garret, between the walls.' He sipped at his cup. 'Years ago our ancestors were smugglers. They often had to hide themselves as well as what they smuggled. I used their secret galleries. I heard every word said.'

'And the writing daubed on the walls?' Grantham asked.

Lord Roger rolled the cup in his hands. 'I knew the murderer was one of you,' he replied. 'I knew there would never be another opportunity like this. I burnt the bridge. I left the writing on the wall and, when the outlaws attacked, it was I who defended you.'

'And where did you hide your horse, your armour?'

Emmeline sat down beside Richard.

'In the woods, at the far end of the island, there's a secret pathway impenetrable even in summer, it leads to a cave, warm and dry, which can house a man and his horse and I had provisions to withstand a siege. I was with you from Colchester,' he remarked. 'Then I left before you. Everything was prepared. I won my horse and armour years ago from a knight at a tournament. I kept them here. Sometimes I returned to the island, once or twice Buthlac nearly saw me.' Lord Roger sipped from his cup. 'I'd come back here,' he whispered. 'And then I realised I wasn't the only one. Oh, I was aware of the occasional pedlar or curiosity seeker but these I could drive off. After all, the manor is haunted.' He grinned sheepishly. 'And I was not above helping the stories. Other times, however, I was aware that someone else had returned: someone connected with this mystery, as if he was looking for something.' He shrugged. 'But I didn't have the time to lay any traps and, even if I had, what would it prove? A man like Ferrers would simply lie, declared he was returning to pay homage.' Lord Roger leaned over to pat his son on the shoulder. 'And, of course, you were always waiting for me in some tavern or castle hall. So I'd leave the island in disguise, be out of Essex before anyone recognised me.'

'I doubt if they would,' Grantham intervened. 'Lord Roger, the years have changed you. Only sitting here watching you carefully, do I recall the man I once served. But why all this?' he asked.

'It was the only way,' Lord Roger replied. He grasped the cup between his two hands and lifted it to his lips. 'But the day draws on, the house is now quiet. Let me tell you from start to finish.'

Chapter 3

'Most of the story you have correctly guessed,' Lord Roger began. 'So I will not plague you with repetition. Baron Simon Fitzalan and I believed, most reluctantly, that one of my household knights was selling secrets to the French.' He spread his hands expansively. 'But who? Suspicion fell on this person or that according to our whim.

'But, if that is true,' Richard asked, 'why did Ferrers strike at that particular time?'

'Of that I don't know. Remember, it was only a matter of time before the truth emerged. Lady Catherine might have brought matters to a head. She may have become more insistent, more public in her adulation of Ferrers.'

'And did Lord Simon know?' Emmeline asked.

'He began to suspect,' Lord Roger replied. 'But, there again, he was a gentleman. He thought the problem would go away.' He paused. 'Just before he was killed, Lord Simon mentioned he wanted to discuss something with me. He alluded to evidence but hinted it concerned a personal matter.'

'But surely he saw Ferrers wearing Lady Catherine's colours at the tournament?'

'Which in itself was quite innocent,' Lord Roger replied. 'It's not enough to hang a man.' He pulled a face. 'After all, it's not uncommon for a knight to wear a lady's colours.' He smiled thinly. 'On one or two occasions Lord Simon wore my wife's. It was a courtesy, a compliment though, I admit, Lord Simon was not happy. Ferrers was a lady's man: Fitzalan nicknamed him "Bold Eyes".'

'Of course!' Richard interrupted. 'Buthlac heard you talking about "Old Eyes": he only half heard what was said?'

Lord Roger smiled grimly. 'Yes, I suppose we were both assuring ourselves that Ferrers was an honourable man. No.' He leaned forward. 'The real danger was Lady Catherine herself. If she admitted to having an affair with Ferrers, then it would only be a matter of time before Fitzalan began to suspect his wife had allowed Ferrers access to secret documents.' He sipped from the cup, eyes narrowed as he recalled the past. 'But there was something else which Ferrers might have overheard. The situation had become quite serious. Baron Simon had agreed that we couldn't spend the rest of our lives in a guessing game.'

'Is that when you and he had a violent altercation?' Bremner asked.

'Yes, yes, it was. Baron Simon did not like what I suggested but eventually he agreed.' Lord Roger drew in a deep breath. 'Forgive me, sirs, when I say this, we decided to send to London for troops and put you all under arrest.'

His words created an outcry. Lord Roger held up his hand, shaking his head in apology.

'What could we do? What could we do?' he murmured. He ran his fingers down his seamed face. 'Once you had returned to your manors, the treason would have continued. I decided to send my squire, Gilbert Savage, with a letter asking for these

238

troops. Savage never left the island. Someone lay in wait, killed him and took the letter. I only learnt that after the tragedy had occurred. Once Ferrers had read my letter, bearing in mind Lady Catherine's growing insistence, he decided to act. The murders were simple. Lady Catherine was invited to meet him. She was killed. I was struck on the head and dragged to the stables and made to look like the assailant, a drunken sot who killed both his lord and his lady.'

'And so it wasn't a servant who killed the Baron?' Emmeline intervened. 'We thought it might be.'

'Oh no, Lord Simon would allow Ferrers in. Perhaps he hoped the knight had come to explain how his wearing of Lady Catherine's colours was something innocent. He would be an easy victim. As Baron Simon lay dying on the floor, he must have seen my family arms and realised what had happened. Hence his final words: "Nothing new under the sun", a cry of despair,' Lord Roger sighed. 'Fitzalan was referring to the iron bar on my family escutcheon, a pun on Ferrers' name.'

'You told us,' Grantham said, 'that Gilbert Savage, your squire, visited you in Colchester prison.'

'Yes, yes, I did. I'd already formed a plan to escape. Let's be honest, gentlemen, I couldn't trust any of you. One of you was a traitor and a killer. I was visited in Colchester gaol by two people.' He glanced sadly at Emmeline. 'Your father Hugo, a good friend and ally accompanied by a young verderer.' He pointed at Barleycorn. 'You see, when Gilbert left the island, I'd also sent a message to Cuthbert to meet him and take him by the swiftest route through the forest to London.'

'I was your father's friend as well as a royal official,' Cuthbert turned to Richard. 'We both attended the Cathedral school in Colchester, been friends since boyhood. When Savage didn't arrive at the agreed place,' the master bowman continued, 'and I heard about the scandal, the murders on the island, I realised something terrible had happened. I took you and your mother away. Nobody paid any attention to me. I then visited your father with Hugo Coticol. I gave him money, a dagger and some drugged wine for the gaoler.'

'I escaped and fled.' Lord Roger took up the tale. 'I met Barleycorn in the forest. The following day we came across a victim of an outlaw attack, a merchant.' He paused and drank from his cup. 'God forgive us but we were desperate. I dressed the corpse in my clothing and made it look as if I had been drowned near a mill.' He wiped the tears from his eyes. 'I shaved, cropped my hair then paid a secret visit to the Lady Maria but her mind was gone. So I went to Hugo Coticol to collect you. Cuthbert returned to his forest. You and I fled, well away from Essex. For years we stayed north of the Trent. Of course, time passes, people forget. You were the son I always wanted.' Again he wiped the tears from his eyes with the back of his hand. 'The Lady Maria was dead and the passage of time had changed my appearance. No one would suspect that the poor knight with his impoverished squire, moving from castle to castle, was once the great Lord Roger Greenele, friend and companion to the King, a member of his inner council, the owner of Crokehurst manor.'

'Hold, hold.' Sir Walter Manning shifted back on his stool. 'Lord Roger, I accept what you say. We did not forget you but,' he shrugged quickly, 'no one ever recognised you?'

Lord Roger shook his head. 'I tell you my appearance was changed. People see what they want to see. Moreover, I always made sure that I was never in one place for long to excite suspicion. Don't forget,' he added, 'I was supposed to be dead: my lawyer and Barleycorn had identified the corpse.'

'But you came back to Essex?' Grantham asked.

'Secretly. I knew Crokehurst island held the key to all this mystery. Surely I could discover something, some document, anything which could point to whom the real assassin might be?' He sighed. 'But the years passed. Richard grew from a boy to a young man. Oh, I heard the news and chatter about you all. But what could I do?'

'Yet Ferrers,' Manning interrupted, 'knew you were not Gilbert Savage! After all, he'd killed your squire?'

'Oh yes,' Lord Roger replied. 'And that's why I took Gilbert's name. I always hoped, I always prayed, that one day one of my knights would come hunting this strange Gilbert Savage. Whoever did that, would know that the real Savage was dead, he would be the assassin.'

'Ferrers must have been a cold-hearted, cool-nerved bastard!' Grantham snapped.

'Yes, he was,' Lord Roger replied. 'He kept his nerve. I don't know if he realised I was alive or not. However, like the cat in the tale, all he had to do was stay silent and watch.'

'And me?' Richard asked.

'God forgive me, son,' his father replied. 'As the years passed I grew desperate. More silent and bitter, wondering how to break out of the trap we were in. When I returned to Essex, some times I would meet Cuthbert or Hugo. They would tell me the lie of the land and how my five household knights were prospering. Ferrers, of course, was very cunning. Not only did he refuse to find out who was pretending to be Gilbert Savage, he also stopped acting as a traitor for the French.' Lord Roger paused and offered his cup to Emmeline to refill. 'Your eighteenth birthday came and went. And then, as if in answer to a prayer, the Black Prince issued his writs, he was to take a great army to France. Naturally, my household knights did not go: there would be younger men eager to make their fortunes. Cuthbert and I met one night outside Dover and made our plans. Hugo Coticol joined us. I would pretend to die, Richard would return to Crokehurst and the invitations would be issued to my household knights.' He grinned over his cup at Richard. 'At first everything went well. My "death" in the ditch: afterwards I followed you to ensure you were safe. Once you

241

had arrived in Dover, Goodman Barleycorn shadowed your every footstep. Oh, it was a desperate gamble. Either one, or both of us, could have been killed in France but the good Lord smiled on us. At least, until we reached England where two things went wrong. First, the plague breaking out in Colchester. Secondly, Barleycorn's bitter feud with the outlaws. Apart from these,' Lord Roger shrugged.

'How did you know the household knights would come?'

'Oh, we'd come,' Grantham snapped. 'We'd taken that vow and all of us had our own suspicions. Strange,' he quipped. 'Ferrers was the most ardent in encouraging us.'

'Naturally,' Lord Roger interrupted. 'Ferrers must have been consumed with curiosity. Was he still safe? Had something been discovered? He came here intent to murder.'

'And, once we'd arrived,' Bremner added, 'you made sure we stayed.'

'As I said: I burnt the bridge. I also showed myself to my son. I wanted him to know that he was not alone. Above all, I wanted all of you to reflect, hence Cuthbert's attack on me: his arrows were deliberately blunted. There's nothing like superstition to sharpen the wits and put people on their edge.'

'And the footsteps in the gallery?' Emmeline asked.

'Crokehurst is a warren of secret passageways and I used them to the best advantage. I heard my son's confrontation with Ferrers, which was why I was ready and waiting on the tournament field. There's an underground passage which leads from the manor deep into the woods. I learnt everything that was said or plotted.' He smiled grimly. 'Well, most of it, except for Beaumont's death. I could have trapped Ferrers then but I was busy elsewhere.'

'The outlaws?' Manning asked.

'Yes. I knew about Ratsbane and Dogwort: their arrival did alarm me. I used the corpses, the severed heads of their scouts, to increase your sense of fear.'

'What did you hope to achieve?' Gildas asked curiously.

'Oh come, magician and self-confessed warlock,' Lord Roger grinned. 'Guilt can easily be stirred. Perhaps the assassin's nerve would break?' He stretched forward and grasped his son's hand. 'I calculated wrongly. Ferrers had a heart of stone. No soul. It was you who trapped him. Now justice has been done.' He got to his feet and stretched.

'What will you do now?' Richard asked, fearful of even letting his father out of his sight.

'We'll stay here until Buthlac returns,' Lord Roger replied. He stared round grimly. 'You will all stay. I will surrender to the sheriff and go to London. You will accompany me?'

Everyone agreed.

'Do we have some wine?' Lord Roger asked. He then walked quickly across the room, grasped Emmeline and embraced her. 'I am sorry about your father's death,' he murmured. 'But everything I have is now yours.' He released her and gestured round to the rest. 'The same is true of all of you: Bremner, Grantham and Manning. You came and I shall remember that. Gildas, Barleycorn? Crokehurst will be your home as well. The bankers in London still hold my monies. The King will release my lands and issue letters of pardon.'

'And you'll come back to live here?' Richard asked anxiously.

Lord Roger shook his head sadly. He came across and stood over his son.

'Not immediately,' he replied, his eyes full of tears. 'I have business which I must finish. On the night your mother died, I went to a small chapel and took an oath before the statue of the Virgin. If she saw justice done: if I was allowed to see the day when I could confront the real assassin, I would go on pilgrimage to St James's shrine in Compostella and then east to Jerusalem.' He lifted his hand. 'And this time,' he said softly, 'you cannot accompany me. I must go alone. Crokehurst needs a lord.' He smiled. 'And the fiery Emmeline has plans of her own. I will return. Now come, let's drink the last of the wine and celebrate!'

Richard hid his sadness at his father's news by helping Emmeline with the wine.

'Did you know,' Richard sat down beside his father. 'Did you know Buthlac had found the ring?'

His father shook his head. 'No, I kept well away from the hermit. He is not the fool he pretends to be. Once or twice our paths nearly crossed.' Lord Roger waved Barleycorn over. 'Cuthbert, your feud with the outlaws is finished. Ratsbane's and Dogwort's corpses lie freezing in the snow.'

'The boy has gone,' Barleycorn murmured. 'One of the gang still lives on.'

'A mere whelp,' Lord Roger scoffed. 'I saw him cross the causeway. He is not the stuff his father was made of.'

Emmeline now came over with a jug of wine to refill their cups. Lord Roger made room for her on the rough-hewn bench.

'Did you ever suspect?' he asked his son.

'No, not really,' Richard replied. 'When I saw you charge, memories were stirred but I never imagined, I never thought it was possible.'

'And you, Emmeline?'

The young woman shook her head. 'Never once,' she replied softly. 'My father and I were close but never once did he mention you. Oh, I knew there was a secret: as he lay dying of the fever he mentioned your name.'

'A good man,' Lord Roger declared, 'Now, my lady, fill our cups. Let's talk about your nuptials!'

Epilogue

In the refectory of the Crutched Friars the franklin paused:
he stared round at his companions.

'Gentle sirs, ladies, my tale is done.'

'Then did it happen?' the prioress asked.

Despite the late hour, she had hung on the franklin's every
word.

'Of course,' the franklin replied. 'Our good friend here, Sir
Godfrey, he came with the King to Crokehurst. Our chaplain
knows about the burial pits and the Masses Lord Roger had sung
for all those who died.'

'And Ferrers?' the shipman asked.

'Buried like a traitor with the rest,' the franklin snapped.

'And did the squire marry his Emmeline?' The wife of Bath
leaned forward, her face wide in a gap-toothed smile.

'Oh yes, they married,' the franklin grinned back. 'The King
himself was present at their nuptials. Go to Crokehurst manor,
next time you are in the wilds of Essex.' The franklin smiled. 'Go
there in the summer, the dovecotes are mended, the warren is
teeming with rabbits, the gardens are full of herbs and roses.

The manor has been restored to its full grandeur. Lord Roger sits in the orchard and watches his grandchildren playing. Five there are: three boys and two girls, sturdy and strong. Richard and Emmeline are as deeply in love as they were on that first day they met in plague-ridden Colchester.'

'And do the ghosts walk there?' the pardoner asked. 'I mean...'

Mine Host looked at the pardoner curiously. Usually the fellow screeched, clawing at his dyed yellow hair, but now the voice was different, soft and mellow.

'Oh,' the franklin answered quickly as if he was trying to protect the pardoner's slip. 'When winter comes and the lake freezes and the mists seep over the fields of Essex, the stories are whispered round the fireside. How at night, the ghosts of Dogwort and Ratsbane can be seen slipping across the causeway. Sometimes, just before dawn breaks, if you stand on the great meadow, you can see the shapes of men fighting, hear the song of the arrow, the clash of arms, the cries of men in violent struggle.' He shrugged and picked up his cup. 'But these are only stories: Crokehurst is at peace.'

'And who are you?' the prioress asked.

The franklin tapped his generous belly. 'Well, I'm not Sir Richard. Buthlac has a hobble. Oh yes, he still lives there. Gildas, I can't be, and Barleycorn? Well, God knows what happened to him? I am just a friend, a traveller, who knows what happened.'

'Tell me,' the man of law spoke up, 'when I worked in the Chancery, I remember releasing letters for the King's seal, authorising the restoration of Crokehurst and all its lands to the Greenele family. In those documents, mention is made of Gildas and Barleycorn and how generously the King rewarded them.'

The franklin pulled a face. 'Sir, I know nothing of that.' He stretched and yawned. 'But the hour is late. Tomorrow we must travel on.'

'The stories about Ratsbane and Dogwort frighten me,' the prioress declared, simpering at the man of law. 'If Black Hod and his gang are on the road, they may do us a mischief.'

'I doubt if they will,' the franklin replied, looking squarely at the summoner. 'We are well armed. Sir Godfrey here is a great warrior. What Lord Roger Greenele did on Crokehurst Island, Sir Godfrey can do amongst Black Hod's followers. Moreover, they are not made of the same metal as Dogwort and Ratsbane.' He played with the embroidered tassel of his belt. 'Black Hod should be careful,' he added quietly, 'one of these days he will attack a group of pilgrims and realise it's a trap.' He smiled expansively. 'Perhaps a group like our own?'

The Miller stood up and blew on his bagpipes, a loud jangling blast which set everyone's teeth on edge.

'I might be drunk!' he bellowed. 'But I don't give a fart for Black Hod! I carry a sword, broad and sharp, I'll grind their skulls like I grind my flour.' Then he sat down to murmurs of approval from his companions.

The franklin rose, put his cup on the table and went over to talk to the physician sitting in the corner: desultory chatter about the taverns and shops of Canterbury. All the time he kept an eye on the summoner, who slunk out of the door. A few minutes later the pardoner followed. The franklin finished his conversation and went out into the cobbled yard. He stopped and looked up at the stars, revelling in the cool night breeze then he walked across to where the horses were stabled. He took an apple from his pocket and went to where his old horse stood cropping at a bundle of hay. The horse snickered with pleasure and turned its head. The franklin offered the apple, the horse nibbled at it gently, stamping its hooves in pleasure.

'You are still a grand horse, Bayard,' the franklin whispered. 'Like your master, you have a great heart and a noble spirit. I always treasure you as a generous gift.' He leaned his head against the horse's flank. 'Oh, we've seen the days together, you and I,' he murmured. 'I have told them the tale. How you brought Richard from France. Without you, he may never have survived.'

The franklin gave the rest of the apple to the horse and walked back out into the cobbled yard. He heard a sound to his left and glimpsed the Pardoner standing in the shadows.

'Well, well, old friend,' the franklin murmured. 'And what did you see?'

The pardoner chuckled and moved closer.

'Our friend the summoner fair scampered along the road. I heard him whistle in the darkness. Someone met him there. He then returned, looking even more like a frightened rabbit.'

'I suppose he heeded the warning,' the franklin replied. 'He has gone and told his friend in Black Hod's gang to leave us well alone.'

'Do you think he knows?' the pardoner asked, coming even closer. 'Do you think he even suspects, Cuthbert, who you and I really are?'

'I couldn't give a fig!' franklin Barleycorn retorted. He loosened the cuff of his jerkin and felt the wristguard there. 'I am his enemy and he is mine: he has never forgotten and nor have I. I still pay men to keep a watch round Crokehurst. One of these dark nights, our summoner and his new friends may travel north to settle old scores.'

'Should we wait till then?' the pardoner asked. 'Or strike first?'

'Perhaps after we reach Canterbury,' the franklin answered. He stretched out his hand. 'It's good to see you again, Gildas. You haven't changed a whit.'

Gildas sighed and clasped the franklin's hand.

'As the good book says...'

'Oh, don't start that!' the franklin snapped. 'You like your new life?'

Gildas shrugged and stared up at the night sky.

'Sir Richard was kind. I stayed at least two years at Crokehurst but it's difficult to be good, Cuthbert. To keep one's feet on the path of righteousness.' He pulled down his collar and scratched at the red weal still faint round his neck. 'But I make a pretty penny and I hear the news of the roads. When I discovered the summoner was coming on the same pilgrimage you make every year, I thought I should tell you.'

'He's a dangerous man,' the franklin replied. 'He hunts me and I hunt him. However, for the rest of the journey Black Hod and his band will leave us alone.'

'Do you still have your bow?' Gildas asked.

'No,' the franklin replied enigmatically. 'But I know where I can get one.' He clapped the pardoner on the shoulder. 'Buthlac sends you his regards. He works in the kitchens at Crokehurst. He spends all his day making cheese. He's become quite an expert. Lord Richard and the Lady Emmeline send their love. They want you to go back.'

'One day soon,' Gildas replied, 'I will wash the dye out of my hair, get rid of the bric-a-brac I sell.' He grinned wolfishly. 'But tomorrow morning I tell my tale and I'll give the summoner a fright. It's about three ne'er-do-wells, who go looking for Death.'

The franklin clapped his hands and laughed as they turned and walked back to the refectory.